The Cougar Killer

by

Londa B.

Purposeful Publishing and Media Services, Inc.
St. Louis, MO.

The Cougar Killer by Londa B.
www.londab.com

Cover Graphics by Londa B.
Photograph Provided by: © **Dmitry Rostovtsev**

IBSN-13: 978-0-9831739-7-7
Library of Congress Control Number: On File
Printed in the United States of America

FIRST PRINTING

Acknowledgements

I am thankful for my obedience when it comes to allowing The Lord to order my steps. I am blessed to know the purpose of my life. Not every step taken, has been with ease, but with the Help of The Lord- I'm making my way. I'd like to take this time to thank my husband, children and beautiful parents. I truly appreciate and love my literary family. Your support in all of my endeavors means the world to me. To my dedicated readers, I thank you for your faithful and continued support. Without your support, I would not be where I stand today.

Dedications

This book dedicated all to the Cougar's and Sugar Daddies. In the modern dating scene, the way in which individuals seek sex, and companionship, have changed. True, age is nothing but a number, but the manner in which you pursue and conquer your sexual appetites; still cry for the same caution you once (or maybe not) used. **HIV, AIDS, HEPATITIS, SYPHYLLIS, OR ANY OTHER STD DOES NOT DISCRIMINATE!** Take back your lives, re-define your morals, and strengthen your self-esteem. Live, laugh, and learn! Take the time to love yourself. Become proactive, adjust your sexual behaviors within your relationship, and you will dwell in peace.

Life without purpose is a sin!

-Londa B

In Remembrance

Cia-Woo

August 8, 1932-January 14, 2011

I can never pen a book without mentioning this wonderful woman. She was the greatest friend, confidant, advisor, and grandmother. I thank God for allowing such a beautiful and sweet flower to bloom in my life. This beautiful flower delivered sweet lessons laced with love. Her perseverance to bloom in life, no matter what, provided all the love, peace, strength, and courage I needed to live with purpose and passion. No regrets live here grandma- only lessons! Now since the Lord has plucked one of his favorite flowers to plant in Heavens garden, I am at peace.

Love you always!

Londa

FOREWORD

The reason I wrote this book is dear to heart. My grandmother's best friend, (I will call her Bonnie) passed away from AIDS. Bonnie was sixty-four, and the man she dated was forty-three. From the start, everyone felt the relationship was odd, to say the least. No one approved of this man. He was attractive enough to pull any woman he wanted. His smile, his swag, his attitude and great sense of humor; lured Bonnie into his bed. My grandmother continued to warn Bonnie. Bonnie continued to proceed without caution. I remember how much my grandmother despised him. For a while, Bonnie and my grandmother were distant. Bonnie wrote their friendship off because she felt my grandmother was jealous. For about two years, Bonnie and my grandmother only spoke on Holidays and birthdays. My grandmother never asked Bonnie about her relationship whenever they talked.

One day, Bonnie called my grandmother and shared how sick she had been. She told my grandmother how the doctors told her at one time it was the flu and the next, some form of persistent pneumonia. They warned her to be careful of her surroundings, for being older meant a weaker immune system. Being concerned, my grandmother told Bonnie to find a new doctor. The new doctor was very thorough in her examination. During the exam, the doctor had two important questions for Bonnie. "Are you sexually active, and are you having protected sex?"

At that moment- silence revealed the truth. The doctor ordered a panel of STD lab tests and from there- nerves began to rattle. Not long after, my grandmother accompanied her friend to her follow up appointment. The appointment wasn't what Bonnie hoped for. Bonnie's lab results showed she was HIV positive. My grandmother cared for her friend and tried to soothe her soul, but all Bonnie cared for was to join her husband who unexpectedly passed away eight years ago. Life after diagnosis was awful. Bonnie sunk into depression, and only went to the hospital when she was near death. She pushed everyone away, and cried her heart dead.

Bonnie never intended on finding someone, but the thought of being loved, ignited her soul. She paid the price for lack of knowledge.

In a lot of cases, social media dictates the attitudes and lifestyles for many. Forty is the new fifty, sixty is the new seventy, and so-forth. True, it's great to be forty with a rockin' physique. Hell, we all have seen how older men and women of today, threaten the confidence of the fittest twenty-something. Be it young, or old; no one is exempt from the repercussions of their bad decisions. What's your next move? Wisdom, maturity and stability in one's life should be solid.

Lust and money blurs judgment; avoid the mirage. Once it fades, the mistakes made reveal themselves. At times, most things we see, is not reality. Why invite extra drama into your life?

You've been warned!

-*Londa B.*

The Cougar Killer K

By

Londa B.

A Word from Lucah Hunt

"Her essence, beauty, and grace were mixed with an uncontained and crippling power. Such power that hypnotized me into forsaking all others before I could exhale. Gleaming as if she was the sun, she displayed devout willingness, in showing a man how love, real love, feels. To sum up the whole equation- minus the need for re-calculation, Brooke's body modeled a serene image of perfected landscape. It was as if God's unchanging hands created her one section at a time. Her spirit was sweet, kind, and bitch free. This combination made the strongest man, her love slave.

It seemed others had issues with our fifteen-year age difference, but we loved it. We shared vibes stronger than any airwave signal. Yeah, the bedroom is a nice place to spend time, but the best way to win my heart is through my mind- she won. A smart woman is the ultimate turn on for good old, Lucah Hunt. Answer this- who desires to be in a relationship with a dummy? How long can a relationship as such last?

I love how women fool themselves by thinking if they throw down in the kitchen, and fuck until the bedroom furniture re-arranges itself; the man will roll over, beg, and obey her every command. At the end of the day, a man chooses who he wants. Fuck the tricks; we know every one of them. I hope you ladies are paying attention. You're more valuable when you know your worth.

There is a certain art involved when watching a woman. If a man positioned himself in an inconspicuous spot without compromising his cover, focused, and paced his breathing; he would find himself slow dancing with her every move. Within full circle of the clock, the ability to learn many things about the woman he fancies, presents itself. Women are remarkable creatures.

The thought of being with an older woman never sent me on a detour to love. Older women know how to value, and return love. It is unconditional. The ones I chose to engage with were mature, confident, and great in fulfilling their role. Stability in their life was the welcome mat I had no problem crossing. True, there are some women, no matter their golden age, will die a fool's death. It's truly unfortunate how many women live-without learning from life. Understanding the importance of self-love should be the first lesson a young woman receives. It builds confidence and helps her understand what's best for her life. With self-love, the notion of settling with another woman's, man, would never find comfort in her heart. Who wins in a relationship as such? The man does. He has the best of both worlds, and he will never relinquish either one as long as both women continue settling.

Now young women- they *scare* the hell out of me. The look of *lost* plastered upon their faces, revealed disturbed spirits. Lives filled with emotional baggage; forced airlines to charge them triple just to carry their drama-filled luggage. For the few I've dated, caution was exercised with every turn approached in the relationship. Holding my breath as I traveled through their emotional smog, while hoping to arrive at destination *happy*; depressed the fuck out of me.

Why in the hell does it take women forever when it comes to *getting to happy*? What in the hell is *happy*? I mean, are there any *happy* women out there? Seriously, they always seem to have something to bitch about no matter their position. If the man works long hours and is away from home often, they're pissed. On the other hand, if he is fired or in between jobs- *no matter how long and well he has provided prior to incident*- she will find a way to break his spirit in half. Now where do you find *happy* in all that shit?

Here comes a block of questions. Why do women settle when it comes to their personal lives? Why do women love men who refuse to love them back? Why do women still love us, when we *pretend* to love them? Maybe I need to pen a book on these topics. Listen ladies, if you want *happy*, stop the bullshit from rolling into your life! Everyone knows how shit looks and smells; don't act surprised when you step in it.

Many young and beautiful women have accessorized my arm on numerous outings. Smart enough to know better, I steered clear, of those who lacked self-esteem. Their character lacked luster and for me, manual labor is not a good fit for, Lucah. No matter how hard you polish some gems, flaws remain. True, no one is perfect but the question of how well you handle the person's flaws speaks volumes. As I said, manual labor is not for me.

Youthful age combined with the lack of experience in life, lure young women to take bed with any man. Premature delivery of the *pocket book*; doomed their chances of having a successful relationship. Young women lose out when they fail to understand the power and wealth of the *pocket book*.

Some men never intend on leaving anything in a woman's *pocket book* except empty promises, STD's, or a seed that would grow into an abandoned love child. I'm always fascinated to see how women play games when it comes to finding Mr. Right. Trying to find Mr. Right on the same night they meet AND fuck the guy; is as lucky as finding a winning lotto ticket on the ground, unsigned, and still intact after a fucking tsunami. That's some type of fucking luck!

Confidence, self-esteem, and knowledge; skyrockets *pocket book* value. Ladies, don't give *every* man you meet, the chance to dive into your pocket book; one day it will be bankrupt and you won't have shit to offer.

If you haven't noticed, I'm on a rant. Be patient, for the *real* Lucah Hunt will emerge! I'm sure you will understand what my deal is, by the end of this intro. I truly want you to know who you're fucking with; there's many like me out there.

Women who leave nothing to the imagination disgust me. Men actually care about a woman's intellect. If women choose to dress below a *real* man's standards; they should understand that they are rewarding him the ultimate chance to hit it and split!

You are what you speak. It's important to learn the power of the tongue. I hate to hear women speak deathful tones. It only excels me to evaporate like the last drop of moisture, on the dawn of a hot summer day. This type of energy has never existed in any of my relationships. Again, it is the airlines job to carry the baggage- not Lucah's.

When a man knows what he wants, he goes after it. If the universe or the dick- speaks it, he conquers it. Men know what they want and women *think* they know. Let's face it, women know what type of guy they're dealing with right out the gate. However, the "mother" in them appears and tries *saving* or *changing* the guy, instead of accepting the fact that he's for someone else- not them. If you're in the saving mood, save yourself or visit an animal shelter.

Back to my Brooke. She loved to rave about how much of a priceless gem I was to her. Being younger, she was happy that I didn't require a *second mother.* I knew all about life and was very responsible. She loved my independence and drive. My ability in achieving my life goals by the end of my twenties; turned her on. I have made myself a millionaire many times over. There's no doubt about her love for the dick, but I'm sure, the previously mentioned things were at the top her list.

Back to the dick. Brooke enjoyed our lovemaking sessions. I vividly remember Brooke working relentlessly with a hell on wheels, client. To break the tension, I sat in her office lounge pleasuring myself with the door half ajar. Her taste for sex dominated her thoughts. Watching her fight temptation made my dick harder. Not a fan of panties, I could see right underneath her desk as her plush and lustrous damn of wetness winked silver beams. Her shivering turned me on. It was as if crushed ice flowed through her veins. From one extreme to the next, her body temperature rose, and she became flushed with a panic-filled heat. To no avail, she flashed and the buzzing from her fan whispered temporary relief from the onset of heat. Laughter pained my stomach as I watched her stutter a million times over.

Sniffling away as if allergies seized her nose, Brooke's narrow nostrils failed to release my scent as her nipples swelled with a crazy wanting. Every time she closed her eyes, the color of her NARS, Super Orgasm pink blush converted to a frostbitten, wind- burned shade of, *Winter Rose*. Brooke hated when I watched her conduct business, while pleasuring myself. Don't judge us...everyone has a game.

The bedroom, ah yes, our *Arena of Love* is where it all goes down. Once I'm up, I always perform above standard. Taking deep dives into Brooke, as I maintain rhythms of long, slow, and powerful strokes; delivered shame, not gold medals, to Michael Phelps. A man willing to give his woman ultimate pleasure before self, is a strong lover indeed. Hands down, selfish lovers fail in the bedroom.

If you are trying to figure out what's going on, please stop. You have no damn idea what's going on. It gets deeper.

The psychology of pleasuring a woman is one lesson young men need schooling on before they engage in relationships. Even though, some tactics of lovemaking seem best learned through experience, it should start with mental stimulation. Provoking thoughts turn women on. Let her know you have more than her panties on your mind.

Brooke was not my first relationship with an older woman. There had been many others but it seemed as if their mindsets were underdeveloped or delayed. As I stated earlier, no matter the age, some will die a fool's death.

Noticeable downsides with some older women pinched

15

me here and there. They too, were found mingling in the clubs, drinking heavily, and cursing more than a ship of sailors. Some acted as a loose as a pack of hookers on a Friday night. All of these issues compounded with the lack of self-love, fracture their souls. Pretty was nowhere to be found.

What is hard about relationships? I almost lost my mind to the cosmic regions after trying to fathom sensible facts as to why people fail at monogamy. Men, if a woman cycles through too many friends or has issues with family members, know that there is something biting on the line. You choose- reel it in, or drop the line and run as fast as Hussein Bolt. I am sure I have beaten his record on more than one occasion.

A relationship lacking monogamy is full of greed, and has an insatiable hunger for the unknown. Hunger occurs before greed. Once fed to a fulfilling point, the time to digest the relationship should occur. Greed erupts when the individual has not rested after fulfillment. The digestion of life issues and or circumstances should process in a natural form. If this process fails, the thought of being monogamous fades away. Fulfillment in *every* area of a relationship is important.

Monogamy fails, when you fail to commit.

Once a man fucks up, he learns his lesson and moves forward. Women? They'd rather assemble to talk shit about men, when in all reality; they should spend time trying to figure out where they fucked up in the relationship! Women have so much fun talking about us, but remember to talk about your lousy asses too! Surely, we can't stand alone when it comes to fucking up the relationship. It's never one person's fault! The truth takes no sides!

Brooke was my gem because everything about her was priceless. As the cure to cancer was good for a dying patient, Brooke's love made me whole. The best part of her medicine was the lack of side effects. If hunger pains for her loving were the only side effect experienced, I held on. I knew it would be a matter of time before we would once again, be the silk between the sheets.

Fast forward five years later and I retract every-damn-statement; I ever spoke about "Brooke the Bitch!" Because of her, I am devoted to burying as many Cougars' seeking pleasure from, Lucah Hunt! What I'm about to do, gives a whole new definition to- *Getting it in.*

Never in all-of-my-life would I have thought good old Lucah would become a statistic. To say I am bitter is an understatement. Stripped and violated inside and out-vulnerability unpacked all its shit inside my soul. No one could do anything to make me feel as if was ok to consider giving hope a seat in my future. My manhood and pride were swallowed and consumed by one bitter, dirty, insecure, empty, depressed, selfish, vengeful, and deceptive bitch!

I still find it hard to believe the degree of pain she inflicted upon me. She injected her powerful, hypnotizing, and tainted love into my blood stream. From there, it was a matter of time before it reached my heart. Her wicked act forced a weird and inevitable mutation of my DNA. My soul left me. In the mirror, I was Lucah, but on the inside; I was a science experiment gone wrong.

In my mind, the crisp winter day matched the bitterness I harbored, as I mixed the concrete for her tombstone. The cruelness of January matched her vengeance-filled tone when she delivered the news. Her announcement took control of my mind and the image of how my own corpse would look at my funeral; knocked me to my knees and a hell awful panic attack hi-jacked my body.

The bitch must have borrowed her nerves from a dozen

of insane criminals. Leaving a death sentence on my voicemail, from an untraceable number, was beyond low. My stomach pain intensified when my lungs collapsed on top of it. Air escaped my body as I rolled about on the floor. In and out of consciousness, I heard that bitch laughing her sins away. I never heard Brooke laugh in such a crude manner. It was evil, dark, and quite deserving of a rocket launch to hell. The bitch recited, "You're welcome my precious gem. Welcome to the hellacious world of AIDS!" Evil shit from the mind of a bitch gone bad. For a while I refused to believe Brooke left the message. It was as if someone was playing a trick, but her absence in my life rang truth.

I was prepared to live the rest of my life with Brooke. She was beyond beautiful. Her spirit filled mine with divine love. If she were honest with me, I would have given myself to her no matter the price. We could have worked through it. Are you capable of loving someone like that? If you thought longer than five seconds, don't bother answering.

We were together five years and she never changed until the end. I'm devastated about her choice in sharing herself with another man. Learn the lesson- you never know your lover; people change.

Thinking back, there were times where Brooke told me stories about her need to travel for business, or to see family; so all was fine with me. At one point, Brooke lost a significant amount of weight; but blamed it on a new diet trend. Now that I think of it, Brooke's body was perfect, but nonetheless, I supported whatever she wanted to do. I just figured she wanted to improve upon herself. She never looked sick to me. How in the fuck is AIDS supposed to look? More importantly, how long did she have it?

Maybe the test results were a false positive. Maybe they mixed up the results. I can't remember how many times I had my blood re-drawn. Each time, I grasped onto the fact that accidents happen. Can you imagine how many ways I tried to pray this evil off my life? I hoped God would look at how devout I was in our relationship and deliver me from evil, since I never cheated on Brooke. Let it be known, Lady Luck was on vacation, and that bitch, Karma was working overtime.

The bitch removed herself from the *top-shelf* when she pulled this shitty stunt. Her act requires nothing but the best brand of revenge accompanied by one succulent, tongue-burning plate of evil. Of course, I would never discriminate. I am open to serving all customers seeking pleasure from my delightful menu.

From time to time, Brooke would leave these dry messages for me. They were sad, depressing and at times, downright mean. It appears after her diagnosis, Brooke's willingness to participate in the game of love with vibrancy and faithfulness, burned hotter than hell. The chances of her life sustaining any sense of normality burned to ashes and her dust was ready to be returned to the earth. She turned evil in the midst of her pain, and on next watch, a killer came forth. I wanted to hear her side of the story. I wanted to sit down with her to gather some type of reasoning, better yet- a simple *why,* would have sufficed. On the other hand, would her explanation bring back my good health and happiness? We all want to know *why* in the end, but sometimes, the reason is still not good enough.

I tried to focus on life, but my mind was too busy picturing and framing the end of my own life. The bitterness embedded within Brooke turned foul after her young lover, showed his dirty hands. He never knew who gave him the disease, but I guess he didn't give a damn who he gave it to either. Ah, the price we pay for seeking love from people we know are no good for us. Do you see how this vicious cycle binds someone into being a statistic? Hell, the web of revenge should be as big as the earth itself!

I am bitter and giving a damn about love has expired.

Don't pray for me. Save your breath and reserve your scriptures for your next bible study session. Watering down this brand of payback would show nothing but weakness on my behalf. No need to worry about the end. The Lord and I will have that talk when the time comes. I'm sure regret will occur once I see the thermostat in hell. Who has the definite answer on if heaven or hell even exists? Heaven- it doesn't exist for me! Apparently, I've been deemed not worthy of it and I haven't even hit the damn dirt yet. His mercy runs dry for, Lucah Hunt. God has shown how he feels about me. Normally people would talk about being spiritual, but my soul has wandered too far away. I'm sure my former pastor would be upset with me for what I'm about to do. But hey, this was all by God's design. Nothing else to be said.

The question of should I shoot, or cut the Devil in Prada, as deep as the blue sea; outweighs any chance of Brooke seeing a happy ending. If I find the bitch, she's dead! *The Cougar Killer*, suits me finer than Armani! Who is going to blow the whistle? Who is going to alert the media? This death sentence has literally fucked away my chances of living a quality life.

Fuck what people say! Sure, people are living longer with *tons* of medicine and *millions* of doctor visits, but a lifestyle as such, lacks quality and it fucking sucks!

You watch, fucking around with me will lead to the demise of any cougar who struts my way. You better damn well takes notes, because the class on Cougar Killing- 101 with Professor Hunt as your instructor, is about to start. Call me Mr. Post Man because I intend on delivering my 'package' to every area code possible."

Bitter until the fucking end,
Lucah Hunt
-The Cougar Killer

Londa B.

Isabella

Chapter 1

"Why turn off the lights in my life, Lord? Help me out! If life was going to be this damn unfair, I would have never married!" Isabella cried foul into her wet lap as she continued applying pressure to her husband's blood soaked gauzes. Her husband's mutilated face demanded another changing of the gauze.

Deep lacerations attained from shattered glass; defaced the once handsome man's image. The patchwork of gauze started to take on the semblance of a mummy. "Baby, open your eyes. Look at me- tell me something with your eyes. Blink for me Miguel!" Her face, swollen with sadness, released tears, which gleamed like black diamonds. Tears of sadness were the beginning of her heartache. Frustrated, Isabella circled and peered over her husband's face bobbing and weaving; hoping to witness his toughness and will to live, give way to her commands.

"Who said twenty-five years of marriage is golden? This isn't fair Miguel! We were supposed to go out hand in hand on our porch of *Southern Comfort.* You remember that?" Isabella pushed thoughts of spending her golden years alone, far away. Grandchildren and all, she knew it was going to take more than loved ones to help her blues sing elsewhere. *Southern Comfort* was the mansion Miguel and Isabella purchased on their tenth year wedding anniversary. The home, beyond beautiful, was awarded with placement in an abundance of interior design magazines. Isabella was proud of the home they created.

Spectacular and massive in space, the home was large enough to hold lavish wedding ceremonies, and golfing events from time to time for their high-profile friends. A twelve room, eight bath, four car garage, home, with a mini golf course, Olympic sized pool, waterfalls and ponds filled with some of the world's most exotic aquatic species; was everything the couple desired. A large recreation room, a theater, and huge ballroom were a few of the extras the home offered. No matter what section of the home you walked through, it was obvious the both of them created it out of love.

"Baby, do you remember us stepping for hours on the ballroom floor? Do you remember serving me dinner while serenading me? You have always been a smooth operator. Whew!" Isabella shook her head.

"Miguel you couldn't wait to get on that floor. You threw in some good old R. Kelly, and *baby-* we stepped to love as if it were our first time!" Isabella tried to lure, as many special memories she could think of to sit beside them, hoping a sweet memory whispered into the air, would pull Miguel from his coma.

"It seems I've prayed about a million times, but don't worry, I won't grow faint. I refuse to live without you!"

"Mrs. Valdez?" A tall, and hardened looking doctor with faded green scrubs and disheveled white hair, called for her attention. Isabella taking notice of the doctor's appearance prompted her to raise her eyebrows. Isabella was big on appearances and she wondered if the doctor was good enough to take care of her husband. He looked as if he missed days of sleep.

"I'm Dr. Tobias. Sorry we have to meet under these circumstances. I want to make sure we have answered all of your questions."

"Will you please inject some hope into this situation, Doctor?"

"Mrs. Valdez, the next four hours are going to be tough. I have to remind you that he will not survive this trauma. At your wish, the patient will remain on the ventilator until the rest of your loved ones arrive. We are working relentlessly to maintain his vitals." Isabella's ears shifted to mute. Listening to the pompous Doctor recite her husband's *death script* tore Isabella apart. With his voice unwavering, he continued to recite her husband's demise in a cold and sterile habitude.

"Why can't you look me directly in the face? Why are you talking in scripted tongue? *Why* are you talking about my husband as if he is already dead and tagged for the morgue? Where is the comfort? Why do you call him, *the patient*? His name is Miguel Valdez! You do *know* who my husband is, don't you? You'd have to be crazy not to know who my husband is!"

"Mrs. Valdez, please accept my-,"

"What- your resignation? Physicians like you, keep people from seeking medical attention. Go back to school, and find where you lost your bedside manner! Leave the damn papers on the table and let us be. Once the rest of the family has said their good-byes; you have permission to obtain his organs for donation."

"I'm sorry for not being able to deliver good news. Nevertheless, the team and I are continuing to exercise on every avenue regarding your husband's care. Right now, there have been no changes in your husband's status. He is losing blood faster than we can infuse it. We are trying to keep him hydrated to avoid his electrolytes from going out of range. In all honesty, we are prolonging his death, not saving his life." The doctor explained as he lowered his head in defeat. Weary, tired, and stressed from the events at hand, Dr. Tobias refused to take further witness of Mrs. Valdez' deflated spirit.

"Please, do not hesitate to push the call button if you need anything. Your nurse will come right in to assist you. We intend on doing everything possible for Mr. Valdez." the doctor quietly ushered himself out of the room.

Grief ran Isabella over about a million times and she herself was starting to feel deserving of her own casket. Her eyes displayed a certain coldness that even the coldest winter ever, failed to top. The life she once knew was over. Conquered by a gang of loose minded and reckless thugs; Isabella's King had fallen from his throne.

    With rosary in one hand, and gauzes in the other, panic rushed her into applying more gauze to her husband's face. The deep gashes poured cups of chilled blood into her hands. The deep lacerations over his entire face posed as escape routes. Looking at his pale and mangled face with any hope for successful reconstruction deemed to be a hard match for even the best cosmetic surgeon. The temporary stitches in his face were as weak as levees in Louisiana.

    Stomping one foot to the ground with eyes closed, head bowed and voice low, Isabella tried her best to work a deal with the Lord.

    "Lord, you have to reveal this one to me! Father, please...please, release my soul from the burden of burying him! This is too much to bear. I know you won't forsake me, but *please* bring him back." Pleading for his life, Isabella took seat by her husband. Dizzy spells came and went, but she continued to ignore them.

Chapter 2

Thinking of losing her life, and Miguel all within the same blink was a thought she failed to process. Her life turned into a horrid nightmare. Now it was Isabella's turn to become a statistic for the books or maybe have her story featured on some A&E Crime or Lifetime program. Two hours ago, the horrid nightmare that attacked them in the still of the night, would be no easy task in escaping permanent etching in Isabella's mind. No matter how tight she held her husband's hand, his responses proved to be as faint as his pulse.

Bowing her head and squeezing his hand, she bellowed out another prayer that was bound to heal every ill person in the ER.

"Lord, you gave me a heart the beat but this man here- he gave it rhythm. *Please Father*, please make this the miracle story for us to share with all we know. Sometimes we need reminding of your grace, mercy, and power! Only you can make a way out of no way! *I need you, we need you!*" Isabella prayed, as her grasp on her husband grew even tighter.

"Mrs. Valdez, please- please stop! Some of his chest leads are coming off." The panicked nurse shouted as she tried to regain control.

"We need to monitor your husband's heart and other vitals. Would you please give the staff enough time to come in and do more vitals and other procedures?" The thin, blonde haired nurse with huge, moisture-deprived lips, asked as she hurried to replace the chest leads and oxygen sensor. Without pause, the nurse turned her attention to Mrs. Valdez.

"What? Why are you looking at me like that?" Isabella cried.

"Mrs. Valdez, I need you to calm down. I know it's easy for me to say, and hard for you to do, but you are going to kill yourself."

"Well when that moment comes, will you get the hell out of here and let me die next to my husband?"

"I have ethics! You know doing something like that is not right! I do not play God! We all have to take what the Lord delivers us. None of us are exempt from the trials of life. As for you, we are monitoring your heart with a portable heart monitor. Please restrict movement that would loosen your chest leads."

"I'm heartbroken, and emaciated. Shot in my arm, glass trapped in my face and these old bones are sore as hell." Isabella exhaled as she leaned onto her husband's stretcher resting her head on his arm. The nurse tried to embed relief into Mrs. Valdez's back with a salon-inspired massage. The nurse hoped her next question would not cause an eruption of anger. Since her arrival to the E.R., Mrs. Valdez scolded every worker who stepped into her sight. Her tongue was the sword that tortured all who lacked the courage to stand up to her.

"Mrs. Valdez, we need you to come on back to your room and take a break. We need to re-check your vitals and look at your wounds to check on the bleeding and to see if more swelling has progressed. I instructed you to not pull or lift your husband, because of your injuries. Refusing medical treatment is not a good thing for you to do. The liability is on you, not us. Will you please allow us to give you the attention you need?"

"No! I am not ready to leave his side. Take the vitals and check the wounds right here! The doctor said the bullets entered and exited without any major damage! I am not leaving his side! Keep the pain meds and antibiotics rolling this way! You're right; I need plenty of dope to help me get high enough to feel lifted from this mess!" The alarms and chaos around them continued as they stared each other down.

"*Devil, you ain't gone piggy back me today! Get-off-my-back! Dealing with this woman is hell enough! You done lost your* way if you think I'm going to go there! You are powerless! Get lost!" Exhaling, Lisa regained her sanity and professionalism.

"Mrs. Valdez, I have to remind you of your injuries."

"No need for that! This pain is awful" Mrs. Valdez barked as she nursed her arm.

"You need to rest! We have given you potassium, as well as placed a nitroglycerin patch to help with your blood pressure and heart. We understand your pain, and we are trying to oblige your every demand, but we cannot continue prolonging *your* care."

"Why haven't you retrieved my meds young lady?" Without regard to what Mrs. Valdez said, the nurse continued with her lecture.

"May I also mind you, the morphine we gave you places you on fall precaution. You cannot be up and around, high on morphine. I need you to stay in the stretcher next to your husband. You were shot, and the debris from the glass caused serious lacerations to your face and chest area." The nurse stated, as she stood solid with both arms crossed against her full chest.

"I don't hear a word you are saying right now! I know my patient rights!"

"I think you don't hear me." The nurse mugged Isabella without a blink of fear. "As I said, hospital protocol requires every patient, under narcotic influence to be in a secure bed. Now, the consultations with the plastic and orthopedic surgeons need to take place soon. Our time is limited and we need to start repairing your facial lacerations." By this time the nurse had taken knee, cocked her head to the right, hoping once again to lock eyes with Isabella.

"I know you're in there. Try to remain strong. Your husband needs to hear the woman he knows, not the distress. Continue talking to him. Now, if you will excuse me- I need to tend to your husband."

"Do you think I lost my damn memory?"

"Excuse me?" The nurse responded as she stepped back. Mrs. Valdez' defense attacked the witty nurse's offense. It was clear Isabella wanted the nurse to know she was mentally capable of comprehending everything discussed. "Do you think the horrid thoughts of what occurred early this morning escaped my mind?" Isabella screamed as she forcefully pointed into the bloody bandage wrapped around her head. "Hell, all I know is some thug bastard and his stupid ass partners shot us up! Look at him!" Isabella pointed to her husband's bullet riddled body. Now you tell me, who in the hell looks worse?" Scolded like a child, the nurse bowed her head.

"Your husband does Mrs. Valdez."

"Well then, there's your answer, Lisa."

Growing tired of Mrs. Valdez, Lisa applied another layer of strong face, hoping it would be enough to pull through her hellacious shift. Lisa closed the curtains behind her as she prayed for a barricade to protect her from Isabella's sharp, ear piercing voice.

"Don't you worry about me, I'm tough. My husband needs you and every bit of your staff more than I do!" Isabella yelled to the curtain. Isabella began crying into her weathered and blood tainted hands. As the tears moistened her blood stained hands, one would have thought hard labor was her calling in life by the sight of her hands. Isabella's willingness to take the back seat by avoiding her own healthcare, for the sake of her husband was indeed an honorable act.

"Lisa, I know you have a lot going on in that brilliant mind of yours, but please work with me. I'm sorry for acting out. I know where this whole thing is going- so please bear with me. This is hard to deal with."

"I understand." Lisa replied after entering the room. She placed her focus back on the monitors and IV bags. Upset with Lisa's inability to focus her mind on what Isabella shared, Isabella became pissed. It seemed as if Lisa took some type of make believe, field trip to the land of *whatever*.

Frozen in time, Lisa watched the monitors, and charted in the computer. Within the next moment, Lisa lowered the head of the bed. "Why is his bed in that position? What is wrong with the monitor and why are all of these damn alarms going off? Get some people in here to silence this chaos!" Isabella cried as she grabbed her chest hoping the new onset of pain would kill her dead.

"We are trying to keep his pressure up Mrs. Valdez!" Seeing Mrs. Valdez's emotional distress, Lisa decided to call help for Isabella. As Lisa and three other nurses worked in stabilizing Mr. Valdez, Isabella prayed as pain assaulted her body. After the pain subsided, she took a moment to gather the feelings that fell out of her spiritual self. No one's soul was more bruised and battered than hers. After a few minutes, Isabella was able to stop her eyes from watering her face. Feeling pain in her right arm, hoping to avoid head jerking, she used her left hand to comb through her long, disheveled, golden blonde hair.

Lisa clicked open Mr. Valdez's chart on the computer and reviewed his stats. She placed her hands on her hips and started rocking side to side, as she reviewed all of the charts notes. One minute, her eyes were on the monitor, the next, Mr. Valdez, and back to the computer. She repeated her unorthodox antics about five more times, as if she had some form of OCD. Compelled to query, Isabella zoomed in on Lisa's nervous and aggravating antics; she hoped good news would flow from her full, and now-shiny peach lips. After reviewing Mr. Valdez's vitals, Lisa felt it was time to prescribe Mrs. Valdez with news that would go beyond making her sick, risking the chance of complicating Isabella's health.

"Mrs. Valdez?" The nurse called as she locked eyes with Isabella. Lisa knew it was time to prepare Mrs. Valdez for the end. She pulled up a stool, removed her stethoscope, and reached for Mrs. Valdez's hand.

"How long does he have Lisa?" Isabella asked with a blank stare.

"At best, we may have one, maybe two hours." She released the truth hoping Isabella's reaction would not beckon Lisa to admit Isabella to the psych ward. Lisa was never good at coping with the trimming of a family's tree. Pacing her breathing, Lisa explained every option available regarding Mr. Valdez's care while she passed on more Kleenex. Isabella's blank stare at Lisa's name badge, went into an abyss of no return.

"If he does not go into arrest, let us be. I do understand the transplant needs to occur before his heart actually stops." Isabella knew her chances petitioning for more options had met its end.

"Mrs. Valdez, I know this question is one that many hope to never receive but I must-" Lisa stated as she tapped her multi-colored nursing clogs on the floor.

"Yes, take what's left. He signed his license and I agree- you will have no argument from me. I'll sign the papers." Without wasting time, Lisa handed Mrs. Valdez a clipboard with the attached forms to sign. Her signature would deliver a new breath of life to whoever waited to get the call of a lifetime.

Isabella knew the importance of organ donation. Her sister received a kidney about a year ago. Isabella knew a host of people were close to walking into new seasons of life, because of her husband.

"It's not like he will be able to do anything with them. I hate people who do not care enough to sign the damn license! I've seen first-hand how donating organs is a blessing. Everyone deserves a chance to live."

"You are right Mrs. Valdez."

"The end of it all is sad. After all the visits, and hoop jumping, the end of life rears its ugly head. Their spirits fade, as the chance of a second life seems bleak. In the end, if they're lucky, a chance alerts them with a single phone call."

"What a blessing." Lisa stated.

"At that point, the faith the person has in the Lord, is rewarded. Having faith is the only thing we have." Isabella smiled as she looked toward the ceiling.

"Never thought of it like that." Lisa said as she continued changing IV fluids.

"Does your work allow you to develop immunity from pain?"

"I can't lie. It's all work, until it happens to me or a loved one. If you allow every situation to get to you, you won't last long in this profession. I care about the people and what I do, but I have to draw a line somewhere." Lisa was honest. Isabella's hand tremors were uncontrollable and her tears dissolved the fresh ink on the permission forms.

"Here, you go." Isabella handed the papers over. "I know a blessing is about to come forth. Sad it had to happen this way."

"Mrs. Valdez, I see heartache every time I clock in, but I try my best to stand strong. Sometimes it's not easy. I lost my parents in a car wreck when I was eight years old." Lisa shared her pain.

"The day of the accident, I decided to stay with my grandmother because I loved being with her on rainy days. Whenever the weatherman said, rain was coming, thoughts of her warming the oven, brought a smile to my face. She knew I anticipated her strawberry rice crispy treats! What made things so great was how we both were nuts about cartoons. Funny, we managed to eat the entire pan of the crispy treats before the cartoons went off. To drive my grandmother nuts, I would run around the house stark naked the eating crispy treats. When she caught up with me, she gave one heck of a tickle."

"How sweet."

"Wow, I'm sorry, I guess that was too much info!" Lisa reminisced as a smile of comfort took form upon her face.

"Keep going Lisa." Isabella found delight in Lisa's story.

"I was raised by my grandmother and although she was the best, nothing replaced my mom and dad. It is painful at times-more so around the holidays."

"There's nothing worse than the Holiday's when you are missing loved ones." Isabella said.

"Yet, I still stand by the grace of God and trust me; he will get you through as well. It's going to take time for all the vile and confusing feelings to exit your spirit." A smile stole the frown from Mrs. Valdez's face.

"Now, this will be the last time I say some cliché which is never welcomed in situations like this because you and I both know, no one wants to hear it when they are going through. Even though people are as sorry as the day they sinned, the other person on the end refuses to allow words to comfort their souls. I know for me, I was too busy trying to hear Gods explanation as to why things happened the way they did."

"Oh child, I feel like that right now. I need him to explain himself."

"I was waiting on the Lord to show up and show out. I was waiting on some spectacular vision to lead me on. I know where you stand right now." Lisa confessed with the same painful and absent look Mrs. Valdez, had on her face.

"Ok, sorry about that. This isn't about me!" Lisa apologized as she stood to wipe the tears off her cracked foundation.

"It's okay sweetie. I'm not the first or the last to experience this. Please, tell me time will heal, because this hurt is severe enough to make me doubt Gods power. Lisa, this man was everything! I knew deep in the pit of my stomach, that I was created for Miguel." Isabella confessed sweet whispers as she looked to her husband. "This man could never be duplicated, yet along, imitated without a million faults rising. No man is worthy enough for comparison to Miguel. No man, I mean no man, can provide what my Miguel has given me. You have a love like that

Lisa?"

"Not yet."

"Well I spent most of my young life waiting for that *right* fit. Now mind you, I'm not talking about the right jeans or cute shoes either.

"Yes, I know what you talking about."

"I witnessed how my mother and father loved each other and I was awed at how their love for one another could grow deep feelings and appreciation in my own soul. I was happy about the love my parents shared. I knew one day my husband was going to love me in the same respectful manner as my father did my mother. We are all Queens, and we all have a King out there preparing a home for us. Sadly, my King's reign is over."

Lisa jumped up with her hand raised as she begged for pardon.

"Oh no- I need to correct you Mrs. Valdez. Like a President, once he moves out of office, he is still considered *The President*. Now the same rule applies for your King." Lisa responded in a proud manner as she tried to smile some portion of happiness back into Isabella's heart.

"You know Mrs. Valdez; there are people who never re-marry, because they feel they have already experienced perfection. I guess there is no sense in trying to see if the universe has better to offer."

"Well you are right, there's no need for me to try to experience perfection twice. It won't be the same."

"Yup, I hear those confessions from many of my elderly patients."

"You're right... and the thought of a second marriage, hell- a relationship period- is barred from my mind. I know you have not had that man, but trust me; you will feel him before he even appears. The closer he gets, the dizzier you become. Your knees will weaken and your heart will pause. That moment will give you a chance to inhale the blessing that God has placed before you! You will have to thank God repeatedly as you praise him for him blessing you with a special man."

"I want to meet him now."

"His heartbeat will work overtime to ensure happiness never skips over you. Love is real and love is deep! A good man's love is a love which wraps you in comfort and warmth when the cold and bitterness of the world tries to beat the life out of you!" Isabella preached with an unwavering voice.

"Ok, Mrs. Valdez, you making me wish the next man in sight is the man for me!" Lisa laughed as she continued to hold Mrs. Valdez's hand while monitoring her husband.

"Don't you go off and get a throwback!" Isabella teased.

"What is a throwback, Mrs. Valdez?"

"Oh honey you're too young. If you wait on the Lord, you won't have to worry about throwing some sick dog back into the pound he escaped from!"

"Oh-my-goodness! You are right. I just threw this mangy mutt back into the pound this past weekend."

"Well good! Don't make a mistake thinking that he was good for this and that, because his foul shit will knock you out! You are no fool; don't cry about how good his *thang* was either! That *thang* is what gets young women caught up and screwed-literally!"

"Ok, I had you penned for a savvy and sweet Diva!" Lisa teased. Lowering her voice to the basement, Mrs. Valdez bellowed out as she raised her right eyebrow and smized a sexy, Tyra Bank's branded smile, and whispered, "Young lady, every Diva gets *down!* Hell, I ain't dead! You know me and that man there-", Isabella pointed towards Miguel as she raised one eyebrow, while biting her bottom lip, "could make the walls round us crumble!" Isabella reminisced as a grin drew upon her face.

"Ok, you know you are too much for me to handle right now, right?" Lisa laughed as she got up from her chair admiring

Mrs. Valdez's witty sense of humor.

"Ok, I will take your lesson to heart. Now I have to get things moving, excuse me while I deliver these papers. The transplant team and the recipients will be notified now."

"Lisa, please take care of him and make sure they don't mistreat him. Please treat him with the utmost respect. I've heard the stories on how people treat the dead."

"You have my word. Lisa promised as she tapped twice against her small chest in devotion.

"When the children come back, please send them to me."

"No problem- will do. Now here, please take a drink of this tea. I will be back in a few."

"Lisa-"

"Yes."

"Thank you."

"No problem, I love what I do. This is my assignment from the Lord."

Chapter 3

Silence as low as Miguel's heart rate fell in the room. Every time Isabella spoke to her husband, his heart rate played peak and trough. It was as if he could feel her pain, her tension, her worry, and her grief.

"I wish I would have kept my mouth shut and let you go the way you wanted. I thought a romantic drive home through the park would be a great finale to our anniversary celebration." Isabella started to cry, but decided to swallow her tears. Her order for silence and privacy took away the nurses, doctors, lab, and radiology.

Alone, Isabella's sensitivity to every noise in the room started to vex her. The sounds of the IV dripping turned into a loud flushing sound as the fluids spiraled and looped through the multiple and tangled lines of IV tubing. With almost no husband left to claim, Isabella tried her best to hold onto her husband.

"Sweetie, do you hear me? Please give me a sign that you want to stay. Damn it Miguel! Why didn't you get out of the car like he asked? I know the *Leo* in your ass wouldn't allow anything to be taken from you without a fight but damn you, Miguel. Things can be replaced!" Isabella muttered deep regret as she patted his face. He shivered, but the movement was involuntary.

"Shooting me dead is the one thing that will get me out of this room. Hell, it's not a bad idea, because we can go out, side by side." Isabella's hope and strength were leaving her body. Isabella prayed for the end of her own life to be quick and silent.

"You know people say when you are around someone who is in a coma, they should speak joyfully." Encouraging words by Isabella yielded no results. "Baby, please take hold to my voice. Please tell me there is no light and that you are not walking through a tunnel. Squeeze my hand, baby!"

Not one hint of a comeback presented itself. The room now

filled with signs of life nearing its end; scared Isabella. The noise re-entered the room as alarms beeped in a disharmonious manner. The alarms were welcoming death.

Isabella took to her feet and stared at the man she shared her life. Flash backs to their lavish wedding, the birth of their children, and the sensual thoughts of how they showered love upon each other; made her feel as if she'd taken in an intoxicating cocktail of sweet memories.

"Mrs. Valdez, sorry to interrupt, but your children and other family members are back."

"Lisa, I can't look my children in the face again. I cannot do it. Seeing their faces will tear me apart. Will you please take me back to my room?"

"I will take you back in a minute. I will be there right by your side as well as assist you the best way possible in sharing the update. You know they are going to want to know details. It wouldn't be fair to them."

"Excuse me." A tall woman, with flawless skin, interrupted as she invited herself into the room. Isabella's sister was one to envy. A tall, voluptuous woman of exotic origin, with a body certain to receive more hallelujahs than a Sunday morning church service; made her presence hard to deny. The sisters connected eyes and the transfer of feelings charged them both to erupt into tears.

"I need to speak with my sister, Lisa. She will be with here when the children come in. I know they will want to see that I'm still here and doing ok, so I will stay. Afterwards, I will go to my room. My chest hurts; will you bring me more pain medicine? I've been hurting for the last hour."

"I'm not happy with this news! You have to alert me when you are in pain Mrs. Valdez! Ignoring your pain will not help your situation. I will be right back with some more medication." Lisa gave Isabella and her sister a moment alone as she fetched more medicine.

Isabella was concerned on how she would talk to her children without breaking down. The Valdez family was strong and now- the rope that held the family together was unraveling at a record pace.

"Sissy, I'm hurting- I need you."

"I got you Bella. Do you want me to do anything?"

"Yes, help me with the kids. *Please*, keep Devin under control. You know y'all gone have to call security to keep an eye on him, right?"

"I called big brother." Isabella stated between tears.

"Which one?" Sissy abruptly asked as she pulled her head and shoulder's back with her infamous look.

"Big Rico, you know that! Why you ask me like that?"

"I didn't feel like dealing with jackass, Tony. Our last argument was about him cheating on Olivia sent me through the roof. There is still smoke around that damn scene. He's a lousy ass dog. He's lucky Miguel didn't know about that shit. Olivia is the best thing in his life, and it's time she leaves his ass."

"Yeah, you're right. Miguel did not play about that cheating shit! You know, there are some damn good men out there, if women would take the time to see things for what they are; it's possible to take home a winner. Take what fits, is that too hard to do?" Isabella smiled over at her husband.

"Yeah sis, you right. How do bitches want a Dwayne *"The Rock"* Johnson, but they look like Esther from Sanford and Son in the face, T-Pain by the voice, and Razfuchsia by the body!"

"Oh Sissy, no- you- didn't- go there!" the sisters erupted in a laugh that was long overdue. Isabella wiped the tears away.

"I sure in the hell did take a trip there! People need to know God wants us to take care of our bodies. I know mine is the temple of *oh-my-damn*! A lot of sister's need to take a trip there. Once they get there....they will not go back to fat! Hell, I work out two times a day and I down about 1500 calories a day; and it serves this body fine! People have gotten out of hand with the way they eat! Folks are in love with food, like I'm in love with my vibrator."

"I guess you and that toy of yours got married huh?"

"You damn right, our anniversary is coming up! I need a new one really."

"Oh wow! You know- special people exist all over the world! And my sistah, your mark of being *special*, is present!" Isabella grabbed her sister's hand hoping to shake the shame out of her.

"Stop it Bella!" Sissy snatched her hand away. "Yeah, I am as special and serious as a no trespassing sign! People can go to hell with a leather flight jacket on for all I care! If they don't love themselves, then they shouldn't anticipate love from anyone else. Hell, you want me to feel sorry for someone, let's go back and talk about all he blacks being gunned down. Black Lives DO Matter!!! Let's see a change in the way our people are treated and then, only then I will show sympathy, compassion and understanding!"

Not caring to hear her sister go on with one of her infamous speeches, Isabella releases herself to sit bedside with Miguel.

"I'm done with you on this topic! You and Tony had better sweep that bull under someone's rug! I know you two better not cut up in this hospital! Lord knows I done cut up enough for these people to ban me from this damn place, shot or not!"

"Ok Bella! Damn, now will you calm the hell down! You can be damn mean at times!"

"Yeah, well the ice storm is about to settle on in, so you better wrap up. Hell, me and *mean* dated for a long time, didn't you know?" Bella barked.

"Listen up chick, tell the nurse, to give your ass some *get right pills* before you get too damn loose! I'm close to knocking the hell out of you."

"Don't play with me Sissy! You know how sensitive I am

about you or anyone else for that much, talking about us, *crazy* folk. Outside the PR firm, my advocacy for mental health is serious! You play around too much!"

"Oh shit here we go." Sissy bitched as she removed her jacket."

"Are you going to look at Miguel, Sissy?"

"No. Bella, you know how I feel about that. He's not here and I don't want that image sketched in my brain. You know I love him, right?"

"Yes I do. I'm sorry for that."

"What was I talking about?" Isabella queried."

"Yo ass talking crazy." Sissy laughed.

"Like I was saying, play with me 'bout money... wait- not money, but anything else, and I will move on, but mental health; I am *not* having it! Keep on messing with me and I will drop some Seroquel in your drink and have you casting for one of those "*Walking Dead*" episodes!"

"Ok, yo crazy tail ain't serving me a damn thing to drink or eat ever!"

"Here, drink this tea. I didn't want it." Isabella teased as she slid the cup of tea to her sister.

"You know- people who abandon their prescriptions at the pharmacy; outside of financial reasons, are the ones who are crazy, right?" Isabella laughed at her sister.

"Well hell, the Doctor had to say they were crazy in order to get the script in the first place, right?" Sissy smarted off.

"Bitch, crazy is someone like you. You know damn well your doctor was not lying about your ass being bipolar. You only take the medicine when your nerves are rattled. Hell, don't you know it's too late at that point, dummy! Going on and off your medication is not smart!"

"I got ya damn dummy!" Sissy waved Isabella off.

"Look here- *crazy* is when someone like *you*, is given a diagnosis but refuses to take the medicine. I hate it when you become all nervous, moody, manic, and funny acting when you spiral out of control! Hell, at least I'm smart enough to listen to my doctor!"

"Whatever! Damn, did you see that doctor walk by? Fine as hell! Somewhat young, but I'm sure he can be tamed." Sissy opened the curtain, hoping to catch the young Doctor's eye.

"I'm not listening to you, Sissy.

"Look, Rico said once he was done at the crime scene and talking with a few detectives, he would get here soon." Sissy said as she kept eyeing the young doctor.

"Who's in charge of the case and why in the hell is Rico at the scene when he should be here with you?" Isabella quizzed.

"Your guess is better than mine."

"You know your brother and nephew have heads hotter than the inside of a motor! Think about it- you got one who gets his *street justice* legally and the other...well you know how Devin gets down!" Isabella reminded her frustrated Sissy.

"He dispatched a car to trail Devin. Leila and Miguel Jr. are on the way." Isabella was concerned that her youngest child, Devin the Rebel- would use his time grazing the streets like a hungry, ravaged fool looking to bag the bodies of the losers that assaulted his family like dirty laundry."

Devin was Isabella's tough, do no good, unless he felt good, kid. If he wasn't looking for trouble, trouble was looking for him. Seems Devin's union with trouble was destined. Devin was prepared to set anyone crooked- straight! He was the one kid who hung close to his father. He helped his father operate his promotions company as well as manage his chain of nightclubs. His father opened his first club when he was twenty-three years old. His vision of creating the ultimate club experience was something he dreamed. Being a natural at socializing as well as known for throwing great parties, Mr. Valdez was not going to live far from his passion- his dream. After years of hard work, his dreams became reality. Celebrities, athletes' and entrepreneurs kept his nightclubs full. Receiving the golden stamp by household celebrities was the birth of his brand.

"Handle it all Sissy! Right now, I can't deal with a dead husband *and* a dead child! Devin will not put anymore gray hairs on my head! I'm tired of dying my damn hair!"

"How long will it be before Miguel Jr. and Leila arrives? I was sure they were out of town."

"No, Miguel's case load has been light since he and Jacqueline had the baby. Your jet setting, storytelling, world renowned journalist, and photo snapping niece is in between assignments. They should be here soon."

"Ok. Anything else you want me to do?"

"Yes, Father Ortega was supposed to be here about an hour and a half ago, I had the nurse page him again. Could you call him again? He knows the timeframe we are working with. If he cannot make it, we can use the house Chaplin." In the midst of Isabella and her sister talking, the flat screen television centered inside the nurses command station, reported the horrid incidents Isabella and her husband fell victim to.

"Early this morning philanthropist, promotions mogul and international nightclub owner, Miguel Valdez, along with his wife, Isabella Valdez, owner of the Valdez PR Firm, was gunned down at the corner of Skinker and Forest Park Expressway, in what appeared to be an attempted robbery. Sources from the St. Louis City Police Department and a local EMS crew, reported the scene as a blood bath." The reporter told the story with great detail.

"Behind me is the bullet riddled Bentley owned by Mr. Valdez. Reports made, show four suspects approached the car, two from each side, with their weapons drawn. After Mr. Valdez, refused to exit his car, he reached for his gun and began shooting. His wife, still contained in the vehicle started shooting her weapon as well. Killed at the scene were two suspects. There is report that two other suspects, escaped with injuries. Both victims are in treatment at a local area hospital. No update report is available on the couple's progress.

"Ricardo Valdez, a St. Louis City police officer and the brother of Miguel Valdez, delivered a potent message for the attackers at hand. Officer Valdez promised that rest was no longer on his agenda and the SLPD will not cease until the remaining attackers are behind bars. Officer Valdez prays the thugs turn themselves in and confess their actions, before payback lands on their doorstep. Strong words for the hardened criminals at large."

"Them motherfuckers! Sissy cried.

"Officer Valdez, now on leave to attend to family affairs; urges the public to help by calling the tip lines. If anyone has information, please call the crime stoppers hotline to provide information. The police department sends a reminder, that all calls will remain anonymous! Please call the hotline number at the bottom of the screen. In addition, a one million-dollar reward for the arrest of the suspects at large, is on the table. Law enforcement needs your help in washing these criminal off the streets. I will continue to cover this story as details surface. For now, this is Eric Bennington reporting from the intersection of Forest Park Expressway and Skinker, for *News Channel Six*."

"Girl, they don't waste time putting stuff on the news." Sissy voiced in a disgusted tone. "Are you guys listed under the black-out unit? Your names and the hospital's name should remain private. You never know if those fools will try to come here and shoot up the place. I need to speak with the hospitals communications director to ensure your privacy remains intact! We cannot afford any slip ups. Damn, one million dollars, Sissy?"

"Well Cicely what you want them to do? Now if they failed to put it on the news, you would be bitching about that! Yes, one million is enough to make anyone snitch on those thugs! I am not playing around! You think we gone get somewhere with a five thousand dollar reward?" Isabella stared at her sister with disgust. She loved her big sister, but she hated how she ignorant she acted at times. No matter how pissed she became, Isabella could not stay mad long because she knew her sister was dealing with her set of mental issues. Nevertheless, urges to slap the hell out of her sister for refusing to follow her psychiatrist's instructions were constant.

"Hell, a cheap reward like that is the same as income tax season coming twice in one year! Whoever turns them in will blow through that money like wind, through fall leaves! No, I'm sticking with the million-dollar reward amount."

"Look Bella, I see you're pissed when you call me by my birth name, I'm sorry. You know the reason why they put your story on the news, right? You and Miguel have done a lot for this lousy ass city, and well...your money and celebrity helps! Now, they know damn well black folks get shot up and bagged like groceries all-the-damn day long, but do you hear about that crap on the news? Hell, it's sad when blacks have to hire a damn PR firm, go on marches and start a movement to introduce their missing children to the world. It's as if black children don't matter. They write our children off before they get out the fucking crib. Thinking way back, that damn Shawn Hornbeck story made it to every television with a satellite signal. Our stories only matter when we kill one of their own." Too tired to answer her beyond crazy, big sister, Isabella dismissed her sister's bullshit with a roll of her eyes.

Isabella's mute button was now activated.

"You know how I feel about this lousy state! The *Show Me State*, will show your ass how much they living in the past. Last to exit slavery-"

"Get your facts right on that!" Isabella Laughed.

"Hush, you know what I'm getting at! Majority of the streets on the Southside was named after former slave owners and the whole feeling of segregation still surviving and striving in this state like dope; makes me sick as hell!" Isabella hung her head as low as an Ostrich and released a deep sigh. Isabella knew no amount of money could ever extract the North side from her Sissy's DNA. At times Isabella had a hard time telling if it was the bipolar disorder, or her sister being the worst bitch ever.

"Please shut the fuck up!" Isabella snapped.

"Nope, you got me going now, Bella. Police pulling black folks over in record numbers in Ferguson, West County, and other grimey municipalities should speak volumes to you. They're lightning fast to lock your black ass away, money or not! Slavery still exists; it's more mental than physical now."

"I see the *hood,* still has your address!" Isabella spoke with added sickness.

"Right on! *Hood* keeps me sharp and able to shoot down any bullshit traveling my way! Baby sis, you know bullshit does not have flight rewards over here." Sissy responded as she pretended to dust off her shoulders.

"You better go find a new pair of shoes and take those two, goody-goodies off! I respect white people, but the way they have treated us since we were tricked into slavery...,"

"Oh shit, here we go with the slavery spill! Shut up!"

"Ok, what's this shit with white folks getting *their* country back? For the first time in life, we have a black President and the country is off the rocker and treading hell all over the earth. They got their guns out, bleaching their hoods all while looking for the lighter fluid and matches."

Clueless, Isabella was afraid to ask, but her deer in the headlight look, gave the right ahead for her Sissy to continue talking trash!

"Burn the cross....white hoods...the KKK!" The entire ER watched in shock as the two sisters exchange words for at least another five minutes. Tired and embarrassed by their show, Lisa ended the chaos by announcing a trauma call. The naturalistic chaos and urgency of the ER returned.

"You never cease to embarrass us. You need to grow up and release that anger, Cicely." Focusing on the situation at hand, Cicely calmed down and focused on her sister.

"Bella, do you want to see Miguel once more? Sissy asked before she called for the nurse to bring the rest of the family in.

"I don't know what I want to do."

"Look Bella, you are going to mess around and have a heart attack! Why are you standing? I thought you were to stay off your feet."

"I'm ok. Give me a second Sissy." Cicely left the room with her head bowed, appearing to be engaged in deep prayer. Even though her sister proved to be the Devil's roll dog at times, she proved to be a powerful prayer warrior. Through her rough humor, Cicely always mentioned how she was the hardest cookie in the batch. She knew it was tough for folks to deal with her at times. Yet, she was a firm believer of Christ's love for her. The judgment of others never got to her. She tried her best in using discernment when it came to speaking or acting out on things.

Yet, no matter how hard she tried at times, the worst of the situation managed to pull away her best. With that, she contained good in her heart and toted hell around in her expensive handbags. The girl was a true work of art. Hell everyone needs a touch-up here and there.

"Miguel, if this is the last time you hear my voice; know that I cherished hearing yours for ten lifetimes. Don't hold on for me. If you're ready, go. I trust you with the big man. Whether he takes you or send you back to us, I know it's all his will." Isabella released pain through her cracked and weakened voice. Before she knew what was going on, her knees buckled, and her arms crossed her chest. The words and tears lodged inside her throat caused a burning pain in her chest. She began pounding her chest hoping it would help release the rest of her goodbyes as well as the breath taking pain she was experiencing.

Trapped pain continued snatching each breath away making it harder for her to breathe. With each attempt to inhale, her lungs stabbed her heart. She opened and closed her eyes more than a dozen times, praying the next time she opened them; she would find herself traveling to eternity with Miguel. Dying together was better than living alone.

Falling onto the bed of her husband screaming in a bewildered mode, Isabella found herself trying to steal her husband from deaths grip. With pain still centered and radiating throughout her entire chest cavity, she found a way to release her anger, her fear, her depression and what she hoped...her last breath.

Finding her center, Isabella took to her feet.

"Who am I fooling? Lord, forgive me for acting as if you don't know your child. It's hard giving way to your will sometimes." Crying over her husband's frail chest for the last time, she wiped his face, and added more Carmex to his chapped, blood stained lips. His once exotic and envy invoking skin, whitened by the minuet. She squeezed his hand once more as if some of her energy would revive him.

"I love you baby! Thank you for the kids, the love, the good, and the bad. Go home." Isabella gathered up what strength she had left, and called for her Sissy as she waivered alongside her husband's bed. Her frame wavering like a flag at half-staff was a signal for help. Her hands trembled as her heart tried to find a normal pace. She felt her aura dissipating into the air. Isabella tried to go one way, when she was going another way... face forward onto the floor.

Chapter 4

"Mrs. Valdez...Mrs. Valdez, can you hear me?" The nurse yelled while batting her bright blue eyes. Yelling louder than necessary made it seem as if Isabella was deafer than deaf itself. Moving from one routine to the next, while popping her gum like an insignificant hooker on a truck stop, seemed to be the nurses natural manner of being. Isabella was dizzy and confused. Murmuring and shaking her head as she shied from the bright lights above her bed; was all she could do. As Mrs. Valdez tried to raise her head, a quick choke slammed her back onto the pillow. Her eyes filled with tears and fear. Her breathing filled with panic as she tried to free her hands. Each attempt to raise her head brought forth pain. During surgery for the gunshot wounds, the doctor decided to keep Isabella on the ventilator, due to her heart rhythm converting several times during surgery.

"Mrs. Valdez, you had a heart attack. Now buttercup, I am giving you some pain medicine, and a new nitroglycerin patch. The doctor took care of your wounds." Isabella eyes searched for freedom. Blink once if you understand me sweetie pie!" The nurse continued yelling. The nurse proved to be the difference in what a day makes, compared to Nurse Lisa. Hair greasy and wet with sweat beads rolling over her body, the nurse continued working her country tail off. "Progression from here sugar pie!" The nurse chimed out.

Isabella's stubbornness returned to an unusual extent. Destined to set fire to the nurse, Isabella's eyes zoomed in, and released laser beams hot enough to melt gold, while violently shaking and bucking her body like a wild horse.

"Calm down beautiful. Don't force me to put you back under. I want you off the drugs long enough to get that tubing out." Isabella was once again, living in the world of mute.

"Stop bucking Mrs. Valdez! Oh Lordy be! Don't make me get orders to put you back under. Now you choose sweetie! What do you wanna do, huh?"

Isabella motioned enough anger to raise her middle finger to salute the nurse and resumed her rodeo. The nurse disappeared and quickly returned with a glass vial filled with liquid, a syringe, alcohol pads, and saline. Isabella knew what was about to happen, but giving a damn was the last thing on her list, and she continued bucking away. The nurse and Isabella connected eyes as they each took a mental snapshot of the bitch they battled.

Isabella's wild bucking transformed into a slow, slumping pump. The drugs pushed into her IV line ended her rodeo. With Isabella defeated, the nurse snapped her fingers as she walked out the room.

Chapter 5

"**H**ey there sweetness!" The hungry looking nurse called out. Do you know what today's date is?" Isabella remained silent. "You know you were out for a while. Look at ya, a new day and I still find you, raising all kinds of hell."

"Look here heifer, are you hungry or something?"

"What? Who are you talking to like that you train wrecked, Diva? I don't care about who you are. No one disrespects me like that!" The nurse said as she took a defensive stance.

"Look here hungry Jill, you been calling out every food dish you can think of, since I first saw you! Will you please call me by my name? Not after some sugary snack you inhaled at lunch." Numb from Isabella's stinger tongue, the nurse continued humming while assessing her hell patient.

"How in the hell am I supposed to know the damn date?" Isabella hissed through her sore and raspy voice. The intubation tube left in her throat for two days contributed to soreness and a change in her voice.

"Why you want to know? You know what damn day this is. Quit playing with me, and go find some food to eat, and stop insulting my intelligence! Where is my Miguel?" Isabella asked as she searched the room. A quick jab to the heart motioned for a quick pause as reality walked back into her life. She fell into a sick, depressing, and heart-wrenching crying spell.

"Mrs. Valdez, I am sorry," the nurse explained as she hustled to close the sliding glass door. The nurse gathered her composure and tried her best not to cry. With her patient's pain transparent, the nurse rushed to hold her. "Do you remember your husband passing away Mrs. Valdez?" the nurse questioned as she grabbed a wet cloth to dab Isabella's tears away.

"It's been three days since. The moment you fell ill with

another heart attack, your husband coded. They were able to revive him to perform the transplant surgery."

"What? Why did they have the funeral before I could get out of here?" Isabella asked as she turned to the side, making a new crescent in her pillow; giving her tears a new place to puddle.

"Remember...think back Mrs. Valdez. Your husband's licensed gave consent for organ donations. You signed the papers in the emergency room. Once your husband went into arrest, the ER staff worked very hard to bring him back for the surgery. Do you remember how hard the staff worked to keep him alive while you were there with him?"

"No, I don't."

"To answer the other question, your family has not moved forward with the service. They knew you would be upset if they did that."

"Where is Nurse Lisa?"

"Oh yes, Lisa has been here for you and your family. Your family has taken a liking to her."

"This is the ICU. But none of that matters, because Lisa said she was coming to see you today."

"Am I good enough to go home?"

"Dr. Martins, our ICU doctor, will be here to talk to you in a few."

"Oh come on, tell me!"

"That's the doctor's job."

"How 'bout this- if I give you a cheesecake, will you talk then?"

"Is there something else you need Mrs. Valdez?" The nurse said in an annoyed tone.

"Where's my family?"

"They are in the waiting room. The doctor has given your sister a report and she is aware of your special care instructions. You need to focus on getting out of this ICU, move forward to the step down unit. Your loved ones have stated that no services for your husband will occur until your discharge."

"This *is* a dream, right?"

"I'm afraid not, Mrs. Valdez. I wish your visit was due to a bad fall,"

"Really, a bad fall?" Isabella was pissed.

"Ok, how about the flu?"

"To late to clean that shit up."

"We both know that is not the case. Now you rest, the plastic surgeon will be here to consult with you about repairing the lacerations on both sides of your face. Your lacerations were freed of glass and cleaned out properly. Right now, there is gel-like glue on your face, to help mend the laceration until surgery. Please try your best not to pick at it. They wanted to wait another day or two, to see if you are strong enough for the other surgery."

"Sleep is all I want, Nurse Betty."

"Nurse Betty? Are you talking about the movie, Sugar? You think we look alike?" The nurse smiled.

"Only in the face. Go to lunch, and stop calling me out like food at the market. Do you talk to all your patients like this?"

"Ok, fair enough, I apologize. My southern upbringing is hard to dissolve."

"Oh wow...I hit it on the head!" Isabella stated while nodding. "So, you're a true country girl, huh?"

"Born and raised in good old Georgia. I moved to St. Louis three years ago because my husband's job laid him off. Two job offers came a month later, and it was either St. Louis or Wisconsin."

"Gotta do what you gotta do." Isabella sighed.

"I'm ready to sleep the rest of my life away. I'm really tired, but my brain won't shut down."

"You hush now. Let this sleep grab you." Nurse Betty comforted Isabella as she pulled out another cocktail. Holding the syringe to the light, the nurse re-checked the dosage and thumped the syringe a few more times with her index finger to rid the air bubbles. Before she counted to three, Nurse Betty had injected unconscious peace into her patient.

Chapter 6

"Look at these damn people! Death and tragedy surround them, yet they stand desensitized to the value of human life." Isabella bitched while shaking her head in pity as she watched staff members walk past her room. In a moment of wonderment, she was curious in knowing how people could become immune to their work and the circumstances surrounding them. She wanted to know if they would be able to digest Gods main entrée of life, served with a side plate of grave deep grief, if devastation visited their doorstep.

"Hey, why in the hell are you looking in here? You know damn well your wife looks nothing like Sally Richardson!" Isabella yelled to the man peering through her glass door. Isabella's bitter sense of sarcastic humor returned for the third quarter.

"Can someone tell me where in the hell do folks hide mirrors in this place? Damn, I guess since folks are sick and near death, they shouldn't give a hot damn about how they look, huh? Lord, get me out of here!"

After calming her nerves, Isabella began to reflect on her own actions. She battled with the thought of being careless and stupid enough to view Miguel as her Savior. She questioned if she was grateful enough for all the great things the Lord bestowed upon her. Now humbled, Isabella sought understanding.

"Mrs. Valdez? Who are you speaking to?"

"The good Lord, I hope he hears me."

"How are you doing? Do you need something to drink?" Lisa asked as she sat her purse and jacket on the chair next to Isabella's bed.

"I'm in deep thought sweetheart. My mind- it's traveled to so many places to where it needs a passport."

"I understand. I am so grateful to see you looking well. Dr.

Bronson did a great job on your face! You look great."

"Yes, he was fantastic. I will have to refer him to everyone, including my sister. Girl gets so many Botox injections; she looks excited when she sleeps!"

"Oh no, there goes that raw and *nice-nasty* humor!"

Lisa and Isabella held hands as they smiled at each other. The bond between the two was unbreakable. Within the next moment, a light breeze laced with a sensual fragrance kissed Mrs. Valdez.

"Miguel?" The scent and soft wind continued brushing along Isabella's neck as she searched the room hoping to see her husband. "Is that you baby? I see you still love to kiss me there." Lisa stood back and decided to go to the back of the room to look out the window. With her eyes closed, Isabella caressed her neck; forgetting all soreness and pain. It was the lips of her husband that drew a smile upon her face. A moment of joy appeared. Sitting up in her bed, Isabella tried to catch her husband, but his presence started to fade away. With that, tears and pain returned.

"Oh my Lord, why did he have to leave?" Isabella was lost and her desire to find a way through her ordeal was in need of strength. They were all each other knew. Marriage in their young adult years was the beginning of their life.

Both had impeccable work ethics, great people skills and were positive about the outcome of their success. Success was a thought they feasted upon quite often. Coming up, the two of them worked as if they were a superhero duo. Miguel worked hard while Isabella controlled the home front; all while attaining her Masters in Communications. Miguel worked hard while saving and investing his money. A former product of the streets, Miguel's hustle instinct never left him. He was relentless in ensuring his family lived the best life possible. His love for his family forced him to leave the game.

His love for music and entertainment led him on another

journey. Miguel opened his first club on the west coast in 1989. His vision for entertaining the best of the best was without limit. By the end of his second year, Miguel was working on opening three more clubs, in Miami, New York, Atlanta.

Isabella was not far behind her husband. After college, she was busy building one of the largest PR firms in the country. The PR firm and the nightclub had one thing in common...rich people. The rich loved to party and at some point in their career, they needed rescuing out of bad situations.

In 1994, Miguel hired his baby boy Devin to help manage and supervise half of his father's nightclubs. Devin's electric and raw personality helped grow the business into a new stratosphere. Devin had plenty of street sense, and like his father, he knew what people wanted. The clubs were successful because people of every age, and background had a place designated for them to party within the clubs.

"Mrs. Valdez, are you ok?" Lisa asked.

"Just thinking of the past."

"I will be back, Mrs. Valdez. I'm going to bring your family in so *everyone* hears your discharge instructions! I asked them in because I do not want you cutting up once you are discharged. Your blood pressure has been stable; don't mess that up now!"

"I'm going to live the best I know how. I will take whatever comes my way. My heart has a block in it and it's only a matter of time before it blows." Isabella cried about her fate as she glared past happiness and took a sharp right turn down the road of darkness. Looking for happiness was the last thing on her mind. If she was given the key to heaven right now, she would be halfway up the stairway.

"Relax, Mrs. Valdez, it's going to be ok, you got me to help you along! I'm not going anywhere. Your family has my contact information! I'm not going to let you go through this alone."

"You are a God send Lisa."

"I will be right back." Lisa exited the room with joy in her heart. Isabella felt blessed to have met a wonderful young woman like Lisa.

"Hey there momma!" Leila cried while covering her face.

"Hey momma!" Miguel Jr. greeted as he extended his long and masculine body across his mother's bed.

"Hey momma, you looking a lot better. When you feel like it, we need to talk." Devin the Rebel told his mother.

"Look here son, I'm not in the mood to discuss anything with you right now. Your uncle has told you all everything there is to know. I do not want to re-live that night. It's bad enough I can't stop blaming myself or wishing I would have allowed your father to go home the way he wanted."

"Sorry momma. I will let it go- for now." Devin hinted. He was not about to release anything into God's hands.

Isabella's baby girl, Leila, cried as she fell into her the chair next to her mother's bed. Shaken, her head took comfort in her mother's lap. Decent and pure at heart, Leila would not fight a midget even if he tripped her. She was soft, and trimmed with poised grace. Her spirit was gentle, open, and willing to understand whatever came her way. Yet, the murder of her father drilled a hole in the core of her niceness, but she found a way to stand strong. Isabella was proud of her daughter. All those years of going to school, one would have thought Leila was going to be a doctor. Instead, she graduated with a degree in journalism. Her daughter's love for photography and writing stories helped shaped her career path.

"What are you thinking about momma?" Leila asked.

"I remember how your father and I had to sneak on our vacations, when we wanted a 'picture free' vacation. I remember every time we came home from a trip you would ask for the film so you could develop the pictures. You remember that?"

"Yes momma! I loved trips."

"Girl, you *loved* pictures." Laughing aloud, Miguel Jr. embraced the memories as well.

"Yeah momma, Leila had a way of describing things. Hell, made me want to go back to a many vacation spots." Miguel Jr. spoke as he thumped his baby sister on her head.

"Yeah, the little devil had gazillions of cameras. My question though, was why did you always have snot running down your nose when you took pictures?" Devin teased as he fell back laughing.

"Shut up Devin!" Leila snapped as she tried to pinch her brother. "Yeah, she would present us with highlights about our trip. Afterwards, she wanted interrogate- oops, I meant interview people about their experience." Devin teased his sister even more.

"Yup, we had our own star in the making. Miguel Jr. smiled at his sister.

"Ok Devin, why did you have to take a dump in *every* pool, on *every* vacation we took? Devin will you ever release information as to why you always walked around the house with a dirty booty?" Leila asked while pretending to be in a one on one interview with her brother.

"Ouch! Sis got you him on that one!" Miguel Jr. blew the heat off his trigger finger.

"You play too damn much! Why you gotta go there Leila?" Devin asked with his mouth wide open as he snatched away from his sister's arms. Harmonious laughter rang from the room. You would have thought Isabella's children were teenagers with the way they teased and fought each other.

"You see how it feels right? Keep it up punk, and Facebook will see the *real* Devin Valdez!" Leila teased.

"Yeah dude, dad even named you, stink pot!" Everyone in the room all laughed aloud as they covered their mouth's hoping no one could hear the circus was in town.

"Ok, it's good to hear laughter." Lisa announced as she came into the room with Mrs. Valdez's discharge papers.

"Oh damn, you looking good today, nurse Lisa." Devin

complemented Lisa as he checked her out.

"Damn, baby *is PHAT!*" Devin smiled as he buttered his lips with Chap Stick.

"Boy shut up! This is a good girl and she does not need your rough neck tail. You got too many women! Plus, you know your little ass is a throwback!" Isabella clapped back.

Thinking back to their conversation they had in the E.R., Lisa and Mrs. Valdez erupted into belly aching laughter!

"Oh *now* I see how that works Mrs. Valdez." Lisa gave Mrs. Valdez a high-five.

"Ok, I see now! Yawl gone play me like that, huh?"

"Devin, please give me some peace! I'm trying to get the hell out of here!"

"Yes momma." Devin whispered knowing how close he was to seeing his mother's bad side. Grown or not, Isabella's children knew where to draw the line with their mother.

"I talked with the doctor and he approved me going over your discharge instructions. He felt you wasn't paying too much attention to him Mrs. Valdez. What was up with that?"

"You know how my mind travels, Lisa."

"Yeah, I need to seize your passport."

"Oh child you are a mess." After Lisa gave strict and precise instructions on Mrs. Valdez's after care, the doctor invited himself in the room, wanted or not. Everyone in the room agreed that it would take Jesus and all his disciples to keep Isabella on track.

"Oh Lord, please help us." Sissy begged.

"Be good Mrs. Valdez." Lisa begged Isabella

"Ok, I will. I'm going to make the best of this mess, Lisa."

"Good. I left my personal information on another sheet of paper in case you ever feel the need to talk. I want you to know that I care and that I'm not treating you or any of my patients for that much, as another chart in the rack!"

"Thanks love."

"Goodbye Mrs. Valdez. I gotta get to work."

"Young lady don't you walk away from me without giving me a hug. Oh yeah, never say goodbye! See you later will do fine."

"Ok, see you later." The women hugged each other and Lisa waved goodbye to the rest of the family as she grabbed her items. Not long after her exit, Isabella sat up in her bed.

"Let me tell you *all* something! First, God has his hand on this. I know we all are hurting and we all want vengeance, but you know vengeance belongs to the Lord. Rico...Devin..., I want you to look me dead center and promise that you will not go on some type of *thug hunt*." Devin and his uncle both nodded their heads and vowed to be on their best behavior. *Devin had his fingers crossed.*

"These thugs do not give one hot damn about your father, or us. If I hear any of you partaking in evil, I *will* turn you in my damn self!"

"Well the Sheriff has spoken!" Sissy cited as she backed her sister up with a dirty mouthed speech of her own.

"Ok! Now everyone get out. Sissy, you bring my clothes?"

"Chanel for the Queen!"

"Cicely I don't feel the runway stuff!"

"Huh? There you go getting mad. We are divas all the time. I got the sunglasses, the scarf, perfume, purse, shoes, and your outfit ready!" Sissy sassed on.

"Ok, do what you want because you always do."

"Good, about time you recognized authority!"

"Hey Leila, grab two thank-you cards from the gift shop. Oh yeah, buy a couple dozen roses." Without question, Leila carried out her mother's request.

"Mom, I'm going to whip the Maybach around."

"The Maybach? Couldn't we be more discreet?"

"Don't worry mom, everything is fine. I will be waiting for you all in valet. Uncle Rico got a couple of undercover cops following us to the house. The private security firm will be there afterwards, patrolling the house." Miguel Jr. announced as he grabbed his Armani trench, with cool ease. Dressed from head to toe, Isabella's oldest was the poster man for *damn fine* and he knew it.

"Junior, I want to go to the Ritz or Chase Park Plaza. I'm not ready to go home. Not alone."

"Bella, I'm going home with you. We won't do anything to the house until you tell us to."

"I said I wanted to get away! Please don't make me raise up off this damn bed!"

"No problem mom." Miguel Jr. interrupted with his hands separating his mother and aunt.

"Ok, I will make the changes for you, Bella. Sorry."

"It's ok. Make sure you tell them we want to enter from the back, and inform the manager, no one else needs to know my whereabouts. Matter of fact; put the room in Leila's name. I am not ready to face the press."

"Hey Bella, I will be there to handle the security details soon after you arrive." Rico said as he grabbed his jacket.

"Rico, where is your brother?"

"*Your* brother is dealing with some mess on the home front, if you know what I mean." Rico responded

"Oh hell, here we go. Tell Tony to get it right! Don't bring that bull near me!" Isabella yelled out to Rico as he exited the room.

"Hey momma, here are the cards and flowers you requested."

"Thanks baby. Tell the head doctor I want to see him in about twenty minutes. Give me time to get dressed."

"You need me to help you."

"Sure, I can use all the help I can get, but let the doctor know, first."

After getting dressed, Isabella was ready to wish her doctor farewell.

"Mrs. Valdez you look great, considering the circumstances."

"Glad I look good because I feel like a zombie."

"Part of it is the pain from your shoulder surgery, and the other part is you're drained- physically and emotionally. Please accept my condolences. Your husband was a great man."

"Thank you."

"Look, please make sure the hospital's CEO gets this card and please make sure Lisa Baker, the nurse from the E.R., receives this card."

"Sure, no problem at all."

"Thank you for all you have done. These flowers are for you and the other dozen is for Nurse Betty."

"Thank you! Now which nurse are you referring to?" The doctor looked confused.

"I'm sorry, the nurse with the deep southern accent."

"Ok, I know who you're talking about." The doctor flashed a warm smile.

"She answers to Nurse Betty with me. It's an inside joke."

"I got it!" The doctor smiled as he finished with his last look over of Isabella.

"You didn't have to buy me flowers Mrs. Valdez."

"I did too, you did great work!"

"Ok, thank you Mrs. Valdez. I wish you all the best. Good luck."

"Thank you, Sir!"

On the way to the main level of the hospital, a smile came across Isabella's face. She knew the million-dollar check she left with the doctor would make the hospital's CEO grin a few times over. Miguel and Isabella shared deep passion when it came to philanthropy. As for Lisa, she wondered how her face would look once she saw the hundred thousand dollar check. Isabella hoped her offer for Lisa to become her personal nurse for the next six months, would lure her from the hospital for a while. Isabella had grown fond of Lisa and she wanted only the best involved in her recovery.

Chapter 7

Funeral services for Mr. Valdez turned out to be a larger than life. His passion for living life to the fullest was the message penetrating throughout the cathedral.

"I love the purple momma."

"Leila, does everything look good? Do you think we are sending your father off right?"

"There's no question about it mom."

"You do know why purple was your father's favorite color?"

"Yup, we all know purple means royalty. He lived the best life ever."

With the casket open from head to toe, visitors were able to admire Mr. Valdez for one last time. Isabella hired a fashion designer to gather his going home attire. His attire- a brand new, white Armani suit with a lavender shirt, accessorized with a deep colored violet tie and a rose pink handkerchief; gave him a look beyond pristine. White Armani dress shoes, with his favorite white fedora tilted to the right finished the look. His favorite brand of Davidoff cigars was propped snugly between two fingers of his smoking hand. This was how people saw Mr. Valdez while entertaining or out and about.

Hands of an anointed individual restored his face to perfection. Isabella was in awe when she viewed him alone. Isabella knew this would be the last time she saw him. At times, Isabella felt drawn to jump in the casket with her husband; nevertheless, she reserved her feelings and continued to model the semblance of a strong willed widow.

Beautiful melodic songs of remembrance echoed throughout the cathedral. Mrs. Valdez went the distance for her husband. The interior of his casket, padded in deep purple plush velour with his name embroidered in thread, spun with gold filaments; was breathtaking. Depending on the angle in which one stood while viewing the casket, the mother of pearl glaze atop of the lilac colored casket, gave a cast of brilliant shine, which revealed small flakes of diamonds within the paint.

Erected at the guest sign-in was a large eleven, by twenty-foot message board. The board, adorned with angels and doves displayed his name, inked in purple and gold. It was a tasteful design. Everyone who came to the service felt compelled to add his or her own sentiment to the board.

Flowers sat around his casket with platinum handles. The abundance of flowers obstructed the casket's view. Before the service started, the funeral director had his assistants load a van with the steady incoming of floral arrangements. Isabella had plans to plant the remaining flowers in garden and throughout their home.

"Baby please let me know when the service will start. I know people want to have the chance to see me, but I'm tired." Isabella grew weaker with each apology and hug.

"Mom, give me a minute and I will inform the Chaplin and funeral director that we are ready to start. I'm going to go find Lisa."

"Thanks baby." Devin sprinted to find relief for his mother.

The seventh guestbook was soon to be full and the crowd continued to grow. Celebrities, political officials, media, athlete's, and people from across the nation came to show their final respects. The card box overflowed and the funeral director informed Rico that he will need to find someone to take the five card boxes with him. Isabella stared at the boxes with sadness because the Lord knew she was nowhere ready to send what seemed to be over a million, thank you cards to everyone in attendance.

After the service, the funeral procession blocked off traffic for endless miles. Five white mother of pearl Bentley's and a fleet of five to six-hundred cars, tagged behind the police motorcade. The city halted in honor of the Valdez Family.

Packed beyond capacity, the cemetery was a maze of hell. The police was busy detouring cars from entering the cemetery.

Weak and tired, Isabella cried for the end to come. Deep within, the service was the only thing allowing her to see her husband for the last time. Deceased or not, the only thing that mattered to Isabella was being close to Miguel. Strength escaped her body, leaving her as lifeless and dry as a lily on a summer grave. Knowing her position and considering how her family looked to her for strength, she was ready for someone to be her foundation.

"Momma is looking bad Miguel. Can we please get her out of here?" Devin pleaded as her nervously eyeballed his mother.

"I'm in route little bro. I need you to handle the rest of things."

"I got it." Devin signaled Lisa for her assistance.

"Momma, you can't do this any longer. You need to get to the car. Devin will stay behind to tie up loose ends."

"How far we have to walk?"

"Not even fifty steps. We are close the outer circle."

"Ok baby."

"Lisa, come with us. Momma's going to need some medicine and her blood pressure taken. You did bring her meds, right?"

"Miguel, don't worry. All her meds are in the bag along with the blood pressure kit. We have everything we need."

"Thanks Lisa. Let's move out." Isabella took one more look at her husband's casket.

"See you soon my love."

Lily Lee
Chapter 8

"Who left this entrée sitting without calling it out? What in the hell do I have to do in order to get some *real* results? People, we are a team and we have a system! If no one is going to use it--- I advise you not to come back after your lunch break!" Chef Lily Lee yelled as she dished out her best Chef Ramsey impersonation; while throwing pots and pans at her kitchen crew. Her kitchen was the second stage set for Hell's Kitchen. Compared to Lily Lee, Chef Ramsey looked softer than Kleenex.

"I don't give a damn if she *is* a top chef, I'm about to knock her to the bottom." Adrienne murmured as she cut her eyes at Lily.

"Wow, did I hear you say something? Lily questioned as she walked towards Adrienne. The tension between Lily Lee and Adrienne burned hotter than the kitchen itself.

"Look, I'm a damn good assistant, I've been here the longest with you, and I'm tired of all the drama and that jacked up ego of yours!" Adrienne flipped into effect mode. Her sharp and jerky movements welcomed confrontation. "Smile for the camera, greet your star studded, fake-ass patrons and you come right back here- full of shit as always; talking about them to us, and us to them! Whose damn side you on?" Adrienne questioned as she threw a pair of tongs down on the kitchen floor. "Shit, never mind that question, it's a given who you side with. You are out of control and I'm tired of this shit!"

"You know today is the last of you, right?" Lily screamed as she snatched her cap off.

"Amen and an *overdue* Hallelujah! Come on and cut my

check now!" Lily was full of rage; her reddened face showed her boiling point. Lily's eyes searched every angle of her kitchen for something to throw. Never had anyone rattled Lily's pots and pans, like Adrienne.

"Get out! Get out now! Clock out, and leave your jacket!"

"Damn, never has a bitch felt pleasure like this! I'm out!" Like a sellout, Adrienne called out those left standing. "Y'all know y'all can't stand her! You bitches are just as disgusting as her entrées! Damn cowards!" Adrienne yelled as she exited through the double white doors.

"Anyone in agreement with her has thirty seconds to get the hell-out-my-damn-kitchen!" Everyone continued working as if nothing went down. "If you have issues, approach me! We can talk and you know that! However, when we are on the floor and those restaurant doors open- its show time! Do you think those people out there give a shit about your personal issues? All they want is something good to eat! Come straight or take your crooked asses' home! I promise...I won't be mad!"

No one wanted to talk, and the kitchen's direction shifted. Assistants moved on to the next station taking on their new roles to cover Adrienne's absence, in silence. Lily threw all of her anger onto each of their chopping boards. It was her way of letting them know how easy their head could land on the chopping block.

"Good, glad we all *love* each other!" Chef Dezi, come on over and take command. I will be back in a few minutes, I have a table request." Lily stepped off the floor and into her office. She checked her make-up, kicked off her flats and stepped into a fierce pair of chili pepper red, Jimmy Choo's, changed jackets and strutted onto the dining floor.

"Ok, let's move to the groove. Full house and the Chef Lee's depending on us to knock shit out! Only one take back order yesterday, so let's aim for ZERO today! Is everyone on time with production?"

"Yes, Chef Dezi!" The kitchen staff sang in unison as their bodies loosened. Vegetables were being chopped; beef, lamb, salmon, and chicken sizzled on the grill. The smell of vibrant seasonings mixed with the scent of charred hickory smoke teased the stomachs of the hungry patrons as they entered the restaurant.

"Damn, now this smells like a kitchen fo-sho!" Darrell yelled out as he did his favorite James Brown dance move across the kitchen to the sink to rinse his vegetables. Everyone was finally able to start laughing again! Poor fools, everyone working for Lily knew with every shift worked, the feeling of working in a pressure cooker for eight hours, felt worse than third degree burns. Yet, giving a damn deemed too much of an effort for the crew, because they knew the rewards they could reap from cooking beside Lily Lee. It was a great learning tool as well as another way to add power to their resumes.

Even though Adrienne and Lily battled through many head butting sessions; Lily was not evil enough to ruin someone's chance at getting a job elsewhere. Adrienne had lost her head for the last time, and it was time for the union to end.

Lily, a celebrity chef, was proud of the dynasty she built. A poor girl from China, Lily knew cooking was her calling.

Her entrée dishes were unbeatable. Junior's in New York was the King of Cheesecake's and Chef Lily was the master of grilling exotic entrée dishes. Her specialty meats and seasonings were the key to her success. Unconventional methods of mixing the unthinkable together for a meal; won her many awards and several guest appearances on Oprah, Rachel Ray, Martha Stewart, and other major cooking shows.

Lily was beyond beautiful. Jaded gems trimmed in 24-karat gold adorned her neck, ears, and wrists. Her long silky black hair waved with every step she took. Far from passing as the ordinary Chinese woman; Lily's body was conditioned and toned by the best trainer money could afford. Her complexion was vanilla with hint of ginger.

In pursuit to her request, she focused her eyes on the suave and masculine man who required her attention. With each step, she felt her nipples hardening, and her heart fluttering. It had been two years post divorce, since she had seen a man that whispered wet sex to her hormones. *This smooth bastard is probably trying to complain his way out of paying his bill.* Lily continued to ponder while she scanned her guest from head, to torso, to groin, to shoes. Lily was not a fan of men who dressed poorly, or those wearing shoes which looked like they were ran over in rush hour traffic.

"Hello, I'm Chef Lee. Glad you are enjoying your visit. How can I help you?" The man locked eyes with Lily, and for a moment, only he existed.

"Mrs. Lee..."

"No, it's Ms. Lee." Lily crossed her arms.

"Ok, Ms. Lee. Please, have a seat with me." Lily sat with caution.

"I love your restaurant, and I truly love how you give back to the community. I want to offer several proposals for your services and I hope you like them all. I have eight events coming up and I need your catering services at each event." Still engaged in scanning the mystery man over while trying to figure out his angle; proved to be a tough task for Lily. His scent lured her into a trance.

"Wait, first off, what is your name? Second, who told you I catered?" Lily, now knocked out her trance, became irritated with the concept of catering someone's event she barely knew. She only catered for known celebs, and in her downtime; she delivered foods to shelters. Having no idea of who sat before her, Lily cautioned her wording. The man smiled, and lifted his wine glass to take a sip. He smiled at Lily and parted his thin, buttery lips.

"I'm Lucah Hunt, owner of Hunt Enterprises. Hunt

Enterprises is a global company. We touch hands with many prominent industry companies and professionals. We offer services in real estate and property preservation, stocks, public relations, company branding and marketing.

"Sounds fantastic, but I will have to review your company information and proposals. I am a ..."

"Yes, a busy woman." Lucah interjected as he returned some of the same looks he caught Lily passing at him.

"Ms. Lee, I promise you will not be disappointed. I predict your client base to increase greatly after you and I have bonded on a few projects. I love building new networks."

In and out of trance, Lily took to her feet and initiated a stare down of Lucah's groin.

"I have my doubts about your ability in doing something that hasn't already been done. But, with your attitude, I will review your *little* offer."

Lucah took to his feet.

"Ms. Lee, I'm six foot seven, I wear a size fourteen shoe, and my arms are long enough to wrap around you twice. There is nothing little about me. My homes, bank accounts, and lifestyle are all..."

"Stop right there! Nothing is much bigger than that overgrown ego of yours!"

"Ouch, that stung." Lucah joked as he tried to rub the stinging sensation off the side of his well-groomed face. Lily found herself enjoying their conversation.

"Good! Now if you don't mind, I have work to do. Thank you for coming and I hope you enjoyed your experience."

"Wait, you forgot my proposals."

"Thank you. Is your card and contact information included? Chasing potential clients is not my thing. My time is important Mr. Hunt."

"When I make a move, it's always right." By now, the entire dining area managed to glue their eyes on Lucah and Lily. Their game of warding off the obvious chemistry between them provided comedy to the onlookers.

"Well, I guess this is where I should be preparing to make my exit." Lucah said.

"I hope you keep your phone on."

"Why is that Ms. Lee?" Lucah asked.

"I work *all* hours of the night. It's the only time I can unwind to review records and other business. I may text or call you."

"Ok, great, I await your call. I am sure you will love everything you see Ms. Lee. There is nothing about me or my company that you would dislike." Lucah hinted as he smiled through every pore of Lily's body. Lily felt what he was saying but tried her best to remain planted. Lucah knew Lily would be interested more sooner than later and her smile proved so as he continued checking her out.

"Ok, I will." Lily was shocked to see how Lucah towered over her petite frame. Suddenly nervous, her body language became that of a newborn deer. Her hands shuffled Lucah's proposals as her knees repeatedly buckled. Lily felt kidnapped by Lucah's powerful sex appeal. Lily was a knucklehead for men that took pride in the way they presented themselves. Nice shoes, slacks, shirt and tie, and a perfected haircut along with the right cologne; sent Lily into a field of sweet, *what if's*. Her taste for Lucah grew more intense for every moment he was in her presence.

"Good Lord you are too tall! Wow, I need a chair to shake your hand." Lily joked.

"My assistant will greet you on the way out. My private number and other info will be on the card she provides you."

"I understand, thank you for today!"

Before Lily could make it back to the kitchen, the dining area bellowed a loud chorus of joy.

After she consulted with the Maitre d', she discovered Lucah decided to pay for everyone's lunch!

"OK- I see who I'm dealing with, but does he know who he's dealing with?" Lily laughed as she quickly added Lucah's numbers into her iPhone.

Virginia
Chapter 9

"Dr. Arlington, Mr. Gibson is on the phone! Sounds as if he's having another rage attack! What do you want me to do with him?"

"Patch him to straight to devil! I cannot do that man today. Forward him to Dr. Greene and inform him that I'm out of state attending a conference."

"OK, will do! Do I need to call you back with his sentiments?"

"Doing your comedy stint on the clock Mackenzie is not a good look for you.

"Oh, do you think I'm funny?" Mackenzie giggled.

"Um, just make sure you clock in everyday we're open. You are not ready for big time!"

"You could have at least given feedback. Dag! OK, I will patch Mr. Gibson to line 6-6-6!" Mackenzie joked.

"Oh wow, now Mackenzie, I will give you a bonus for that one. That was actually funny! Now please get rid of that man. Unless he's talking about suicide, I do not want to hear, what he has to say. I'm going to do my online therapy today with Dr. Tucker for the next thirty minutes. Continue to take messages for me Mackenzie. I will check with you when I am done."

"Got it!"

Dr. Arlington was over her limits and the demands her patients posted had her requesting dosage increases of her own medications. Psychiatrist by day and night, was the life Virginia lived. Widowed with no children, Virginia found herself at the crossroad of deciding if she should dive into the crazy world of dating. The nights home alone, mixed with cold showers, failed to extinguish the five alarm fires down below. Joy turned to pain, when she visited the mall or the movies. No matter where she turned, the sight of love blinded her. Detaching herself from those outlets would reduce her depression. She missed true love and intimacy in her life.

Virginia hated consulting with Dr. Tucker. His advice was sterile and cliché. Making matters worse, Virginia knew what she needed to do to turn things around, but her strength was almost depleted. She was the world's biggest procrastinator.

"Dr. Tucker?"

"Hey there, Virginia. How have things been?" Dr. Tucker waved as he positioned himself in direct view.

"They could be better, but I'm ready to go on that long break I've been talking about. I am starting to feel a little toxic. These patients, Gibson included- are driving me nuts."

"Hey, I feel you. Sometimes the patients forget we have our own lives and own set of problems.

"Yeah, well I hope someone creates a *give a damn* pill real soon! The world might become a better place."

"I love that humor, Virginia."

"Next to The Lord, my meds, my Smith and Wesson, and the gun range; it's all I have."

"Have you been out? Have you tried planning a night out on the town with the girls? Better yet, how bout with a man! Please tell me you've tried doing something besides work, Virginia!"

"You know what my answer will be, so why don't you stop trying to make me do something I'm not ready to do?"

"Look, if Daniel were here, and *you* were gone; he would have moved on by now."

"How in the hell could you say something like that

Raymond?"

"Virginia, your husband and I could have been brothers. I knew him too well. Now you know, sitting inside a box will not heal your spirit! Daniel was about living, Virginia. Didn't you learn from your husband?"

Virginia was close to tears. She closed her eyes hoping to trap them. All she could do was flash back to the times she and her husband shared laughter and many nights making love until the both of them passed out. It's been two years since her husband passed and the sun hasn't shined since.

"I hate this Skype shit!" Virginia bitched.

"Why? Is it because you hate that I can see you choking on those tears?"

"I'm dropping you as my therapist!"

"Why would you do that, Virginia?" Dr. Tucker leaned into the camera.

"I feel as if you don't listen to me anymore. You say the same shit every time!"

"Oh, I'm sorry. I'm tired of hearing *you* say the same shit every time!" Raymond blurted as he lounged in his chair while smoking his cigar.

"Let me say it again V-, stop with the bullshit, and move on. You get new, when you *do* new! I hate seeing you give up on yourself! Ugly, just damn ugly!"

"That hurt Raymond!" Virginia walked away from her laptop.

"I hope it hurts *real* good! Go find the remedy for your pain and get back to me."

"You are a man bitch Raymond!"

"Oh you are darker than a basement without windows, V-!"

"You know we all have a dark side." Virginia gave Raymond the middle finger while sipping on her smoothie.

"Be sure to keep your flashlight close and your generator charged. No one needs to see your darkness, Miss. Lady!"

"Ok, I promise to stand in the light. Raymond, let me ask you something."

"Go ahead."

"Is it truly time to let go?"

"Yes Virginia." Raymond whispered in a low and sincere tone as he scooted closer to the screen. He knew his friend needed consoling and he knew she needed to hear how life was awaiting her return. He knew her work hours combined with her grief would speed up the procession to her funeral. "Please let go. Don't forget, you can remember what you want, but let go of what's killing you. Life isn't easy but we do have some control of it! Do you love yourself Virginia?"

"I guess." Virginia sobbed into her tissue.

"Self-love mixed with perseverance will get anyone through anything! You are not the only person who has lost a spouse. There is not a day where I fail to think of Elizabeth."

"Ok, I promise to get up and go out this weekend. Don't expect me to call you Monday talking about some gorgeous guy I met while hanging out with Darlene."

"Hey, speaking of Darlene..."

"Stop it Raymond! She does not want you."

"Ok, you remember what perseverance will get you!"

"It's called a rape case, Raymond."

"Woman, you're darker than the night sky without a moon! See, darkness dwells deep within!"

"Oh yes, while I am thinking about it. Will you be able to make the fundraiser event for, Mind over Matter next Saturday night at the Ritz?"

"Yes, I look forward to that event every year. I love the auction items, the food, the music, and drinks."

"Um, what else do you like Raymond?"

"Well since you asked, looking at the Founder, Mrs. Brown is always divine."

"You do know you called her, *Mrs.,* right?"

"Oh there you go trying to melt my chocolate dream."

"That woman is not tripping off you Raymond. No matter how much money you throw into her organization, she is not looking for a rendezvous. She's happily married to that fine…"

"Oh now, look who's caught in the rapture."

"Damn, I see why Anita Baker made that song." Virginia laughed.

"You think she likes white men?"

"That woman is truly in love with her husband." Virginia answered with a smirk.

"Oh well, on to the next one."

"I hope you find love real soon Raymond."

"I second that with a shot of this Brandy!"

"It's not even one o'clock Raymond! I hear AA calling you!"

"It's Friday and I'm feeling good!" Raymond partied as Virginia died in laughter.

"Hey Virginia, did you know Mrs. Brown is up for several service awards this year?"

"Really, when did you hear about this?"

"I found out last month when I lunched with Cheryl. She's been awarded a few hometown service awards from Dr. Huxley and Attorney Jay Brown for community service and activism on mental health."

"That's great! I wonder if she would be open to the idea of adding us to her network. I wouldn't mind servicing some of her clients. This is why we do what we do. All too much, people take their mental health for advantage."

"No, they choose not to think about it Virginia. Think about it. The hardest group of people to reach, as you know; are African Americans. The stigmas, their friends, their family, and more painfully, their pastor's, scratch off mental health issues like a bad case of shingles. In the end, they always blame the *devil*, calling *him* a liar."

"Raymond, I wish we could get more pastors' to view

mental health issues like any other health issue."

"Virginia, don't preach to the choir, preach to their leaders! Sometimes they need to hear the sermons *we* preach."

"Good idea Raymond. I will have to call Mrs. Brown to see if we can set up meetings at local churches."

"Sounds good, just say when!"

"Hey, Raymond, if you are going alone to the gala, let's team up?"

"Sure Virginia, but don't anticipate us leaving together. If one cutie, halfway winks at me, she's going to find out why thy really call me, Doctor."

"Forget it Raymond! You are too much to handle." Virginia waved Raymond off. "Good bye Raymond. I will talk to you next week."

"Good bye Virginia!" Raymond heckled away like a crazed hyena. Taking stance by her office window, Virginia layered her stresses onto the window as she sighed a lifetime of pain and depression onto the glass. As soon as her breath clouded the window, it quickly faded away.

Hmm, here one moment, gone the next. Why my problems can't go away like fog on a window leaves me clueless.

Lola
Chapter 10

"Listen Baylor, don't call me again! The next time you show up out of nowhere, I *will* take you down. You cheated, you had your fun, and apparently- it's clear you know what you want. Now why are you still here bothering me?" Lola was full of rage and looking into her husband's eyes allowed more venom to build in her mouth. The disappointment her husband delivered tore her into a million pieces.

"I can't believe how stupid you were for sexting! Did you not learn from that ignorant Mayor from Detroit? What else have you been doing wrong, Baylor? Do I need to have you investigated for other shit? You smell real shitty right about now! Get away from me!" Lola yelled as she covered her nose with the back of her hand.

"It wasn't special at all Lola. She isn't worth losing all I have!" Baylor was close to being out on his ass. Guilt was heavy. Not being able to look his wife in the face was convicting enough, no jury necessary.

"Oh, and you couldn't do that at home with me?" Baylor did everything he could to stop his wife from walking away. Baylor knew his dog days of cheating had met its cycles end. The dawn of reality was blinding. His marriage was over. Life without the woman he cherished and loved like no other was equal to a death sentence. His marriage ended many lovers ago and he knew his time to serve in hell was close. Baylor thought money was the fixer of everything.

The wind tagged Lola as she tunneled around her car. She relentlessly pounded all her fury, shame, and naïve thoughts onto the car, one punch right after the other.

"All the damn signs were right in front of my face like a red light, yet, I proceeded with this damn marriage knowing damn well some shit like this, would one day pull me over. This stuff, this stuff you have done here, will take the Hand of God *and* his Son to rid the evil, hateful, and vengeful thoughts from my mind. You damn well ain't worth me going to hell- or jail, you lousy bastard!" Filled with everything but the Holy Ghost, there was no one, at least in his or her right mind- daring enough to stop her from unleashing her pain in the middle of Downtown Clayton.

No other way to describe his fright, Baylor was double scared. He tried to pass the lumps in his throat; hoping the right words would flow from his mouth.

"Lo-Lo, I don't want to do this anymore. She is not the woman I want to be with for the rest of my life. I admit how wrong I was, and I am sorry. Listen, I'm not expecting you to take me back today, or tomorrow; but know how much I love you Lola Springfield." Lola's eyes felt like a busted damn, but like the levees in Louisiana, she mustered up enough strength to apply another quick fix, to hold the tears back.

"Lola *Jameson* sounds much better! Don't you ever call me by your last name again! Once a cheater always a cheater! I'm not going to hold my breath for a million years, waiting on you to get your shit right. I want to exhale your drama right now! Only dumb bitches stay in some shit like this!"

Laid up drunk in his office one evening, Baylor felt the need to be dirty. After many failed attempts to talk with his lover, Baylor decided to send her a picture of his dick. He also texted that he was on his way to their special spot. He made sure to note that he wanted to see nothing but pink. And he wasn't talking about the clothing line. Baylor did not realize how tight he nailed his coffin shut, until he looked at his phone around three the next morning. Not only did he see 8 missed calls, and a whole book of text messages, he saw the last person he called and texted was his wife. This fuck-up sent bubbles to his stomach faster than a pot of his mother-in-law's greens.

"Are we done? I need to go shopping! I'm tired of listening to your whining ass!" Lola sighed as she took seat inside her car. Shopping was Lola's past time in happiness and sadness.

"Shopping? What in the hell do you think shopping will do? I mean, can't we talk this out like two sensible adults?"

"Your nerves are fried harder than burnt chicken. Here you stand, still attempting to use what's left of them to make your sorry ass story seem opposite of what it is! Answer this, do you think Jesus will accept your reasoning for cheating on judgment day?" Baylor hated when Lola jumped on the Holy ramp. "Well hell, if he does, then this marriage is back on, in prime-time." Lola waited for Baylor's response.

Baylor shied away from his wife's comment because he knew damn well if he spoke out of order, the Lord might reach from above and pluck him from this earth.

"Let's relax, and take some time apart. I want to do this the right way."

"The right way?" Lola cried as she released the steering wheel. Her exit from her car matched the force and quickness of a county cop. "Excuse the hell out of you! I have done right since the moment we met. I've given you what you should have given me! I made the money, I gave you a child, and I gave myself to you one-hundred percent! Who helped *you* get to where *you* stand today? Hell, I almost lost myself while trying to help you with your career. Don't forget who stayed home to care for Grace!" Lola arched over her embarrassingly short husband as her breast smothered his chances of oxygen exchange.

"Straight to hell you go, Baylor! I need a man I can look up to. It would be a change of scenery from your short, insecure, and anatomically small..."

"Ok, I know you pissed and all but what's the need in going there? I never heard you complaining." Baylor looked around to see who was taking in the scenery.

"Oh Yeah? Well that's because I held it all in. The little thing is hard to hold in when wet. You know how many Kegel exercises I had to do to hold little man in. Hell it's a wonder I wasn't cheating before you were."

"You are a cold bitch!"

"Well if you took more time warming me up, versus your mistress, maybe we wouldn't be standing here today!"

"You never wanted me, Lola."

"Look don't stand here and play games with me *Lil Man*! Psychological games won't get you anywhere but committed! Don't make this out to be my fault. You and I took the same vows and you...yes you, messed this union up! The small things- and I do mean the small things, are doable, but cheating? You have lost your mind and I suggest you take an ad out in the *lost* section of the Post-Dispatch."

"You know you wasn't perfect either!" Lola wasn't about to allow, Baylor to stand firm in his shitty pile of reason. He was a cheater and that was that. The emotions traveling throughout Lola's body brought on a tsunami of dangerous thoughts.

"It looks a lot bigger on a cell phone picture more than it does in real life. You are sad, Baylor. I have no one else but myself to blame for this mess. I should have seen the signs, but working full-time, going to charity events and speaking at engagements nationwide, will allow many flyovers. Sadly, you knew all of this and you played me because you knew my attention was parked elsewhere!" Lola was tired. Leaning against the car, her body displayed her weariness wrapped in a shell of bitter emotions.

"I have to ask again, are you that dumb? What made you send that picture over your phone? Do you know any better, Baylor? It makes you look stupid! I see, God finally ran out of mercy, and pulled the curtain on your whack ass! You see how slick catches up, right? Just when you thought your game was 'air tight', you forgot to check for the leaks dumb ass."

"Lola, I'm going to leave you alone." Baylor blurted as he

paced back and forth. Making a scene in the middle of Clayton County's court district was the farthest thing from his mind. He didn't care about all the police officers, judges, attorney's, civil servants and the other patrons of Clayton County getting a window seat to the rush hour feature of his marriage in destruction.

Lola and Baylor practiced as successful attorneys. Their client base featured all of West County's old money gang, prime-time thugs and, pro-athletes. Now it seemed they were going to be in need of legal services of their own.

Leaning on the car, Lola studied her soon to be ex, from head to toe. Before Baylor spoke, Lola was circling and sniffing him like a hungry animal.

"Wow Baylor, you must have scored with some high-society butterfly."

"Lola what are you talking about? I told you she means nothing to me!"

"Oh yes she does. I mean look at you. Hmm, damn, you even smell different Baylor. What is that? It's definitely a scent I would never think you'd wear. A little too strong for such a soft man like you. Oh wow, love the shoes. Gucci, right Baylor? Oh damn, what a nice suit. I see this one isn't from the men's exchange. Damn, another change I should have seen." Lola pointed to the temple of her head, as she bit her bottom lip. "Good luck chasing that ass Baylor. Don't you know how hard it is chasing young tail?"

"You have no idea what you're talking about!" Baylor answered as he stared his wife down. The smirk on his face was insulting to Lola. It was almost as if he felt good that his wife saw the new him. It was almost as if he was happy that someone other than his wife loved his short and pathetic looking self.

"Enjoy chasing that young thang. She got low miles, so pace your speed. Oh yeah, don't call me from the hospital when your little blue pills kill your ass. You know you can't do more than one at a time." Lola laughed as she leaned onto her car while slapping the roof.

"Got tired of the old lady, so you went and got a young thang, huh? Well guess what dumb ass- those young girls want *all* the attention! Do you think she's giving you that attention for free? Good-bye, Baylor. The world is yours *and* Nino's. I want you to be at the house around five and gone before seven. Make sure you bring help or send movers! I'm not paying for this divorce and you better believe you will be paying big in alimony and child support! I know every dime you have and I know about the other two homes! Now get the hell out of my way!" Lola sped off in her black Audi A8, with her arm extended out the driver's window, waving her middle finger.

Chapter 11

"Daphne, let's get together for lunch and shopping today. I need some help with a few things. Are you available today?"

"I'm here for you! What in the hell is going on? I heard you arguing with Baylor. Your phone must have been in your jacket because it kept calling me."

"You heard right, girl! Baylor has been messing around and I caught him big time!"

"How did he do it, Lola?" Daphne questioned her longtime friend of forty-five years.

"I heard something about a cell picture and something about going to a special spot." Lola felt okay talking to Daphne about anything. She knew her friend would tell her when she fell out of order, like a private in the army. On the other side of the wall, Lola knew her friend would hold her up and celebrate when she was on point. From the playground to the college dorm, the two were eternal sisters. Not sharing would go against everything they knew.

"Daph, he was stupid drunk one night in his office. He stays overnight when he's had too much to drink at the office. Anyway, out of nowhere he sent me a picture of himself releasing a trifling lust. It was disgusting seeing it half dead, still clinched in his hand."

"HUH! Come...Ok, I didn't mean it like that, repeat that for me." Daphne pleaded.

"You heard me. He thought he was sending the texts and picture to her, but it was me. I'm sure when he sobered up the next morning, his heart dropped in his ass. We've never done no shit like that over the phone. Bedroom only."

"Ok, are you on the way to pick up the kit? Daphne asked.

"Girl, what are you talking about?" Lola was aggravated.

"The *kick his ass out,* kit!"

"Oh girl, you're crazy!!!! Sure, let's do it. All at his expense too!" Lola giggled because she knew could not wait to hear the clerk tell her that his card was over its limit. "Be ready in a few, and we will ride to my home from there. I gave him a seven o'clock deadline time to get his junk out the house. The movers will be there this weekend.

Lola's mother always thought it was was necessary to give her lessons on how to kick a man out in style. Maybe those lessons were preparing Lola for this weekend. A mother always knows. Lola's mother shared how it was important for the man to feel the pain, shame, disgust and mistrust, he poured over the relationship. Lola's mother felt every woman should kick her man to the curb at least once in her marriage to check on her own self-being. Some women need reminding of how they looked, and felt before the relationship. Deep down, Lola didn't agree with her mother because she felt there were other outlets in reclaiming one's own self.

"Remember the real you, before he came along-" is something her mother recited quite often. Her mother knew how easy it was to lose one's self when boggled down with career, family, and life.

"How may I help you, mom?" Lola answered in a depressed voice. She knew Baylor had already called her mother to tell his half-assed side of the story.

"That so-called husband of yours called me and tried to recruit me into talking you calm, but I told him once the fury was unleashed, it's not worth me getting killed! Not-for-no-damn-body and I meant that!"

"Good, I'm glad you know your place mother. This is happening to me, not you. I did not call to hear "I told you" or the "You should have seen it" lectures."

"Good! I'm not in the mood to preach like your daddy. Did you go shopping?"

"Not yet, but Daphne is coming with me."

"Pick me up something just for the hell of it sweetie!"

"No mom, you live like a Queen. What in the heck can I buy you?" Lola shook her head as she pulled into Starbuck's for a caffeine fix. Her nerves were rattling worse than a bad muffler.

"I'm always looking for something new."

"Mom you're a star."

"Shut up Mitchell! She is a grown woman and she doesn't need to hear you speaking according to the word of your jumbled gospel!" Lola's parents were a pair of mismatched socks. A young preacher from the south and a young Diva from the west, should have never crossed paths.

"See, you're the reason why people skip church, and go straight to hell! Let me speak to my daughter!" Lola giggled as she listened to her parents argue on whose idea was best fit for her situation.

"Lo, are you there?"

"Yes dad, I'm here."

"Be a woman and take the high road. You are a child of God and you know there is no one whose able to hand down a butt whipping like The Lord! I know you are hurting and I know the devil is dancing all around you while whispering sweet paybacks; but you have to rise above and send the devil back downstairs!"

"Dad, it's easy for people to say the right thing when wrong hasn't been done to them! It's as if you are telling someone how everything happens for a reason, after cancer has invaded their body. Who in the hell wants to hear that while infested with disease, fear and uncertainty? I can't sit here and agree with the will of The Lord right now. I'm not you and I haven't graduated to that level of faith and forgiveness!"

"I understand, but don't cut your life short. Don't bring ill will into your life. God has a way of paying us all back and Lola, I don't want to be around when he decides to repay you. I know it hurts, Lo. Do dad a favor and let-it-go!" Lola wanted to cry something awful but once again, she found herself inhaling tears.

"Go and prepare your Sunday sermon Mitchell!" Lola's mother chimed in."

"I can't wait for the Lord to give me the signal to cut you off. Damn nerves so bad, I gotta hide the good ones before you kill those too! If Lola listens to anything you say, I am going to hold it over *your* head! You know better Diane!" Mitchell mumbled.

"Ok, whatever you say Mitchell! In one ear and out the next! Lola, your father is getting the best of me! Thank the Lord it's time for me and the girls to take our annual trip! Sweetie, after you clean up all the mess your husband has made, you want to join me and the girls on our annual trip?"

The image of her mother and friends frolicking around in whatever; forced Lola to spit her coffee out.

"Mom, this cub does not want to hang around you cougar's! I'm not in the mood for any socializing."

"Don't forget you're out of the cub club. You got some years on yourself Miss Lady. I'm not the cougar of the group and you know that! Do not forget, I love your father more than he will ever know, but it does not mean that momma can't enjoy whatever dances in front of her eyes. Don't let me come home and find you drowning in work. Overworking will kill you! Matter of fact, are you able to turn some of your cases over? You need to focus on you and Grace right now!"

"I'm going to turn over two. The one left is a slam-dunk! It's the remaining two thugs that shot down the Valdez' some months ago."

"Oh-my-goodness, there's some good news for a change! How did that land on your desk?"

"The family came to us. I'm ready to shred those bastard a new one. They deserve everything the judge and the state and throws their way!"

"Who got the reward?"

"The person, of course, wants to remain anonymous! Hell, do you blame them? I wouldn't want anyone coming after me because I snitched!"

"Lola, you be careful. I don't think it would be wise for you to handle that case. It's too high profile."

"Mom, I will be fine. If threat arises, Baylor will take over." Lola figured it's better for Baylor to deal with the case, keeping herself out of the line of fire. She smiled at the thought of Baylor stretched lifeless on a stretcher.

"Now you're thinking like your momma!"

"I agree with dad, we need Jesus!"

"Child, he is with me every day. Ok, onto cleaning Baylor out of your life. Lola, make this break up, a damn symphony! You are the conductor and it's time to turn the music up! Make sure you have bottles of chilled wine in every room as you dance throughout your home in the sexiest outfit. Buy some damn Kleenex, but never let him see you cry. Let him wonder, what your next move will be. Buy the best damn music, including the classic soundtrack from the movie, *Waiting to Exhale*!"

"Mom, I'm too tired for all that extra mess."

"When he comes to get his shit, you better believe you and Beyoncé need to be throwing his shit as far as to the left as possible. Don't let him go any further than the foyer. The house he once called home will now be a memory to him. Oh yes, have some young and sexy eye candy helping you rearrange the house. Honey, if he sees all that going on, his head will swell with regret! Your glow will not be because of him." Lola beamed as she smiled at the thought of getting back in touch with the woman she once knew.

"Mom, I'm going to be classy. If he witnesses anything crazy, our drama will graduate to another level. Did you not hear how tired I was? This is too draining."

"Get *you* back. Get the life you missed while you were too

busy making his life a success! Oh yes, a nice pair of heaven high stilettos, with a sexy outfit, with your long red hair hanging mid-back is enough to send Baylor right to the therapist- hell maybe the psychiatric ward."

No matter how Lola tried to shift her mind out the drama zone, Baylor's dick pic, intended for another for another woman, pissed her off. Her mother's idea of ruining a man's life was just as sinister as the plans men construct to cheat on their women. For every thought of pain, a new ingredient fell into the *'kick his ass out'* kit. Lola toyed with what she wanted to buy.

~~Checklist:~~
~~Saks~~
~~New Handbags and shoes from Louis Vuitton~~
~~New cocktail ring, bracelet, and necklace from Tiffany's~~
~~Daphne's Birthday gift~~
~~Something for mom~~

~~Target~~
~~Bleach- Destroy all his shit!!!~~
~~Scissors- Cut the zippers out of his pants. If a dog's dick hangs, his should too!!!~~
~~Construction trash bags-Stuff his clothes in trash bags, not luggage! Good men travel with luggage!!!~~

~~EYE CANDY! He will act like a damn fool on fire!~~

FUCK IT!

The good Lord will have to deal with me later on this one! It's time Baylor saw the real Lola!

Chapter 12

"**D**r. Arlington, Isabella Valdez is here."

"Ok, send her in." Isabella had been in treatment with Virginia for the last four months. To Isabella, the four months seemed more like four days since Miguel passed.

"Hello Isabella. How are you doing, love?" Virginia asked as she greeted Isabella with open arms. She'd known Isabella since the birth of wild child, Devin. Isabella suffered from severe post-partum depression after the birth of Devin, and she was referred to Virginia. As Devin got older, he worried Isabella to the point of insanity. Virginia knew it would take The Lord, and a great psychiatrist to help her.

Isabella and good old, Maxwell House- black, no cream or sugar- sat up a many nights, waiting for Devin to return home. She knew what a stick of dynamite Devin was, and she always worried who would light it.

Since his father passed, it seemed Devin's uncontrollable flexing' seemed to cease. He was more relaxed, and his attitude was much better. Deep down, Isabella felt Devin was boiling a pot of revenge.

"I'm trying to hold on. Lisa, my nurse has been wonderful to me. I credit her and the Lord for bringing me this far. I'm not sure what God has in store for me, but I want to see it."

"There we go! I am glad to hear you talking happy, girl. What brought you to this point?

"The grief was killing me. Issues with high blood pressure and crazy sugar levels set-in and tried to take claim. At first, I wasn't bothered when Dr. Williams made the announcement on my failing health. I embraced the idea of death. But when I thought about it, all I wanted was death from my emotional pain, not life."

"I remember all too well." Virginia stated as she jotted

down notes.

"I thought of the conversations Miguel and I had when we vacationed last." Isabella spoke as she gazed into emptiness.

"He always spoke as if he knew he was going to pass ahead of me. Miguel knew how hard I loved him and he knew I would be devastated if he left me. I take comfort when I think back to how he expressed his desires for me to explore the depths of life without the association of guilt. He didn't want me to stop living life and to me- that's real love."

"That's beautiful Isabella." Virginia commented as she and Isabella shared box of Kleenex. Both women dabbed their fiercely beaten faces, hoping to avoid an expensive meltdown.

"How do you think you would want to start with your re-introduction to the world?"

"Work is my life now. I have many clients, old and new in need of my services. I guess you see where I'm going, right?"

"Oh, I see you're in the mood for a lecture."

"Not now, Virginia."

"It's not that easy to shut me up, Isabella!"

"Please give me the secret on how to do it!"

"You are not funny. Since you know today's sermon, be sure you learn your lesson, and avoid acting out of your natural self. Do as I advise Isabella."

"Who's gonna tell you if I don't?"

"I have my sources!" Virginia laughed.

"Look Virginia, if working my blues away is what I choose to do, let me. You know better than anyone that we all work through grief differently. Matter of fact..."

"Oh no, don't you go there!" Virginia warned as she dismissed herself from sitting position. Isabella finally had one up on the good doctor and for a moment, Isabella discharged herself from the status of patient.

"How have you been, Virginia? You don't talk much about how *you* are progressing. Here you are giving advice, but you too have failed to move on, Ms. Lady. When will you move on?" Throwing her hands in the air, Virginia knew the charade was over.

"I know, I serve the advice quite well but I sure as hell fail when it comes to living by my own words. Isabella, I hate the idea of starting over. Getting to know someone all over again, dealing with his little quirks, finding out all his lies, bit by bit, irritates the shit out of me."

"I feel you. The simple things such as the way our men held us, kissed us, made love and cared for us, is something no other man can duplicate."

"You're right Isabella. Simple things from opening doors, ordering food, making decisions without disregarding my feelings is something, Daniel never did. I felt equal. I stood beside him, not behind him."

"My Miguel was wonderful in consoling me during the hard times. He taught me how to make it through anything." Isabella and Virginia looked as if their devotion to their beloveds would live on.

"Isabella, don't forget the age factor! I mean, my body is as great as a seasoned thirty year old, but our men loved us for us, and we knew it. I don't have time trying to wonder if I am fulfilling some man's fantasy! We never had a worry about where our men were and what they were doing."

"Yaaasss honey! If money wasn't growing in the bank account, somebody was bullshitting. You can't get rich by playing in those streets." Virginia said as she and Isabella fell into laughter. Laughter rang so hard, a race to the office bathroom started.

"Oh damn Virginia...I got five years on you. Let me go first. You know my bladder is stretched out. Come on out of there before you need housekeeping to come clean your carpet."

"Housekeeping quit, now you will have to clean up after yourself."

"You think quickly on the toilet don't ya? Isabella joked as she walked to the office refrigerator hoping to wet her whistle. Virginia emerged from the bathroom appearing to be refreshed.

"It's all yours!"

"Bout time." Isabella raced to the toilet.

"Tell you what. We will go out next Saturday to this fundraiser, and afterwards, we will go have dinner at Lily Lee's. Sound good to you?"

"Yes! Anything you say will sound better once my bladder is empty!" Virginia stood by the bathroom door and continued her conversation while she filed her nails.

"Who's throwing the fundraiser?"

"The Mind over Matter 2 Day, is throwing their annual gala, to help raise money and awareness for people who live with mental illnesses. The agency provides funds to help people afford their medication, therapy, and psychiatric visits. They help the community a lot. The founder is looking to go nationwide with her efforts."

"Ok, sounds good." Isabella sung as emptied her bladder.

"Plus, I have someone I want you to meet." Returning from the bathroom, Isabella connected with Virginia's face and shone a disapproving look.

"Oh hell, I knew it was coming."

"He's a great man; please listen before you sound off Isabella."

"Speak quickly woman."

"You two have plenty in common. Sadly, he lost his wife about four years ago but now, he is excited about venturing back into life. He is a great guy Bella! I must admit, he is quite the character but truthfully, he is best friend material. I dare not lie about that."

"No thanks. I do not need a new friend. Humph, ready to venture out my butt. He needs to venture elsewhere! I want to heal my own way, minus the pressure of some strange man's expectancies. No one will ever match Miguel. Do you get where I am going?" Shrugging away from Isabella, Virginia gave her word as she zipped her mouth shut. Isabella proved in ten seconds that she was nowhere near being ready for any form of companionship.

Gabrielle
Chapter 13

"**W**hy are you in my bedroom Dale?"

"Baby, come sit next to me." Dale begged as he patted on the bed motioning for Gabrielle to sit.

Sitting half way close to her husband, Gabrielle was ready to spill the truth one last time.

"Look, you need to understand that you and I are no more. Your senses must be on vacation if you think we are going to be roomies with benefits! We made the agreement to pay our share of the bills, wait for the twins to finish their last year of high school and you move out!" Gabrielle was beyond upset with her cheating husband of twenty-two years.

"I thought therapy and talking things out were going to help re-build our marriage, Gabby. I have been faithful ever since, and I damn sure make it a must to go to therapy. I say this because it's more than what you do."

"Look Dale, truthfully, the therapy helped me from catching a felony. It barley killed the urge to toss you out on the streets in front of all your fancy, arrogant friends and colleagues. You've brought nothing but shame and tons of STD's my way! Your desire for me to pretend happiness lives here, proves you are nuts." Gabrielle belted as she dug into her husband's stubborn and scarred forehead.

"Gabby, I asked you to keep your hands off of me!"

"What if I don't? All those years of ass whippings and you up here acting as if you don't know any better. I guess I don't kick your ass enough. To me, I think the more I beat you, the more you love it!"

"If you think you've hurt me Gabby, you're..."
Gabrielle picked up a crystal vase and held it firmly. Dale knew the impact the vase would have if Gabrielle made contact, so

walking away was best. "I'm going to my bedroom and I'm leaving this shit here."

"Yeah, walk away you coward." Before Gabrielle could turn around to sit the vase on the dresser, Dale pounced onto her backside.

Gabrielle's body kissed the wall, leaving no room to move. Tired of fighting, she gave out like captured prey. Dale ignited a forbidden, body-burning grind against his wife's backside. The intense heat sizzling between them delivered an illegal form of passion. You're right Gabby, maybe we need to figure out a way to split." Dale whispered into Gabrielle's ear as he pinned his solid frame against her supermodel thin physique.

"Bitch, I swear your days of hitting me are over! I've endured enough of your drama."

"You Mr. Tough Guy now, huh? You better hope I don't get loose." Gabrielle tried once more to fight Dale off while trying to free her face from the wall.

"Yeah, maybe I deserved some of your shit, but you need help in more ways than one! You pushed me out there Gabby! Your heavy drinking, cursing, abuse, and crazy demands drove us all crazy! I'm going to put the house on the market, and talk with the accountant to see where we can liquidate some of our other properties, and investments. I'm tired of faking! This marriage *is* over."

"If it's over, why are you still on me, Dale?"

The pressure Dale applied to Gabrielle's petite frame labored her breathing.

"We had an agreement! We were to stay together until the twins left for college." Dale was tired of his wife, but he knew his sins of the past had a lot to do with the possession of his wife's spirit. Both of them were the greatest magicians ever. Both succeeded at faking pain and their magic shows proved to be better than any Vegas review.

"Gabby, you are damn confused. The kids have lived in this

hell as well. What makes you think they have no idea of what's been going on? Do you think it was fair for them to live through this? Sure, take your issues out on me, but our children. I would bury you quick if I ever caught you mistreating the girls! I've told you that a million times."

"Oh now you want to sound holier than God! Are you playing the game of *forget it all*? Come on Dale! You are lower than low, to sneak women in the same house your children live. Did you forget about the time the children caught you chasing after another woman in our home?" Gabrielle screamed as she scoured enough strength to kick Dale off her. "You can't stand here and point the finger at me hoping it will exile you from all the wrong you've committed Dale. You smell like death! I blame *you* for how I am. You have left a dirty, vile, and evil spirit inside me. I never thought I could have such hate in me.

"It's the damn alcohol woman!"

"Well what in the hell do you think drove me to the vineyard? Momma was right! If a motherfucker brings the worst out of you, it's time to get away!"

"Gabrielle, the girls knew this so-called, smooth sailing of a marriage, shipwrecked years ago!" Dale yelled as he shut their bedroom door to contain yet another fight. Turning around, he found himself covering his face to protect it from Gabrielle's fist.

Dale was beyond tired and he was not in the mood to deal with another tantrum from his wife. "Let me go you dirty bastard! I hate the day you came to be! Your daddy should have aimed for your mommas face!"

"There you go, talking all mean and dirty. I know what that means!"

"I want no part of you on me- yet alone, in me Dale!" Gabrielle screamed as she spat into Dale's face.

"Listen here, you know you want it as bad as I do. I told you I was willing to do what it takes to repair this marriage, but you keep fighting. Why do this Gabby? I still love you and I don't want this to be over." Dale whispered as he stripped his wife's bottom half free. Gabby opted to look away from her husband, but her body danced to a different tune. Her thighs parted like enemies and her breathing intensified. Dale did not hesitate in hoisting his wife upon his waist.

With his arms wrapped around her tiny waist, and her arms around his neck, a magnetic force sealed their position. Dale greeted an uncontrollable wetness, and Gabrielle, met a firm awakening. Bouncing his wife on and off his cemented pleasure intensified as Gabrielle matched his forceful stroking, with a slow winding motion. Her return signaled Dale to increase intensity. Gabrielle groaned in a crazed pain as Dale slammed her back into the wall. Her nails scratched the textured wallpaper as Dale shifted into overdrive, as he suckled his wife's breasts. Dale was in full mode and was determined to perform everything his wife loved from her menu of orgasmic pleasure. His forceful thrusts of passion, blended with many years of apologies, made it seem as if it was their first time. Her body overdosed on all he was giving her.

"Talk to her." Gabrielle slurred in a drunken state and Dale obliged.

One would have thought Dale missed breakfast and lunch on purpose the way he served himself.

"Oh I guess my loving is good when you can't find any of your lousy hoes."

"Don't go there. You too wet to be through with me." Coming up for air Dale saw the pleasure in his wife's face.

"You know what that's telling me, right? You can't fake *everything*, Gabby! Are you ready to stop fighting?"

"What in the hell are we doing? Dale stop, we can't do this." Gabrielle kicked Dale off her.

"Get back here!" Dale snatched his wife by the ankles and slammed himself back into his wife. With her eyes searching for glory, she released moans as high as mountains, while her husband fulfilled his hunger. Soon after, they separated themselves on the bed, wondering about their next step.

"Gabby, this marriage has not met its end! You get mad, I get mad, but we see right through each other and there is no questioning as to how we do it because it is natural." Dale stared to the ceiling hoping a ray of hope would beam down on the both of them.

"Naturally fucked up is what I think!" Gabrielle laughed.

"You never find the good in the bad do you?"

"Is that supposed to excuse the bad you do?"

"No. Gabby, we both have our issues, but I want to be happy and move on. I'm convinced you feel the same way- I know you do! Come here, baby." For the next couple of minutes Dale and Gabrielle held onto one another as if drama never took a seat in their life. As long as they held on, neither one of them did wrong. The problem, what would happen once they let go?

Lucah
Chapter 14

"Mr. Hunt, do we have an understanding about everything we've discussed?" The doctor asked while Lucah affixed his clothing to their original state.

"Dr. Helton, It's amazing how you physicians' talk about shit you all think would improve people's lifestyles."

"Have you been to your psychiatrist? Are you engaged in a personal relationship as of now?" Dr. Helton asked as he examined Lucah's face hoping a dab of truth would free fall from his bitter lips. Lucah was the doctor's most challenging patient. Lucah's rage was bound to escape and wreck havoc upon the lives of the innocent. Dr. Helton sensed Lucah's bitterness and tried everything possible to rid him of it.

"No, I'm not in the midst of any type of relationship. I'm in no shape to do that doc. I deal with this shit the way I can. To answer your other question, I went to see the psychiatrist and she was nothing close to great. Truthfully, she was more of a bitch than anything, but I tolerated her. Does anyone understand my need for privacy? I'm dealing with this in my own way. I'm not too cool on this psychiatrist you have me going to."

"I understand Lucah."

"No, I don't believe you do." Lucah argued as he snatched his blazer off the coat rack. The room suddenly became as cold as a container of dry ice. The look in Lucah's eyes was a hard portrait to view. The Dr. stood quiet as he searched for words that would help- not hurt. Sad enough, Lucah was too far-gone and too unpredictable.

"Look Lucah, I empathize with you! My son is HIV positive and hey man...I know the deal. Sadly, he became too comfortable with a woman he hardly knew. He knew better, but he did what he wanted. You would think all the talks' parents have with their children, would be enough to help save them from life's hardships. Damn, I wish he would have listened to me about that woman!" Dr. Helton confessed as he rested his weight on the wall. The pain and weary, glazed across his face proved he was not talking from some, get well script.

"The day my son and I sat to talk about his test results, was the last day I saw the *real* Robby. Here was this new creature in front of me and man- all I wanted to do was cast all of his pain, grief, and illness upon myself. I cried many days. I couldn't breathe, talk, or see anything but my son's pain and depression. A leave from work had to taken. It tore me up that much, Lucah." Lucah paused and leaned onto the examining table and as he listened to the doctor.

"I knew deep down that I had to take a stand, I had to be the strong one, the leader, the comforter; so I revived myself and pressed on for my son. I would have been less than a man to let my son nosedive into hell.

"I am sorry. How he is now? Lucah asked hoping, Dr. Helton's son would still be an ill-hearted maniac, unleashing his brand of hell upon earth. Lucah was looking for a man made confirmation to make him feel good about his plan to kill every cougar possible.

"He's better. He started back practicing law and he found a beautiful woman- HIV free- may I add, who loves him unconditionally."

"What? You mean to tell me she's HIV free?"

"Yeah man! I was shocked when he told me. Turned out she was the counselor at his support group. He was about to stop attending until she begged him to stay. She was tough on him, but it was because she cared. Once he opened up. The connection was instant. I think, she saw how bitter he was and I think she truly wanted to show him that the good side of life still existed. She never wanted him to become a statistic...in the criminal sense. She never gave up on him. She saw him for what he was and that was it."

"She saved him."

"Yeah man. It was divine intervention. I didn't like the route Robby was traveling. The darkness he shared with the devil was scary! You two shared that same look."

"I will be fine." Lucah failed at convincing Dr. Helton.

"I've rode on some hellacious roller coasters a few times myself. Hell, it wasn't a port large enough to harbor the things I felt. I'm just grateful for prayer. I'm happy the Lord healed Robby's heart."

"Doc, I'm going to do better. I'm meeting with my Pastor soon."

"I'm glad to hear that Lucah. Just look to the future. Lucah, I'm not giving you some text book statement! This is real life. My son speaks about this all the time and he is always open and willing to speak to people I send his way."

"I'm dealing with my way right now. Maybe I will talk with him later."

"That's understandable, just wanted to throw that your way."

"I know God has a spot in his heart for me, but it needs to be a hell of a lot bigger! I'm not feeling any love right about now."

"Well, how big was your spot for him prior to all of this happening to you Lucah?"

"I'm not going into all of that, what I do know is I'm not cool on what he's thrown in my lap right now. I can't focus on anything but myself right now."

"When in bad times, focus on Christ, his will, and his purpose for you. Some people never make it to the next phase in life because they focus on self too much! You would be surprised to see how helping someone else can make you feel.

"You're pouring it on me more than my Pastor."

"Well I guess I should, since I know it's going to be a few minutes before you visit the House of the Lord."

"Damn right on that."

"Lucah, I'm not ordained but the key to life is living with purpose, not regret! Now you know his mercy and grace is limited. Even the Lord gets tired! Brother, you need to focus and pray until your faith overflows. Faith in The Lord makes it all possible."

"I know who is in control, but I am not ready to deal with that right now. It's whatever right now. Look, I will follow up with the psychiatrist and go from there."

"There are bad people everywhere, but you don't have to be one of them. Don't let this diagnosis define you. Don't let it control you, Lucah." Dr. Helton's last comment stung Lucah to his core.

Lucah turned from the door and extended his hand for the doctor to shake. "Point well taken Doc. Thanks for the talk today. I promise to follow through."

"Enjoy the day my man. God is going to see you through. Think of Robby whenever you get low. If he made it, you can too."

"Ok." Lucah was moved by the story the doctor laid on him, but by the time he got to the parking lot, his mood shifted and he was back to feeling as if he was a five star general in the devil's army.

"Ms. Lee, this is Mr. Hunt. I received your call and I will be more than happy to meet you this evening. Call me with details. I look forward to hearing from you."

It would be nice to find a woman, no matter the age, who is willing to love unconditionally. If my lips fail to kiss love again, what is the use in living a righteous life?

Chapter 15

"**M**rs. Valdez, will you please inform the court of the tragic events which wounded you and ended the life of your husband, Miguel Valdez?" Baylor questioned as he tried his best to focus on the case at hand. He was a wreck. Since the spilt, he was drinking heavily, sleeping in, and his partners were carrying more than their load. Even though the law firm belonged to Baylor, his partner's did not care for the lowlife he came to be. "Please be patient with me. My thoughts are certain, but a little slow coming to me. I remember everything clearly, but talking about it..." Baylor saw pain gliding across his clients face. He touched her hand to confirm if she was strong enough to carry on with her testimony.

Isabella was not sure if she could hold herself together. She had lost about three days of sleep prior to the trial. She wondered if she should've brought a gun to kill the thugs' front faced, or allow the system to dish out whatever brand of justice they thought the thugs deserved. Shooting them sounded better but she was out of bullets.

"My husband and I left the Jazz Bistro after celebrating our anniversary- sniff, sniff- oh Lord..." Talking about her last moments began to overwhelm her.

"It's okay Mrs. Valdez. Please, take your time. Do you need water? Do you need a break?" Baylor asked as he grabbed the silver water pitcher and poured his client a glass of water.

"No, I'm fine. The quicker, this is over, the sooner I can move on. It's time for those bastards to be sent to hell. Let's move on." Isabella hardened her tone and sat up in the chair fixing her outfit. She had a rose pinned to her suit and a button with Mr. Valdez's picture on it. Baylor knew what to do to pull at the Jurys heartstrings.

"Counsel, have your client to refrain from obscenities in my courtroom."

"Yes, your honor."

"Mrs. Valdez, you are doing great. Let's go through the rest of this without incident. I know you can do it." Isabella nodded and squeezed Baylor's hand.

"Mrs. Valdez, please proceed with your testimony."

"That night I felt like driving through Forest Park versus driving down highway forty. Miguel didn't want to go that way, but since it was our night, he gave way to everything I asked. We exited the park onto Union, and from there, we made a left onto the Forest Park expressway. Once we came to the light at Skinker, we paused. Miguel and I were talking about the events of the night, and that's when Miguel stiffened up."

"Stiffened up Mrs. Valdez? Could you elaborate?"

"Miguel could sniff out trouble better than a blood hound. He checked both rearview mirrors and he cited the number four, and told me to pull my piece...,"

"Your piece? Please elaborate for the court please." Baylor asked to eliminate confusion within the jury. It seemed as if some of the jury members never knew St. Louis had north side. The language barrier shone on their faces.

"My gun, that's what I meant, sorry. Miguel and I obtained our licenses to conceal and carry as soon as the State lit the green light. I pulled the gun out of the side door compartment. I knew what was about to happen and before I could cradle my gun, that punk right there, had his gun to my husband's neck." Isabella screamed with conviction as she pointed toward the shameless thug.

"Your honor, I would like to cite that my client has identified Lamont Edwards as the shooter of Miguel Valdez."

"Note taken. Please proceed." The judge responded as he shuffled through his papers. Baylor shifted his eyes to Isabella and questioned with his eyes to ask if she was okay. Isabella acknowledged.

"Okay Mrs. Valdez, please go on."

"Miguel asked him if he could slowly unbuckle his seat belt, and get out of the car. He told the boy he could have the car and the money we had on us. Next thing I knew, another punk was on my side with his gun pointed dead in my face."

"Is the young man who pointed the gun in your face in the court room?" Isabella's face almost gave rise and similarity to the look of a Joker's face. It was evil and over the top. "No, that bastard was delivered to city morgue that night. Proud to say my gun range classes paid off because his brain turned into a nasty, splatter of matter on the city street." The courtroom erupted with blend of cheer and applause. Inside, Isabella was sad she killed the young man, but for the moment, she felt as stronger than a superhero.

"Order in the court!" The judge barked as he banged his abused gavel several times, while trying to keep his glasses on his face.

"Sorry your honor." Isabella lied.

"I've warned you more than I have cared to. Caution your words Mrs. Valdez." The judge warned as he took to his notes.

"Miguel looked me in my face, told me he loved me, and asked me if I was ready. I looked down and saw he had his right hand occupied with his gun. Miguel wasn't going down without a fight."

"Was driving off an option?" Baylor asked as he paced back and forth in front of the witness stand.

"Now if it was, my husband would be alive and those misfits wouldn't be dead or on trial today. Anyway, we had committed the biggest sin and we were ready to deal with the outcome."

"Biggest sin? Explain Mrs. Valdez."

"In the midst of our pause at the light, we had fallen prey to conversation, instead of remaining focused. There are some places one should remain focused on the elements. Daydreaming, talking and texting on your phone, will get your life jacked in a second.

"Ok, understood." Baylor smiled at Isabella's bright language.

"Miguel gave me that special smile but for some reason, I didn't welcome it. I felt coldness and regret surrounding us. With the heavy onset of feelings overcoming us, I could not yell loud enough to stop the train wreck. Next thing I knew, the punk on my side yelled about seeing a car coming down the expressway, and that boy over there, the one who was on my husband's side became distracted and that's when the night fire turned into the first light of dawn. I pulled my piece and shot the thug on my side in his shoulder, he ran, turned back, and shot at me, and I fired off several more rounds. The other one on my side was shooting and I shot him. I turned back to check on Miguel and he was struggling to get his seatbelt off as he continued to fire shots. I saw another individual, that one sitting next to the other boy."

"You mean Latavion Jones?"

"What? That's his name? Lord what kind of name is that?"

"Stay focused Mrs. Valdez. Latavion is the man sitting next to the defense attorney, Mr. Bills." Baylor pointed out as he did his best not to laugh at Isabella. In business, Baylor and his partners always found humor in some of their client's names.

"Yes, Latavion was the other one I shot. He was at the scene. Lamont was able to get his gun into the car and he shot Miguel in the chest about three times." Isabella told her story with a cold stare. Her look was unpredictable and scary.

"Oh God- Oh no.... he was motionless-" Isabella whispered as her hands crossed her chest. "I fired my gun about two more times and I saw the other two punks limping away." By this time, the courtroom was silent. Not a dry eye in the courtroom. Baylor did everything possible to hold himself together, but Isabella's pain was contagious.

Isabella spoke in a broken panic. One minute she was angry and the next, nervous and whispering the details as if she were a scared child.

"I called 911 and screamed out the location. All I cared about was my husband. The blood pooling in his seat gave me chest pain, but it went away. I pulled him from the seat, stretched him out on the ground, and applied pressure to the wounds. Still alive, all he talked about was our family. He never complained about the pain. Not one damn complaint!" Isabella stuttered through her tears.

"He was telling me the end was near and I cried. I tried, Lord knows I tried to keep him with me. I did all things possible, but he kept going in and out of consciousness." Isabella screamed with her hands out, hoping peace would cradle her. "The blood began pooling in his mouth. I even tried scooping it out because I did not want him to choke on it. Next thing I knew, I saw the cops and the ambulance. I didn't know I had been shot until the paramedics placed me on a stretcher." With her last set of words, Isabella grew faint.

"It's okay Mrs. Valdez." Baylor grabbed her hand.

"Thank you, for the testimony Mrs. Valdez. I know it was not easy. Thank you." Baylor was confident that the public defender would not have one fact to stand on for cross-examination. At least that's what the two of them discussed at Baylor's office this morning over breakfast.

"Does the defense have any questions for the witness?"

"No your honor, the defense rests." The young lawyer added as he scooped his papers up.

"Nigga what! Bitch, you better get yo punk ass up thur and do sumthin! You better ask that hoe-bitch sumthin! Bitch lookin' old and shit. It was dark as hell outside and that wasn't me she saw!" Latavion yelled as he spat into his lawyer's face. Isabella ignored him and allowed Lisa and the Paramedic to escort her off the stand for treatment.

As she left the stand, Baylor smiled and winked at Isabella, because he knew the case was ending by the way the jury shook their heads, at the rejects from hell. The conviction, written over the jury members faces, sealed the defendants' fate. One hour later, the jury confirmed what everyone suspected- guilty. The two thugs were in for a long ride; life without the possibility of parole.

Chapter 16

"I see you are early." Lily noted as she checked her sparkling, diamond encrusted Rolex. Lily could not resist dressing her best for the meeting between her and Lucah. Lily dressed better than the nine's was when she was scheduled for TV appearances, book-signing events, and meetings for her numerous charity events; and as far as she was concerned, Lucah was just as important. He demanded her best without saying one word.

"I see you keep nice time." Lucah said as he checked Lily out from every dimension his eyes snapped.

"I work too hard not to enjoy the pleasures of life. Last time I checked, I work for Lily. Nevertheless, it doesn't mean I fly all over the land flashing my success the way society seduces us to do. I donate my time to certain non-profits by preparing meals and donating checks large enough to feed people across the nation. I know all about being hungry, desperate, and depressed by the circumstances of life."

"Such a strong woman you are." Lucah smiled.

"Thank you. I vowed to do the right thing as soon as I had enough to share with one, two, three, and now- thousands. I hope that number increases to the millions within the next few years. If I eat nothing but humility for the rest of my life, I will never run empty."

"Wow, well spoken." Lucah was taken hostage by Lily's infinite and powerful wisdom.

"Money is not the source of my happiness. I could have this place open and making a hefty amount by 2pm, but I have other priorities and I know my employee's have lives of their own. Sunday's and Monday's belong to them."

"A great boss you are." Lucah smiled.

"I'm a leader." Lily corrected Lucah.

"I value my spirituality. I'm not the type of leader who forces their employees to choose over Sunday morning service or grilling my chicken. Do you know what I mean, or are you the opposite?" Lily talked as she prepared the table.

Feeling comfortable with Lily, Lucah began modeling. Flashing his million-dollar smile while reaching inside his blazer to unbutton it; made Lily think twice about ending the meeting too soon. Lily sighed once she saw Lucah's broad chest.

"No, I certainly value my downtime. Ms. Lee, you seem to be the proud woman."

"Call me Lily. Look, don't confuse my level of confidence with pride. Pride can be deadly." Lily said as she poured Lucah a glass of water and placed two Chef salad's on the table. "Even when I was weak, the lesson was to appear strong, and ready at all times. I had to endure many challenges. The more I learned, the more confident I became. Now, Mr. Big Man, what is *your* deal? You have big companies, big cars, big-" Lily paused. She saw Lucah's face smiling away to devilish thoughts.

"A big what, Lily?"

"Look, don't flatter yourself." Lily said as she waived her hands in the air dismissing Lucah's immature thought. "I am sure every woman you have been with will comment something different about that, so I wouldn't be too bold to boast. Especially, since I didn't ask. Now, for your info, I was talking about your *big ego*, Mr. Millionaire. I'm sure there's a story behind that!"

"Ouch! You bite hard little Lil Lady! What did you think about my proposals?" Lucah asked as he moved things around on his salad plate.

"Answer my question, Sir."

"Ok, I do a lot of work to fill the void of loneliness. I was in a great relationship but she changed. She wasn't the same woman I fell in love with."

"Sounds like my story. Lucah, is there a problem? Are you allergic to something? You never responded to the menu selection I texted to you, so I thought all was OK." Lily noticed Lucah playing with his food.

"No, everything is perfect. I wanted to be sure my mouth wasn't in line for baptism in a pool of onions. I am not a big fan of onions."

"I went light on them. Trust me; we came to exchange business- nothing else."

"You are about as funny as, what's that comedian's name?" Lucah pondered as he tapped his manicured nails on the table.

"Who Monique?" Lily asked giggling. She kicked her shoe off and folded her foot under her bottom. She loved Monique. "She is a raw and in your face chick."

"No, I meant Charlie Murphy. You know, Eddie Murphy's baby brother." Lucah said as he leaned back while loosening his tie. The two chatted as if they had known each other for years. They were comfortable with each other and it showed, because neither one of them knew the cleaning crew had left over thirty minutes ago. Lily sat motionless with a smirk as she tried to think of a comeback to Lucah's joke.

"Come on Lily, you know, the one who's not that funny. You know who I'm talkin' bout, right? He's done a lot of stuff, but he's most memorable for his roles on the Chappell Show."

"Um hmm, I know who you're talking about. Lily grunted as she played in her food. The silence following their laughter was awkward, awkward enough to curve the conversation to business.

"Lucah, maybe I can't go with the business plans you presented me, but on other business affairs- well maybe not business, how about we go out on a date. I don't think it's wise to mix business with pleasure." Soon as Lily allowed her pride to slip out, she held her breath hoping Lucah would not slap her offer off the dinner table.

"Hmm, you reading my mind? Looks like you wanted more than lunch, huh?" Lucah smiled as he leaned onto the table. With his arms rested on the pressed white tablecloth, Lucah flashed his beautiful whites, forcing Lily to blush something awful. Lily had not felt this way since she saw her first crush, Lee Chang, on the school playground. Lily was in love with Lee Chang. Every time she saw him, she smiled on the inside, and the feelings of giddiness and warmth made her pledge her entire summer to chasing Lee Chang for her first kiss. Caught in the moment, Lily could have given a hot flash damn, if Lucah chose to chase the next woman he saw, as long as she got what she wanted first.

"OK, here's the deal-" Lucah offered as he circled his neck from side to side, while biting the bottom corner of his right lip. How about we design a plan to donate to each other's favorite charity, hold some events during the year, and gather sponsors to help us support the community. Our names in the headlines together will produce a lot of buzz. I'm sure your people and my people can make things happen while you and I-..."

"You're smoother than my finest drink of Sake, Lucah! Let's create the campaign and have our people work with one another and let's see how things turn." Lily suggested as she took notes. She did the best she could to give Lucah the appearance that she returned to business mode, but Lily's open and shimmering crevice on her chest; gave Lucah the hint that she signed up for his plan of leisure a long time ago.

"When is our first date, Lily?" Lucah sprung the question Lily wanted to hear.

"You tell me." Lily smiled as she gathered their plates from the table.

Chapter 17

"Virginia, I am happy to see the close of the case. My nerves were ready to jump the edge."

"I bet you were Bella!"

"You know, it's always easy for people to say cliché things, when life is good for them."

"Girl, it's over, so praise God. I'm happy we were able to keep you alive *and* sane in the process."

"I know. I got your messages and texts about the white jacket and the all white V.I.P room being reserved at the hospital in case I wanted to give up!" Isabella said as she rolled her eyes at her good friend.

"Bella, do you feel like much time has passed since Miguel's passing?"

"No. It feels like a second ago. I must admit, each day gets a little better, but then there are some days where I feel being alive is unfair. I talked with Bishop, and I didn't know how heavy my heart was until we talked."

"You have to let it out! Don't try to block it, the pain only intensifies."

"Whew- I could not believe how much guilt surfaces when you lose a loved one. You always think of how things could have been different. I also questioned if I placed Miguel before the Lord too!"

"Look Bella, I understand how you came to that feeling. Nevertheless, you and Miguel did not start at the top of the mountain. You two worked hard, raised your children, attended college, and took advantage of everything placed before you. Winner's operate like that!"

"I know..."

"No- you wait! I have been with you for some time, and I know the Valdez family does not have the 'lazy gene' in one soul.

Think about all the hard times, think about everything you and Miguel sacrificed in order to be where you stand today. All the charities you have helped, and all the community service you provide, has shaped this city. You do more than some of this city's richest snobs have done in a lifetime. Bella- you, Miguel and those children deserved every vacation, every car, every jewel, and everything else the Lord blessed you all with."

"Thank you. I love you Virginia. Bishop was clear on making the same point. My heart is not vain, and never have I felt as if we were bigger than anyone on earth."

"Well good, now kick those Louboutin's off and let me play in them. What size is these bad chicks' right here?" Virginia pranced as she tried to steal Isabella's shoes. Isabella was grateful to have a friend as honest and loyal as Virginia.

Chapter 18

"**O**K, the girl's have been gone about three months now Gabby, what are we going to do? I've been here; I've made myself as transparent as tape. I want you to understand, outside of home, the only thing important to me is you. I'm not looking to add another label of shame to this marriage. All we do is work. We hardly talk and truthfully, it is killing me. I want to live, I want *us* to live." Gabby was nowhere near ready to tell her husband that their marriage was over. Memories of the good old days made her brain smile for a moment. Soon after, the bitterness of the bad days gave her a terrible onset of brain freeze.

"You never went to counseling Gabby."

"Yes, I did." Gabrielle coldly stated as she looked out her bay window into a future undefined. The noise of her neighbor mowing his lawn at seven-thirty in the morning would normally send her into an episode, but the sound of the mower was oddly soothing.

"Dale, what do you want from me?" Gabrielle asked as she turned to her husband whose defense seemed beaten and worn. Dale's shit-filled apologies failed to penetrate Gabrielle's heart. She no longer wanted to be a part of Dale's team. Some people die a fan of something, even if they know it's toxic. Gabrielle no longer wanted to be the housewife who slowly died on the inside, all for the sake of the children. "We have to get back to living and loving. I know you remember when..."

"Not in the mood for the shit Dale." Gabrielle hated the sound of his voice. Neither did she desire his touch. In her misery, she had days where slitting her wrists sounded like the perfect escape from Dale's bullshit. The arguments between them about her career and her eagerness to be alone when she experienced her lows; wore her out. In the end, she opted to self-medicate to help escape misery. At times, Gabrielle thought she possessed super powers, because of her ability to tune out Dale's chatter as she looked him dead in the face.

"I'm not talking about sex Gabby. I remember when you would smile just to see me smile. I remember all the times where a day of nothing turned into hours something with one touch, one smile, or one hug."

"Well not today! You can believe that shit!"

"It's not the time that binds us as one Gabby, it's the love. It's all the 'in between' moments that give this marriage a cause to stand the test of time. To hell with what people think. A good marriage has bad stuff in it. The thing that makes it good is when two people stand to make sure the other never leaves.

"Negro you been watching too many Tyler Perry movies!" Gabrielle pushed Dale away as she cleaned off her dresser.

"Look Gabby, people give up on marriage too easy. I know I dumped some nasty stuff on you over the years, and you have the right to leave, but answer me one question." Gabby stared through Dale as if he were a blurred memory. She wanted to respond but her pride was drowning her. Before she spoke, chunked up feelings forced her into a crazy coughing spell. Dale rushed to help his wife.

"You OK? Here, sit down."

"Yeah, I'm alright." Gabrielle responded as she took down the glass of water Dale gave her. Dale rubbed his wife's back.

"Well answer this, Gabby. Why haven't you left?"

"I don't know." Gabby released as she cried.

"Come on baby, it's OK. I'm not going to judge you. I'm putting the past out of my life and I want the best for us. Do you want the same? Do you want to try one last time?"

"Yes." Gabby cried as she and Dale folded like chairs. Finally, Dale had the answer he was looking for. Gabby leaned into Dale's chest as she stared into the mirror affixed on her wall, and wondered if she was doing the right thing. For years she waited for the girls to leave home and now the fear of being alone and starting over paralyzed her. For the moment, the night belonged to something that was on vacation for way too long- forgiveness.

Chapter 19

"I take everything looks good, Mrs. Springfield?"

"How about calling me, Ms. Jameson?" Lola corrected Baylor's attorney. Three months past, and Baylor put up one hell of a fight during his divorce battle with Lola and her lawyers. Lola wasted no time in sharing all she knew about Baylor's hidden properties and bank accounts. The cell phone bills and the hell awful picture helped Lola's case. Regret tunneled throughout Baylor's heart. He knew he was close to losing the best thing he ever had with one stroke of his pen.

"What is the total reward amount? Only two properties have been awarded, and they are *not* the ones I wanted. I made it clear what I wanted!"

"Mr. Springfield is not…"

"Stop, Kenneth." Baylor interrupted.

"Give her the properties she wanted. I have done everything a man could dream of in the both of them. It's time for a fresh start."

"Easy for you to say that shit now! Why not then?" Lola asked as she left her seat. Face to face, Lola vented hell.

"Your dick swinging, whorish ass should have said that to my face long time ago and all this would have been done and over with. Save me and my daughter the damn heartache."

"*Our* daughter, you mean!" Baylor belted as he took to his feet.

"Don't act as if you care about her! If you cared, you would have handled things like a man. Hell, I guess it's hard for you *little men* to do anything on a *real* man's level!"

"Folks please! Can we remain civil?" Lola's lawyer pleaded for peace.

"Keep it up, and I will make *sweet* on my promise to blast

you.

"Let's wrap this up. I have a dinner date." Baylor snapped his fingers.

"Ok, for the record, the property requests have been switched, citing Lola Springfield- I mean Jameson, the properties in Missouri, and Georgia. Alimony and child support has been ordered and monetary award sums to fifteen million dollars."

"How you loving that, Baylor?"

"It's Ok. I will be fine! Now that the trash has been taken out, it's time to take in some fresh air!" Baylor retaliated.

"Folks please!"

"Reginald, stay behind to make sure the amendments are taken care of and forward me the originals as soon as possible. Friday is my last day in town and I will be unavailable for three weeks. I want things completed before I leave."

"Yes, Ms. Jameson."

"Well Mr. Bachelor, enjoy your daughter for three weeks. Here's the place and numbers to where I will be staying. Rachel's insurance cards, and her medicine, will be in her bag. Oh, yeah, no skank trash around my child! Her mother is alive and well and there is no need to substitute the real thing. If it's not about Rachel, don't call me. Mother and father will have the right to talk with her when they call; so make sure she hears from them." Lola strutted out the door in a fierce fashion ensemble of red, spiked Laboutain heels, white Fendi clutch, with an amazing royal blue, Prada dress to mark the debut of her independence. All the men watched Lola as she strutted out the room.

Chapter 20

"Lucah, this is Dr. Helton. I have left numerous calls for you and to no avail; you have not returned them. I think I need to pay a visit to you. I called your therapist and she has stated the same. I feel inclined..."

"Hello Dr. Helton." Lucah answered the phone from his bed. Lucah had finally had enough of all the panicked messages left by Dr. Helton and Dr. Arlington.

"Lucah, you know this isn't healthy. You skipped your medication refills and you have missed many appointments with me. What is going on?"

"Look doc, I'm sure you would love to turn me into your son, but I'm tired. I want to be left alone. Can you make that happen?"

"Lucah, I'm coming over. That's all there is to it. I'm going to bring some supplies to draw your blood. I will also call the pharmacy and have them deliver you a 90-day supply of all your meds. You're not going down like this." Lucah hung up the phone and started cleaning his room. He knew Dr. Helton wasn't going to sit back and allow Lucah to nose dive into the belly of death.

Lucah made his way to the bathroom and gave the porcelain Goddess everything his body had. He was down fifteen pounds in weight, his eyes, dark and sunken- gave the appearance of a dead man stalking his grave. He knew restarting his medication would take a toll on his body. Grabbing his remote, Lucah opened his blinds halfway, turned on several TV monitors and tuned into his favorite radio station. Lucah's bedroom had been his office for the last month.

"Mother, it's me."

"Oh my goodness!" Son, where in heaven have you been? You know my heart cannot take all this stress. All I do is pray, eat, and dream of sleep. Every time I think I know where you live, or work; I get a dead end. Are you on the run? Have you done something wrong?" Lucah's frantic mother shot out questions like an automatic weapon. Lucah felt bad about leaving his mother in the dark about his life. He was always afraid of what his mother would think if she knew her son was HIV positive. Somehow, today was different.

"Mother, I'm ok. I have something I need to discuss with you and please- let me finish what I have to say before you start shooting off those questions of yours."

"Lucah, whatever it is, you should have come to me a long time ago."

"Well I'm here now, mother."

"Speak son."

"Mother, do you remember Brooke?"

"Oh yes, how could I forget? Did you two get married and make me a grandmother?"

"Mother, please stop!"

"Go ahead son."

"Brooke left and it hurt badly. Since then, only evil thoughts have resided in my head. My life is full of darkness, confusion, hate, and rage."

"Oh my God baby." Mrs. Hunt's voice trembled with fear, sadness, and uncertainty. Mrs. Hunt raised her son to be God fearing and full of love for all. She knew whatever Brooke had done to her son; would require a miracle.

"When she left me mother, she also left me with a *package*."

"A package? Are you talking about a baby? What are you talking about, Lucah! Get to it, I mean right now!"

"Mother, I'm HIV positive." The pause on the line rattled Lucah's nerves. He counted his respirations and on the twelfth breath, he heard a crack in his mother's voice.

"Are you on the down low, Lucah?"

"No mother, I'm not." Mrs. Hunt trusted her son when it

came to him being honest with his responses. Honesty was one of the first lessons she taught Lucah growing up. Lucah knew his mother would disown him for lying to her. She hated liars the same way she hated snakes.

"What happened?"

"She was involved with a young man the same time we were together. One morning when she woke up, she found a nasty letter on her pillow. The first line alerted her that she was HIV positive and the second line stated that she should start planning her funeral."

"Oh Lord. Who would do such evil?"

"I don't know mother. She was dry and limited with her wording to me. I never thought a mean bone was part of her structure. You know mother, I was willing to love her no matter what. I found the perfect woman and we loved each other. I am still trying to understand why she disconnected herself without notice. Nothing was out of order; everything was fine the day before. Normally I could tell when she was upset about something, but not this time. Why did she cut me off like that?"

"Son she was upset. She lost her joy in the midst of it all. If you ask me, she jumped before she got to the edge. She knew she was wrong for cheating on you. She also knew she would have to face you again. Sadly, instead of being a woman about it, the bitch took the wrong road."

"Mother!"

"This is awful news and I'm supposed to remain calm? I don't think so son. I never understood why you loved older women the way you did."

"I loved her mother." Lucah cried.

"Why do this alone, Lucah? Why not come to me sooner, son? This weight is too heavy to carry alone." Lucah and his mother cried to one another as they tried to make sense of everything.

"Mother, I had to tell you. I didn't want you to hear it from the mouth of someone else. I owe only the best to you."

"Do you need me to help you? I can move in you know. How do you feel about that? Lucah's mother once again shot off more questions. Frustrated and depressed, Lucah rubbed his hand through his unkempt hair as he sat on the edge of his bed.

"Mother, I will fly home to visit you soon. We need to talk about the future. I want you to know my plans should I pass before you."

"Lucah, please don't make me cry any harder than what I'm already doing."

"I'm sorry mother. I can't wait for us to be together. I miss you and Greece."

"I miss you too, Lucah. How is your head son? Where is your heart? You know there is a chance of living a good life with your diagnosis, right? Do you take your medicine, how often do you go to a doctor, and do you have a therapist or psychiatrist? Are you depressed?"

"Mother, are you interviewing to take over Oprah's slot?"

"Sorry son, but I wouldn't be a mother if I didn't ask. You will have to keep on stomping your feet until you answer all my questions."

"Write them down and save them for me. I will be there on Friday. I'll be home for two weeks. You feel like cooking my favorite dishes?"

"You know I don't hang around in the kitchen too much, but for you...anything."

"Sounds good to me."

"I love you son

"Love you too mother." The more Lucah thought about all the pain Brooke caused to him and those he loved; his desire to infect returned. He knew before he could hunt, he had to get back in shape- mentally and physically.

Chapter 21

"Lily, this is Lucah. I know you have thought of many ways to express how badly you would like for me to go hell right now, but I have a reason for the long hiatus. Losing my mother was the worst of everything, but I'm ok now. In the midst of trying to grieve and take care of her personal affairs, I fell ill myself. There it is- no lies attached." By now, Lucah told as many lies as a politician, and it seemed he was comfortable with his new line of work.

"I'm praying you return my message. I must admit, I have faced many critical things in my life, and personally, shutting down felt like the best option. Just thinking of you made me realize giving up was not an option. Lily, will you please have dinner with me tonight at my home? Give me the chance to tell you everything about me. If I don't hear back from you I can assume you have moved on; so please send my well wishes to the lucky gentleman in your life." Lucah usually got his way when he pleaded and growled. His best act to date was his famous lip biting and neck-rolling act. There wasn't a woman alive that could pass up Lucah's insatiable sex appeal.

Chapter 22

Many restless nights led Lucah to pay a visit to his former Pastor. Feeling as if his spiritual side had been sold to the devil since his diagnosis, the idea of looking to God did not seem like a bad idea. Driving through Chesterfield Valley proved to be a busy and pleasant day for both shoppers and retailers.

Chesterfield was sensitive to the looks of anything darker than a fortune cookie, but Lucah never gave a damn about people's personal views. Lucah was a hint darker than a fortune cookie and people had always mistaken his bronze glow for every other nationality under the sun. He was one-hundred percent Grecian, and he was proud of it.

Lucah lived life well and thanks to his financial stance. Smiles- real or fake- greeted him regularly. Call it what you want, but a fine man driving a 2015 butter crème Bentley Mulsanne, layered in fine tailor made suits, matched with elite swagger was sizably undeniable. Being a connoisseur of cologne, Lucah knew if he skipped wearing cologne; the scent of his money would do. To some, he knew his riches would never be enough to dodge the ignorance of some people. No matter how rich a person outside the white race, whites still had their way of letting you know that you would never be one of them.

"That's right, keep on looking. I'm sure you would love to pull me over with your busted ass, Mr. Officer. I'm sure there's an order of food somewhere waiting on you to pick it up."
The cop sped around Lucah and stared him dead face, as the cop mumbled an endearing message. Above trash, Lucah nodded his head and shined one of his dazzling smiles. Too pissed to stop, the cop sped off.

Twenty minutes from the church, Lucah finds pleasure in the valley hills as he coasts down the freeway listening to the soulful sounds of Julie Dexter.

Standing outside the church with, Lucah stared holiness in its face. Deep down, guilt, sin, fear, and depression circled his heart. Lucah always prayed about finding a woman who would love him regardless. Maybe the Pastor could pull a miracle out his handkerchief.

"Hello Pastor. Thank you for seeing me on short notice."

"Ah my son, you know I would do anything for you. I requested you to come to many services to speak, but you never responded. With all you have done for the church, we felt a ceremony for you was in order, but again, you never responded."

"Pastor, you know how I feel about awards and things of such." Lucah grunted as he took seat on the cinnamon colored leather couch.

"Well everyone knew who donated the money to assist us with building the new church."

"I am a mere servant. I'm blessed to be the giver. I can't take this money with me you know." Lucah looked to the sky hoping it would not fall on him in the new church.

"True, true my son." Lucah felt restricted and tight. No matter how many times he changed his position, he couldn't find comfort. His heart took off in an unannounced race and a tidal wave of perspiration started seeping through his shirt.

"What is it you need to speak about son?"

"Bishop, I was slighted and something awful came into my life. Right now, it's been one heck of a trip trying to restore my mind and body. Without going into details; I feel there is nowhere other than hell for me to go."

"Are you damning yourself to hell for something someone done to you, Lucah?"

"Yes, no matter how hard I pray or fast, my spirit is not satisfied. A demon is dancing on the inside and truthfully, I want to dance with it." Lucah was as honest as the word itself. The betrayal and sudden discharge from Brooke; was inescapable from his heart.

"Do you want to discuss this with me? You know what happens here, is between us. It won't leave this room." Lucah immediately took to his feet. Afraid of being singled out as gay, or druggie; he shelled up.

"Let's pray Lucah." Lucah took seat as the Bishop rested his hands onto Lucah's shoulders.

"Father, we come to you in a period of darkness. Knowing that you are a God which cannot fail, a God who can soothe the storm in the midst of the midnight hour; we claim victory. For we know father, there is a lesson, and a mission to conquer. Father God, I rebuke this demon; I order it to leave Brother Hunt's spirit. The devil has no victory here nor will he take claim over this child of God. This man is a man of God, a servant who seeks placement on the path of righteousness. Father God, we all know there is always a ministry in misery. Show Brother Hunt, your child, the purpose of your will. Help him accept his role in the building of your kingdom. Lead him from wrongdoing, mend his heart father God, and dry his tears. Comfort him in the midnight hour. Father God, remove this illness, this *thing*, which binds your child into a hellacious world of depression and uncertainty. Bless his family, his friends, his company and every endeavor he sets forth to do. We are victorious coming and going. Stand by him father God, for you will not lead him wrong. All these things we ask in your name- Amen."

With spirit and truth present, Lucah cried away his pain. Refreshed, Lucah and hos Pastor united in a strong hug. "Son, I can try to imagine what has happened, but it wouldn't be fair, but remember judgment day. Remember, everyone is accountable for his or her sins. Saying the *devil made me do it*, won't fly with the big guy, and you know this. Pause and think before you make your move. God hears our prayers. He will answer them, in his time! Lucah, don't try to do God's job. Vengeance is his!"

"Well Pastor, if you only knew, you might feel the same way I do. I don't think he's willing to alter my situation."

"He's willing if you're able Lucah. You know better."

"I guess I deserve it. True, playing God is a large role, so I will decline the part." Lucah grabbed his trench.

"Don't give up on the Lord. He will never give up on you! I love you, and please Lucah, keep the faith and stay in touch! Don't stay away so long."

"I promise to do better with visiting church. Thank you and God bless, Pastor." Lucah lost half the weight his heart harbored prior to visiting his pastor, but the devil refused to move out the other half.

Chapter 23

"Lucah, its Lily. I would love to have dinner tonight at the Jazz Bistro. It's located right across from the Fox. Tonight at seven, Mr. Hunt, or the hunt ends, and this kitty will roam elsewhere in the safari. Oh yeah, bring plenty of Kleenex, if you plan to make me cry. I apologize for all you have been through."

Chapter 24

"Hi, party of six for Withers." Gabrielle announced as she and her entourage followed suit. Tonight was the night Gabrielle planned to finish negotiations on her book deal. Pleased with the schedule for her first book tour in four years; Gabrielle glistened like crystal. Gabrielle was happy to have a book with buzz more than a bumblebee. Her bouts with Dale and depression wore her thin, but she persevered.

"Right this way Mrs. Withers." The giddy host announced as she switched her thin tail about. The Bistro was Gabrielle's favorite place to dine. She welcomed the smooth and calming sounds of jazz. The dark and velvety ambiance mix with the sounds of jazz buzzing through the joint ceased the calling of the night's end.

Everyone knew Gabrielle for her bright personality, beautiful artwork, and wondrous literary works. On the dark side, the news about Dale cheating, and her suicide attempts were talked about more than the Rams and the Cardinals put together.

"Good evening everyone! I hope everyone had a great trip in." Gabrielle said as she pulled out her seat.

"Gabby, sit honey! I have been anticipating this entire trip." Jill said as she continued chain smoking. Gabrielle hated Jill's bad habits. She hated when Jill would turn a business matter into a social matter. Jill knew Gabrielle preferred talking and dealing in a clear mind, and the way Jill was tossing drinks back; she knew something was bound to go wrong along the road.

"Oh really? *You* were hyped about coming to St. Louis? I thought you hated St. Louis Jill."

"I do, it's not New York, you know." Jill smarted off as she lit another cigarette.

"Whatever Jill. I guess everything I asked for is on the

contract. Am I right?" Taking a quick puff of cancer and a swish of Chardonnay, Jill staggered her way back to the conversation.

"Yes, darling, you got everything you wanted! Questioning my skills to deal in the real world of books shows your lack of faith."

"Yeah, well I put my faith in The Lord, Jill." Jill gave Gabrielle the chatter-hand.

"Look, the last book was great, but the fans want more. Since your last episode of drama, your fans really feel you have a story to share. Something they can relate to. I know you have injected a little of your life into the art you create."

"Oh shit, Jill! What the fuck are we talking?"

"The media demands are heavy. Are you ready for this?"

"Oh shit, hold on everyone!" Gabrielle joked as she held her breath and closed her eyes tight. She knew Jill was a kill-kill agent and she knew Jill would never walk away with scraps. If her clients got scraps, well-she got kibbles. Jill Levy never took bits of anything.

"You know all the talk shows are in love with the non-profits you support, they love you Gabby! They love how *real* you are." Jill hinted as she elbowed Gabrielle in the side. "They are curious to see how much of your art imitates your life- or however the fuck that goes. On the eve of your book launch, we can tape for a few live show segments. This way, by the time you wake up the next morning, you- my little book diva, will be bathing in moo-lah!"

"Ah shit! Why you go do that?" Gabrielle was pissed and everyone at the table knew it. Everyone stopped breathing.

"Okay everyone, go hang out at the bar and give us two gals a moment." The crew took off running for the bar.

"Look Gabby, I'm not sure what's been going on, but you have to pull through this if you want to stay on top. Getting to the top is easy; staying there is the hard part!"

"Look bitch, if I may kindly call you by your birth name. I am not interested in having the world sitting in my bedroom. Dale and I are trying to work things out and I just want some fucking peace. I mean, how in the hell can we dress this shit up without it hurting my family?"

"Well first, re-write the whole fucking book!" Jill hissed venom as if Gabby stepped in her territory. "Look, we have worked together for years and I would never steer you wrong. This opportunity is made for retirement. No more book writing. Make a few appearances here and there, a few signings and BAM- it's all done!"

"Huh? BAM? I guess that's the way *your* life works, but you won't be *bamming* a damn thing around here, Jill! I'm going to release this project the way I want. I want say in regards to my show appearances. Next, keep my family out of this shit! They have stressed their desire to avoid the press with this release. The girls have settled in at college and they don't need this mess."

"Gabby, your family is off limits and please, please Gabby, consider Oprah!" Jill nervously released every detail Gabrielle wanted to hear. Jill knew she had to be careful with Gabrielle, because she would cancel a project without the twitch of her lip.

"The book is done, I will go back and add some changes and we can go from there. When is everything expected? I know we need copies of the book to the reviewers; so be reasonable!

"Two weeks sound fair."

"Bitch three."

"Three it is." Jill celebrated.

"Yes, we are covered one-hundred percent! The team has designed a plan if you can have the book done within three weeks, it won't change the book tour at all."

"Good, tell the publisher we have a deal." Jill and Gabrielle dabbed the sweat from their faces, lifted their wine glasses and saluted to another successful deal. "Ok, excuse me Super-Agent. The restroom calls. You have made me perspire more than I desire too."

"Go right ahead. I will be right here getting freaky on this Muscato! Where the hell did this wine come from?"

"Ask Nelly and those Lunatics."

"Figures! Damn rappers grind harder than anyone I know. Hey Felicia, make a note for me to hunt down a few hip-hop clients."

"Got it boss." Felicia responded as she pecked on her iPhone.

Gabrielle was about to pass out from the waves of heat which burned at her core. Sprinting for the front door, she inhaled the much-needed fresh air. Not even a few minutes outside, she inhales an intoxicating scent. Curious to find the source of the wild scent, she put her sniffer to the test and started mingling with the crowd- bloodhound style. Several people recognized who she was and made their way to pay their respects as well as grab a few pictures for their Face Book and Twitter pages.

Still set on finding the scent, Gabby continued her hunt. Lost, she stood still and allowed the air to circulate a second whiff of delight into her nostrils. Head titled high into the air with her neck tilted to the side and eyes closed; the source of the scent arrived.

"Oh my goodness, please excuse me. I didn't mean to bump into you. I guess I got a little mesmerized by the night's breeze and wonderful jazz."

"Wow, I must say that I've seen all I have needed to see tonight."

"Do you start all your conversations off this way?" Gabby played around as she tried to visualize where she'd seen the magnificent specimen that stood before her.

"Wait, aren't you the phenomenal author and artist, Gabrielle Withers?"

"Yes, yes I am." Gabrielle blushed. A new onset of wild

thoughts, vibrant energy, and sinful excitement associated with the chance of getting to experience a man outside of Dale; increased her respirations.

Still staring through Gabrielle, Lucah turned his manners on. "Oh, excuse me. I'm Lucah Hunt. I am a huge fan of your work. I have everything you have done in my home library."

"Really? Even the paintings?"

"Yes, even your paintings. You'd be surprised to know that I purchased three of your portraits at last year's exhibit at the Randall Art Gallery." Gabrielle was nowhere near giving a damn about the celebration honoring her name, occurring inside the restaurant. Lucah had laid yet, another trap, and Gabrielle was falling for it.

"Oh, thank you!" Gabrielle wanted to run to the restroom to see what rose colored cheeks looked like without blush. "I am sorry to be rude, but here's my card. I have a new book dropping soon. Hope to see you at a signing. Oh yes, right after, I will have a new art show following. Please feel free to call if you need custom pieces for your home or office." Gabrielle knew damn well that her days of creating personal pieces were over, but for Lucah, she was ready to paint butt ass naked for him.

"I will do that. If you don't mind, would you like to meet me for dinner after I conduct business with a client tonight?"

Thrown back by Lucah's offer, Gabrielle knew a field trip to stutter land was fast approaching. *Pull it together bitch! He fine and all, but making yourself look like an ass ain't the way to go.*

"Lucah, I will call you when I'm free. My party is expecting me back, and I don't want to mix business and..." Gabrielle unwontedly alerted Lucah of her interest in his company.

"It's ok, I understand. That was rude to ask. Please stay in touch. I would love to purchase something exclusive. Heck, maybe you may be willing to create something for me." Lucah reminded Gabrielle back.

"Ok, that sounds great! Talk to you soon." Running back inside the restaurant had Gabrielle raced to the rest room to see how wet her panties were.

Chapter 25

"**A**re you looking for the gentleman who's been to hell and back?"

"If you been to hell and back looking this damn fine, I guess I may as well saddle up too." Lily greeted Lucah with a peck on the cheek.

"Wow! You looking too good for this crowd Ms. Lady. You think I can get another kiss?" Lucah begged as he grabbed hold to Lily as he wrapped his arms around her body.

"Hmm, are all your kisses so delicious and sensual?" Lily quizzed as she tried her best to maintain her balance.

"Looks like a packed house. Are you interested in going elsewhere? Maybe there's another restaurant open without the wait."

"Ok, sounds good to me. I'm not in the mood for signing autographs or picture ops. Let's scramble like eggs!"

"Ouch! There goes that infamous Charlie Murphy comedy!"

"Ah come on Lucah, why you gotta do me like that?"

"Ok, it's a little better. You are now as good as Chris Rock's little brother!"

"Oh I see you like to crack jokes Mr. Man!" Lily gave chase to Lucah the best she could as she clutched down on her Hermes bag.

"Oh hell, oh my goodness..." Lily screamed as she lost balance.

"I got ya!" Lucah celebrated as he swept Lily up in the air before she kissed the ground."

"Wow, my personal Superman." Lily smiled as she hugged Lucah.

"Can't let you fall sweetness." Lily loved every dose of romance Lucah had to offer. As soon as Lucah attempted to plant Lily back on solid ground; the rain showered them without mercy.

"Where did you park?"

"I parked one block up on the private parking lot. You think we can make it?" Lily quizzed as she did a poor job of protecting her hair.

"Will your car be safe overnight?"

"No *way*, I can't risk it Lucah! I will call Katie, my assistant. She lives about fifteen minutes from here. I will pay her to catch a taxi to pick my car up. She has a set of keys for it. Is it ok for her pick me up from your home later?"

Lucah smiled as he bit on his corner lip while rolling his neck from side to side. "How about I drop you off at her home tomorrow? No sense in her driving all the way out to my home."

"Oh- tomorrow? You talking like you got plans for us. That's fine as long as you promise to be a good boy!"

"I will." Lucah crossed his sinful heart.

"No working on our date, Lucah. Enjoy your downtime!"

"Now that I have you, that's a mission fulfilled!"

Lily was happy thus far and took comfort in placing her small head onto Lucah's solid chest as his cologne provided a quick session of aromatherapy.

"Feel free to make yourself at home. I'm going to check some messages, and run to the cellar to grab a bottle of wine. I called my chef ahead of time and he is preparing something for us, right now. Please, feel free to walk around and check the place out." Lucah informed Lily as he hit a few switches to turn on lighting and music.

"Thank you." Lily loved the décor and the lavish colors Lucah displayed throughout his mansion. It was as if every room had its own theme. The exquisite art, fine furniture, and beautiful chandeliers gave the home tremendous value. A room with color rich, velvet portraits displayed Lucah's family history. Not inside the home too long, Lily had a sense of what Lucah was all about.

Light mail, brought happiness because it meant Lucah didn't have to spend hours reading proposals, and requests for speaking engagements, or sponsorship. Flipping through the end of the mail, a letter fell from the pile. A handwriting known, Lucah ripped the envelope open.

"My Dear Lucah,

How is life treating you? If I may, I have to say that I miss you- I miss us. I know by now your blood is boiling hotter than a pan of water, but believe me when I say that I never meant to hurt you. Lucah, I cannot explain how much all this pain and shame hurt me. I WAS A COWARD! I admit my crime. I was afraid, full of rage, and betrayed. My mind became the enemy. I cried, prayed, and hoped that all I went through was a bloody nightmare. I guess one could say I snapped when I poisoned you.

I did not want to release my diagnosis to you; for I feared you would leave me, or worse- kill me. I knew you loved me more than life itself, but something like being HIV positive changes situations; and I know no one is willing to play that game.

Lucah, I am tired of living. Hurting others never delivered satisfaction to my doorsteps. I didn't understand the animal I had become! The medicine regimen, the depression and all the pain- made me question God with every breath I took. If anything, the diagnosis brought forward a certain doom. Hell, if this were cancer, my feelings would have changed. At least I could have the chance to be cured. On the bad hand, I can't shake AIDS way. I will be cursed if I am still alive by the time you finish reading this letter, but I plead- live life the best way God allows you to live.

I am sure you have sifted through barrels of emotions. I know you feel like lashing out at every woman you meet, but it is not right. Trust me, I'm close to the gates of hell right now and you do not want to experience this. Once you are in route to hell, there is no detour, Dear Love. I've left a few messages on your home phone. I haven't left any lately because your inbox is full. Lucah, if you have started destructive behavior, please stop before it's too late. I am sorry. I will travel to the gates of hell begging forgiveness from you- not the Lord. That's how much I realized the depth of my love for you.

Forever Yours until-

Brooke"

Lucah felt as if someone threw a hundred pound weight onto his chest. He collapsed into his wingback and reached for the phone. Bypassing message after message, Lucah arrived to the one he wanted to hear.

"Lucah, I love you. Would you have loved me regardless? Were you willing to re-structure your life, your business, your leisure; for a life with a woman full of poison? Lucah, I knew you loved me with all of your soul. I felt it miles away. Call it selfish, but damn, the price for love goes way above expensive. Love turned on me. Love became ugly, and I am sorry for ruining your portrait of love. You did not deserve it. I am trying to make all my wrongdoings, right. If the Lord sends me to hell, I would not rebel it one bit.

I sent you an email. My number and everything is included. If I have not passed, I will respond. If not, the end came and went. There are instructions on who to contact. They know who you are. Lucah, I know you need for nothing, but I left everything to you. You are right; we sure as hell can't take it all with us, but I know you will find a way to be a blessing to someone else. I always loved how you gave unconditionally. I love you!"

Lucah stiffened with rage. Every emotion imaginable was on the menu, deciding which one to act upon first; puzzled his brain. His plan to slay every cougar he met became a blurred vision. Thoughts of his conversation with his Pastor and Dr. Helton surfaced. In the end, Lucah's desire to give Brooke or any other woman a chance, fled the scene.

"Brooke, love is pain, love is evil and it moved out my heart, a long time ago. I pray your death comes quicker than the wind wrapped in a tornado. Go to hell! Do not contact me anymore. The grave is where you belong. I should have had the choice Brooke. I could have used protection Brooke. Even if we were having sex, and you became positive, or even after he told you; the choice should have been mine! I would have never done something so mean and inhumane to you! I loved you and I was prepared to stand until the end with you. At what point did your fucking brain melt? You are smarter than that! Harvard educated, and you resorted to stupid, childish, and selfish acts!

The more I think about things, I would have left you had you told me Brooke. I never betrayed you. I never lied or cheated during our relationship, so no, there is no room for me to love you. I think deep down you knew what my answer was going to be and that is when you made the decision for me. Please have someone inform me as soon as you die; I'll come burn your body myself!" Lucah hit send and reclined to think about his actions.

"Lucah, are you ok?" Startled by Lily's sudden entrance into his office, Lucah closed his laptop. Lily felt the moment she walked in on, was indeed a private one.

"Sure, a little pissed right now. Business deal gone bad. Now I have to put on my cleaning gloves come this Monday. I should have listened to myself on this deal!"

"You were not supposed to be working!"

"See what happens when we take a break?" Lucah reminded Lily on why he worked and handled much of his business affairs on his own.

"You have to be able to trust the people around you sometimes. Every great entrepreneur has a great team. No one can be on my team unless they have served others first! A great servant becomes a great leader. That is what makes us damn good at what we do. We all make mistakes along the way." Lily consoled Lucah.

"Sadly, the mistake this person made is costing me big time. Now many others will have to deal with this mess." Lucah said as he looked across his office.

"I understand." Lily responded as she took seat in Lucah's larger than life wingback. Her feet were at least ten inches from the floor. "You are a good man. You give freely and you are good at fixing things. It will all pull together Lucah."

"Your good for my soul, fuck Campbell's." Lucah grinned.

"You damn right, fuck Campbell's."

"What makes you feel good Lily?"

"My charity work makes me feel good. I love to see the look on people's faces when their hearts explode with gratitude. I love seeing people happy. The easiness between Lily and Lucah made it easy to talk the night away.

"How bout you Lucah?"

"Being here with you."

"Too sweet. Oh look at you. You sure do sweat a lot. Are you ok?" Lily asked as she stood to wipe the perspiration off Lucah's face with her hand. Lucah allowed his nerves to calm, as he looked Lily over. His face lit with a bright and endearing smile. It had been too long since the touch of a woman warmed his soul.

Lily felt Lucah's sexual heat and backed off. "Is that your bathroom?"

"Sure."

"May I use it?"

"Use the one on the other side of my room. That one is

having new sinks and flooring placed in it. I'm too lazy to remove the stuff from my cabinets, the other one is equipped with everything you need."

"Thank you. When I'm done, can we eat? We talked so long; my stomach punched my back and reminded me how bad it is to skip meals. I am starving!"

"Sure, I will have Luis bring our dinner to the bedroom. We can eat here if you wish."

"Whatever." Lily sang as she skipped to the bathroom. Lucah smiled when he heard to toilet seat plop down.

"Ah, the sound of a woman in the house, how inviting." He laughed as he stood to stretch. Lucah dashed to his bathroom and wiped his entire bathroom counter clear. His mini pharmacy and pillboxes would give-a-way the hint of bad health. Lucah was determined not to meet death until he himself had done damage.

"Umm, the food smells great!" Lily cheered.

"Ok, go easy on Luis. He's a great Chef, but when I told him who I would be dining with this evening, he turned white as ice."

"Sorry, my name kind of follows me. Tell him not to worry. If it's bad, I will ask for cereal next time!"

"Ok, that humor of yours has been upgraded." Lucah and Lily laughed uncontrollably.

"Lucah, do you mind placing my dress in the dryer for a few minutes on low? It's still wet in spots. Also, do you have a robe or dress shirt I can borrow?"

"Sure, see that door over there?"

"Yup."

"It's my laundry area. Go ahead and place the dress in the dryer and feel free to take any shirt off the rack." Lucah mumbled as he ate his dinner.

"You a neat freak like me, huh?" Lily commented. She was amazed at the order of Lucah's walk-in closet.

"Yes, my lady, I am! Order in my life is a must!"

Lily was slow to dress down, when the scent of Lucah's laundry area hit her. The scent had the same soft, but masculine smell throughout the entire mansion. Lily did not avoid smelling Lucah's shirts. The intoxicating scent seduced her into rubbing her breasts on his shirts. Lily closed her eyes and thought of how Lucah rolled his neck side to side as he bit on his lip. *Umm, that look only means one thing.* Lily whispered as she pleasured herself.

"What would that be my sweet?"Lucah caught Lily in her moment. Without permission, he pinned his half-naked body against Lily's petite frame. Sandwiched between the warmth of Lucah's body and the dryer, she felt her lily pond filling with moisture. Imitating Lucah, Lily rolled her neck from side to side. Lucah grabbed hold of her hair and began kissing and licking her neck as if a sweet pastry fell upon it. Lily surrendered and stretched her short arms on top of the dryer. Lucah fondled her breast until his hunger forced him to engorge her succulence.

Hoping she would allow him to enter without a passport, Lucah went downtown to seal the deal. Much time had passed since the wet walls of a woman's cave cradled his love. Not even three minutes into Lucah talking to Lily's wetness, she cried and moaned for the bed. Lucah obliged and swiftly carried Lily to his arena. Lucah laid Lily on her back and smiled at her, as his fingers took over from where his mouth left off. He continued to double the pleasure as he loved on Lily's breasts. In between Lucah's hand game and his exquisite skills of talking to her breasts, Lily's cave was close to exploding sweet tasting lava. Lucah knew this and began to pace the session.

"Is it safe to say that we both want this?" Lucah asked.

"Are you clean, Lucah?"

"As a baby. Do I look like I'm in to taking risks? I can put one on, it's no problem."

"Just put it in. This feels too good Lucah."

"Good, I'm done talking.

Chapter 26

*H*appy and refreshed from her vacation in Miami, Lola was ready to take on anything that flew her way. With the divorce final, and Baylor's calls no longer lighting up her phone; peace and happiness brightened her forecast. Lola prayed Baylor's immature and child-like manners was just a phase. Surviving it all, the only thing Lola cared about was Baylor bringing another woman around their daughter too soon. Lola sure as hell had no plans on bringing a man around her child no time soon.

"Baylor, is Grace ready?"

"Hello to you too Lola. Yes, she's ready."

"Good, I will be there in about an hour, please have her ready. No drama, the less you say, the less I say. Erupting in front of her will not help. I don't want this mess to bother her."

"There you go, Lola. Please calm down. I want peace Lola. I didn't mean the things I said during the hearing. I'm sorry, and I still love you. I'm always going to be here for you and grace. I think we both grew apart and I'm ok with that."

"Ok, I can take that. I want peace because it's proven that divorce messes a kid up. I want to reduce as much stress and depression as possible. Give me a few; we can talk when I get there." Lola rejoiced as she thought about going home to a peaceful atmosphere. No more whining, crying, or waiting up late nights. The drama was all out the door and Lola was ready to move forward.

"Lola, I take you had a great vacation." Baylor asked as he helped her out the car.

"Yes, I did, truly I did, and did I say, yes-I-did!" Lola beamed a smile so bright the sun decided to settle. "Where is my baby at?" Lola quizzed as she allowed her glittery stilettos and silver beaded cream and gold bandage dress to speak *exactly* how the vacation served her.

"Damn, like that Lola?"

"I know your ass ain't worrying about who fluffed this pillow." Lola teased as she switched her way into Baylor's new bachelor pad.

"Mommy!"

"Hey there! Give mommy a hug. How was everything while mommy was gone? Did you take all your medicine? Did your daddy bore you?"

"Mom, you sound like that lawyer lady I know."

"Ok, you have a funny bone showing Ms. Lady! Let me see if I can put that back in."

"Oh no mommy, I was kidding!" Grace screamed out as her Lola tickled her daughter. "Ok little lady, go grab your bags, kiss daddy and lets go home. I foresee a stop by Stone Cold on the way home."

"*Cold Stone mommy, Cold Stone.*" Grace schooled her mother, hopefully for the last time. "I will be right back! I forgot my laptop."

Baylor's pain froze his thoughts. He did not want to see his little princess and the woman he loved; leave him cold. Regret vacationed with Baylor while Lola was enjoying her own but clearly it was not the night to talk reconciliation with Lola.

"Lola, can we set up business meetings and times around our court schedules and other events? I also wanted to know when you can meet to finish interviewing the three paralegals."

"Fine with me, I want to take lighter case loads anyway. Let the young bloods take on some of the load. They have proven themselves, and I trust them. I would like to plan the interviews for one day. I figure we can break for a couple hours, maybe twelve through two. Then we can run straight through until we are done."

"Great, I'm all for it."

"Mommy I'm ready."

"Ok, tell your daddy good-bye and let's jet super star!"

Lola walked to the door and turned to take in a scene she never thought she would see. Baylor kneeled to give his princess a kiss goodnight and a hug that cried for his daughter to stay.

"Daddy I miss you at home. I'm not looking forward to going home alone. You need to be there to protect me and mommy." Lola's steady stance turned into a weak tremble. Paralyzed with anxiety, Lola turned away hoping Baylor was not going to fold like her.

"You my Princess, you know that right?" Baylor tickled his daughter's nose. "You are outstanding! Look, just because mommy and daddy live in the different houses does not change the way we feel for you. Think of it as you having two cool homes to visit. Our time together will not change. Mommy and Daddy are on different pages right now."

"Well close the book and open it again. I'm sure you guys will eventually get on the same page again." Grace shouted as she stomped her foot.

"Come on sweetie, we don't have long before Cold Stone closes." Lola said.

"There you go mommy! You said it right mommy! See, I told you it wasn't hard to say. Ok daddy, I will see you soon. Call me a lot!"

"You bet baby!" Baylor responded while trying to remain composed. Seeing Lola and his daughter walk out the door had to be about the hardest thing, he had ever had to do.

Lord, I need them to walk back in that door and stay. Can you help me?

Chapter 27

"Mrs. Valdez, I have Mr. Truth on the phone."

"Who in heaven, is Mr. Truth Veronica?"

"That new R&B sensation from the south. You know the one who has the single, "*I Apologize*". You listened to his CD a couple of days ago."

"Oh goodness, yes, yes! There's been a lot of buzz about that young man. Patch him through. Isabella smiled as she readied herself to do what she was born to do.

"Mr. Truth...ok, ML, thank you for thinking of me. Yes, I have listened to your CD and it is wonderful. Please tell me what you want." Lola said as she placed the phone on conference. Her assistant took notes, as Isabella's ink pen recorded the conversation.

"Ok, great! I can help you with the PR campaign. It takes a little more work when you are with an Indie Label, but if you have the right people surrounding you, all will be fine. I do not believe in my clients having to do one thing; that is why you pay us. I want you to understand that I am your PR person. If you hire me, I should be the main person in your ear. Run to me when the funk hits the air. If you have an idea about something leaking, call me quick! This helps with the clean up." Lola stated as she gave her lasso sign to Veronica as she pointed to her phone.

"Mrs. Valdez, you have author Jason Billups on line three." Veronica chimed in.

"Thank you Veronica, tell him five seconds."

"ML, review the contract sent, discuss it with your attorney and manager, and call me back no later than three this Friday. I am glad we got the chance to talk and I look forward to working with you. You have my cell, call with any questions."

"I think the Queen is back on her throne and ready to rock!"

"Ya think?"

"Yes I do! Now I'm going for your latte, bagel and fruit. Is there anything else you want?" Isabella greeted her office window with a smile. "I think that will be all Veronica." After breakfast, Isabella was fueled and ready to take on the day. Before she knew it, a few phone calls, presentations, video reviews, and meetings delivered the end of the day to her desk.

"Oh Lord, what a day! Please don't let this be the way I end my life. An over worked, love deprived widow." Isabella placed her head on the window. Deciding to avoid burnout, Isabella decided to close shop for the day.

"Veronica, you got this?"

"Since when have I not had things boss lady?"

"You are the best. Did you get the gift I sent for your birthday?"

"YES! It was wonderful.

"I sent a thank-you card, did you get it?"

"Child, I have too many cards on my desk, it looks like a damn paper farm. The kids and my family are still sending out thank you cards to people who came to Miguel's service. I still have checks that need to go to the bank for our charities. I know it's been a while, but it's been a tough run."

"I understand. I'm up and down myself. It's going to get better moms."

"It damn well better."

"Since you didn't get my card, let me give you this." Veronica ran into Isabella's chest and gave her a big hug. Veronica was Isabella's second daughter. Early in life, visiting group homes was important to Isabella. She felt there wasn't much attention given to children in foster care. Isabella did her best to reach out to the children to help them vision a happy life.

She wanted to help the children feel as if they were a part of the world. Society seems to forget foster kids and the elderly.

Isabella took a liking to Veronica when she met her on one of her group home visits. While giving a speech, Isabella noticed a bright light circling Veronica. For reasons unknown, Isabella could not take her eyes off the witty, fearless, and independent child. Veronica outshined her peers and her body language signed for a better life, and the chance to be great. About two weeks after the speaking engagement, Isabella completed the adoption process and Veronica was a part of the family. Veronica aced her way through high school and off to Spellman she went. After college, Isabella and Miguel purchased Veronica's first home, car, and deposited a hefty amount of cash in her bank account.

Isabella did not want Veronica to graduate with the worries college graduates of today face once they walk the stage. How to pay off loans and how to find work was not the experience she wanted for her child. She knew Veronica loved working in communications, so the idea of turning the firm over to Veronica was never in question. Ten years past, Isabella's plan on grooming Veronica to run the agency finally came into fruition.

Isabella was happy with the flood of love Veronica showered upon her.

"Veronica, I want you to know I'm not upset with you staying away after your father passed."

"I couldn't do it. I was there to see him on my own before you arrived to the church. It was too much for me to deal with. All I could do was think of my birth mother and I was done for it. By the way, Nurse Lisa kept me up to date on things. You know hospitals are the last place I'd visit."

"I know beautiful. It's ok. Hey, you feel lighter. Have you been losing weight?" Isabella quizzed as she stepped back to snap a few shots of Veronica's new frame.

"Yes..." she paused as she did a victory dance. "My latest

love affair has been with the gym." Veronica beamed as she pulled her gym bag from her office closet. "I can't be in the limelight looking like a hot pot of mess. Healthy is better! I didn't try to lose this much, but it feels good, I look good and my energy levels are through the roof." Stretching to the air as far as she could, Veronica inhaled happiness.

"I take it you and Lawrence are over."

"Yes, it's for the best, and that's all I have to say about that!"

"Don't worry, I'm not going to tell you I told you so."

"Your *look* already told me so, but it's all good! Do you need me to do anything else?"

"Nope." Isabella responded as she walked Veronica to the elevator. "Make sure you review the notes I made for tomorrow's meetings. We have some events to attend and I want you catch me up on some other things I highlighted in the packets. Not a lot of homework, don't sweat!"

"Ok, love you and I will see you tomorrow." Veronica chimed as the elevator doors closed. Isabella felt good about being in the swing of things. The question was how much of her time would be spent working and how much moving forward.

"Excuse me." Startled, Isabella jumped three feet into the air.

"Oh LORD! Sir, you scared Satan out of me! Do you know how to whisper or grunt? Hell, my nerves are frayed enough." Isabella reprimanded the young man as she stared into his green eyes.

"I'm sorry. Are you ok?" The man questioned as she reached out to help Isabella catch her breath. "I did not mean to scare you. I apologize."

"How may I help you?" Composed and back in one piece, Isabella was ready to find out who the man was.

"I am looking for the Valdez Agency. I can't believe I got lost. I'm pretty good about finding my way through."

"You have found us." Isabella said as she pointed to the sign on the glass door. "You probably went to one of the division offices I have within the company. I own this whole floor, but every division has its own suite. This is the office where we meet our potential clients."

"Ok, at least I know my navigation skills are still intact."

"I am Isabella Valdez, the owner. What services do you require?"

"I'm sorry, were you leaving?"

"Yes, but go on."

"I wanted to make face, gather some information, and set an appointment. I know this is not the norm of business, but I wanted to get a head up on the company I'm interested in placing in charge of all my PR needs."

"Come on in. I have about twenty minutes of free time." Isabella fibbed. Far as Isabella was concerned, she was ready to slave out another eight hours of work to avoid pain and misery. Isabella opened the door for her potential client. As she directed the strange man to privacy, Isabella took note of his sharpness and detail for fashion. Isabella's nostrils felt a tickling sensation as she inhaled a strong and sensual scent. The scent provoked Isabella to extend her chest as she inhaled his essence. Hypnotized by the scent, Isabella felt her womanhood dancing, vibrating, and throbbing all at the same time.

"Ok, tell me your name, company and, or project." Isabella asked as she grabbed a new folder from her file cabinet.

"Mr. Lucah Hunt is the name and I am the owner of Hunt International. I am an entrepreneur, and philanthropist. I have backgrounds in investment banking, realty, stocks, and I have patented a few products used in the medical field. My latest passion is giving away my fortune if you want to believe that." Lucah humbly added to his list of facts.

Isabella jotted notes onto the paper. Lucah took in the sites of Isabella and came into the position of crossing his leg and placing his arms over his lap, covering his erect penis. Isabella's long, and curly locks bounced around her entire head. Lucah had never seen the actual color of gold in a woman's hair.

With her last jot of notes, Isabella looked up ready to ask more questions when she noticed Lucah lacquering a fine coat of lust over her entire body. Isabella ignored him and continued her Q and A session. The last time Isabella saw that look was on her anniversary night with Miguel, and she knew what that look meant.

"What do you expect the Valdez Agency do for you Mr. Hunt?" She asked while swaying her chair from the left to right, as she took deep recline in her chair.

"I need a strong PR team who can handle sustaining my corporate image. I need help with attaining more PR ops in the media. The last agency I used fell off the wagon like a bunch of drunks. I am for total order; I I need everything to be in sequence. Mess does not exist in my world."

"Ok, I totally understand. Tell you what, create a plan on your vision. I need to know your goals and provide me with the necessary tools to help position you where you need to be. In the meantime, email your current website and email addresses, business and personal references, phone numbers, local, and international; to my personal email. I need to know if you have any enemies, and I need to know with whom you conduct business." Isabella figured it would be wise to stay on a roll, instead of allowing Lucah the chance to eat her alive, with his eyes. Lucah gave Isabella the jitters, and the feeling of a sexual re-birth in her panties, was on the horizon. The last time Isabella thought about sex was the night of her anniversary.

"Mr. Hunt, if you are surrounded by the right people, you will have coverage at all times. I do not believe in my clients having to do one thing; that is what you pay us to do. If we work together, please understand that I am your PR person. I should be the only one in your ear. You run to us when the funk hits the air. If you have an idea about something leaking, and it has the potential to stain your name, call me! This helps with the clean up." Isabella rolled on with her script as she prepared a contract for Lucah to take with him.

"I love your dedication and professionalism. I see you have done this for a long time."

"It's all I know Mr. Hunt." Isabella kept it professional.

"I'm in love with what I see right now. Can't wait to see how things develop." Isabella did not know how to take Lucah's comment. Not wanting to take the time to think about it, she jumped up, affixed her red pants suit, and put on her black sequined crop blazer. Lucah saw Isabella's work history shine throughout her office. Awards, and pictures with some of the world's biggest celebrities and political figures; proved she was the woman for the job.

"Ok, that will be all I need. I will await your word Mr. Hunt. My fees are included in your packet. I've placed twenty or so business cards in there shall you feel the need to share my services with *quality* people." Lucah knew Isabella was trying to put him out and he knew why. As Lucah stood to adjust his suit, his scent delivered a one-two combination into Isabella's nostrils. Lucah's height, mixed with his strong and chiseled frame reminded her of a younger Miguel.

"You were kind and helpful. I look forward to us working together." Lucah extended his hand to seal the deal with Isabella. Lucah's black hair was full of waves deeper than the ocean. Hair no longer than the bottom of his shirt collar, gave him a mixed appearance of a Greek God. Isabella loved men who resembled exotic regions. His golden sand stone skin had a particular glow to it. Lips finely glazed and cared after, showed how well Lucah took care of himself. Isabella was staring perfection in its face. Isabella kicked the good-girl out and gave way to tempting thoughts of how their working relationship could develop into something else.

"See you soon Mr. Hunt, and thank you for your interest in the Valdez Agency. It was a pleasure."

"A pleasure indeed." Lucah stated as the elevator doors kissed good-bye. Isabella went back into her office, removed her jacket, and turned her fan on. She quizzed herself to see if she was experiencing a flash caused by Lucah or mean old Mother Nature. With nothing to do, she began searching the internet to see what her Google search produced on Mr. Hunt.

"Good Lord, this man is the same age as Devin." Isabella shrieked as she reviewed Lucah's LinkedIn profile.

"Thirty-two years old?" Throwing age to the side, Isabella became pleased as she browsed through Lucah's numerous websites. She saw where his sense of fashion and grooming originated. Lucah was a supermodel in his early teens until his late twenties. All the money he earned through modeling and investments gave him a plush seat in the rich lane. Adding to his fortune was his billionaire parents who resided in Greece. His father was a man who dealt with stocks and other ventures. His mother, a former supermodel herself was a spokesperson for many third world non-profits; geared towards raising money for AIDS and cancer research.

Lord what is this you have sent to me?

Chapter 28

Fed-ex was about to lose their status with Gabrielle. The proof copy of Gabrielle's book was en route and she was eager to start her new book campaign.

"Hey mom. Just checking in to see how things are going. Yes, I know. I will be sure to send you a copy of the book, but not before the release date. You messed up last time and left the book at the salon and next thing I know, my book was flying around the salon. I know of at least fifteen people who did not buy my book. Uh, look mom, love ya, I gotta go! The fed-ex man is here."Gabrielle dropped the phone and raced to the front door.

"Mrs. Withers I have a package for you, if you'd be so kind to sign my pad." Gabrielle signed the pad and snatched the package. The box felt light. She looked at the address on the package and noticed the return address was from Atlanta. "Who in the hell sent me a package from Atlanta?" Gabrielle was never up for surprises. She hated feeling uneasy.

"*Before you find yourself rejoicing, it would be wise if you read some of the letters and cards in this package. Hey Sweetie, go grab a stiff vodka or whatever you drink, and see how much your Dale is dedicated in making your marriage work.*" Gabrielle felt faint as she fell onto her couch with the letter trapped in her moist and shaky fist.

"*I know this isn't what you wanted, not with your new book dropping soon. Dale dropped a few toxic bombs when he confided with me about your abusive behaviors. Are you that fucked up where you resort beating the man who once loved you without any pre-existing conditions? Wow, and women wonder why they can't find good men! Its bitches like you that give us good women; a bad name! Not every man is a dog.*

Moving to a prettier portrait, how are the twins? Last time I saw them, they were beautiful and ready to take on the world. No wonder they left like they did. Luckily, Dale was there for them. No telling what you would have done to the girls if he was not there.

I'm sure your eyes are dancing in a crazed maze as you try to figure out who I am, but stay on the path bitch! Let me cut the game short! I want you to walk away from Dale! Some sad part of him wants to hold onto your lousy ass, but there's another part where he holds me as if it was his first time holding a woman. Why are you still there? If you fail to leave Dale, the media will have a good time with your ass. You and I know that you can't afford any more drama! Play smart bitch or get ran over.

F.B."

"Who in the hell is F.B.?" Gabrielle screamed as she ran to the DVD player. She plopped herself on the couch and grabbed her Kleenex. Gabrielle's mouth gave the same semblance of an opera singer as her bottom lip trembled. Breathing stopped, tears fell and her heart bounced like a kick ball. Numb with anger, Gabrielle punched her gut. She was pissed that she failed to follow her mind and not her heart when it came to leaving Dale.

One more chance my ass. Leave it up to your heart and your gut and you pay. I'm too old to be going through shit like this.

Chapter 29

"Hello Lucah. Thank you for the flowers. They are beautiful. I have never seen an arrangement of Cherry Blossoms as this. I am sorry we haven't been able to connect. My schedule has been hectic and I've been under the weather. You had better believe that I have not forgotten about our night. It's been over a month and you scent fails to escape me. Don't get me wrong though, I love it. Oh well, gotta get back to my kitchen, call me after seven this evening." Lily was crazy about Lucah and she looked forward to seeing him again.

Chapter 30

"Mr. Hunt, this is Gabrielle Withers. Something has come up and I think tonight, around seven thirty is a great time to meet. I forgot I rented my studio out to a private party for the evening. If it's ok, I prefer to meet on your grounds. Please feel free to call if this time does not work for your schedule. Thank you.

Chapter 31

"Mr. Hunt, this is Dr. Arlington. I have received your messages but you know I need to see- not hear, from you. Please call the office to set-up an appointment. We need to get to the source of your depression. I want to help you. Be sure to call soon. If not, I have no choice but to drop you. I have strict guidelines to abide by and complaint patients are a must I hope you understand. I look forward to hearing from you.

Chapter 32

"**L**ucah, it's the doc. Look man, I need to see how you are doing. I requested you to visit the lab last month and you didn't go. You know we need to keep an eye on your cell count. Help me, help you my man! We must keep you healthy. I am here, so call me. No matter the time, I'm here for you. Call my cell when you get this message."

Chapter 33

"Grace, will you please stop shaking the cantaloupe!"

"Sure mommy, should I shake the watermelon? They say we black people *love* watermelon!" Grace smarted off as she shifted her body weight onto one hip. Grace knew she could never get away with this behavior as such with her father. Since the split, Grace lived wild everyday as she rode the fence of her mother's patience. Lola was tired, over worked, and slapped with an onset of depression.

"Look, I will slap all of those ignorant brain cells clean out your head! If you make me raise my hand, you will be going to the funeral home and I will be going to jail. Play it how you want, I'm ready! Do you understand little girl? Look at me, I wish you would cry!" Lola didn't give ten hot damns about going to jail; all she wanted for the moment was for Grace to act right.

"Yes mommy. I'm sorry. Mommy, you didn't have to grab me like that." Grace lowered her head when her mother gave her the look that was strong enough to summon hells angels.

"I know the divorce is hard on you, and I know you miss your daddy, but you *will* respect me and you *will* get back in the place of a child. I am *not your damn friend*! I am your mother!" Lola was tired of Grace and she knew the best way to check her wild child was to get eye-to-eye, on bended knee. It was something about getting on a child's level to certify the warning of an upcoming ass whipping.

"Now shut up!" Lola raised her hand into the air ready to strike. "Say one more word....one more!" Grace knew where her mother was coming from and she did not want to finish the trip.

"You are going to granny and paw-paw this weekend. I need a break! Your Daddy will pick you up on Monday after work! You think being ten years old with some scrawny nipple buds makes you grown, well...SIKE! You better get it straight young lady."

"When will you-"

"Shut up Grace!" Lola's hand started to twitch as she looked around. Maybe Grace needed a good old whop on the butt. "I will pick you up on Tuesday after I have had some time to myself! Your dad will be excited to see you. He has been working a lot, just enjoy the time with him. You better not give him any trouble either."

"Ok, I got it."

"Now, go grab your snacks for the weekend, and pick us out a couple of lobsters. Mr. Danny is in seafood and he has a snack for you."

"Ok." Grace walked off without looking back at her mother. Lola was pissed about Baylor not living up to his terms of the divorce. Both agreed that a nanny was not going to be the primary source of Grace's care. Baylor lost his focus on family and shifted it all right into work. With his heavy workload, and his decision to spend time with the woman that wrecked it all; Lola was ready for war.

"Hello?"

"Lola, its Dr. Arlington."

"Oh thank The Lord. The voice of sanity and divine intervention has called."

"Oh wow, I'm getting my schedule book out now. What is going on Lola?"

"I'm working a lot, trying to be there for Grace and getting pissed with Baylor. He hasn't been living up to his end of our divorce agreement regarding Grace. Grace barley sees her father. He's not even showing up to her events."

"I hate to say it, but welcome to the world of single motherhood."

"What in the hell makes them go beyond south of the border? I don't understand men."

"Hell they don't understand us."

"She is still his child Virginia, and he is supposed to be there for her."

"Is he paying his child support?"

"Yes." Lola was not happy with Baylor depositing money in the account and walking away as if that made everything kosher. Since she came back from vacation, Baylor's cold cycle started and now, he was spinning out of control. She did not understand why he made his child suffer because he was going through some mid-life crisis.

"Seems as if you are getting more than what most single mothers are receiving."

"Come on Virginia! You better not be charging me for this session."

"Okay, I turned the timer off."

"Really Virginia?"

"Naw, I was kidding. Woman you need to laugh! It's all about the live, laugh and learn cycle! Right now, you're stuck on living. If you do not laugh and learn from this shit....you will self-destruct in ten seconds! Oh yeah, move Grace out the way! Kill yourself, not her!"

"Oh that's harsh advice doctor."

"No, it's *life* advice! You can do this! You are not the first!"

"Getting back to your question, he pays the money, but it's the time spent with his child that's important. I am shocked at what you said, Virginia! Welcome to single motherhood my ass!"

"I'm sorry, I'm trying to make you see sunlight in the darkness of your drama. You need to turn the channel."

"Well it didn't work."

"Excuse me for doing my job." Lola was not in the mood for additional drama or jokes.

"You want to come in to talk?"

"Yes, I have time off starting tomorrow. I took down time to catch up and unwind, before the stress finds a way to gag and bind me."

"How about three tomorrow?"

"Sounds great."

"Do you need me to call in a script to help you relax?"

"Sure, I see no harm in that. Can you have it delivered today?"

"I sure can."

"I will be home after five this evening."

"You are covered. Be sure to come in tomorrow. In the mean time, you *and* Baylor need to schedule a joint session. Let's see if we will be able to re-structure a plan that will make things easier on the both of you."

"I think he is finding a way to unwind as we speak! Why would he want to show up?"

"Now Lola, the divorce is final. We need to omit some of that unnecessary drama. Whatever he chooses to do on *his* time is fine. We need to focus on how we will direct him back to the original agreement between the two of you concerning Grace. You know he loves her!" Lola was pissed and close to hitting the end button with Virginia as she browsed over the pasta selection.

"Yes, I know, but he's acting pretty childish. There is no reason for him to act cold and distant to his own child. I don't give a skillet of hot grease who he's screwing; his first priority should be his daughter."

"Well, let's show him everything you spoke, in a grown-up way. Don't feed the dog when he's not hungry. I swear, the dog bastard will bite you *and* shit on your porch when you least expect it! Do your best to never give way to fault."

"Hey, when did you learn how to talk like that Virginia?" Lola dropped a pack of pasta as she tried not to laugh out her ass.

"Hell, you would be surprised by the shit I learn here in this office of mine."

"Oh hell...that was a good laugh. Umm, Virginia, I will see

you soon, this little girl is tripping big time in this store." Lola became enraged to see Grace engaged in a conversation with a stranger.

"Excuse me little girl, why in the hell are you talking to this man? Before Lola knew it, she was shaking the hell out of Grace.

"Ma'am, please allow me to speak."

"Ma'am? Lola was pissed that the man classed her in the *Upper Room*, club. "Sir, your statement is not necessary. I am not interested in what you want to say. She knows better!"

"Mommy, he's no booty man or freak."

"Booty man? Where the hell you learn that?" Grace tilted her head and looked at her mother as if she knew the teacher of bad language personally.

"He was trying to help me. He asked me if I needed help getting the cereal off the shelf, and I told him no. I explained that's a job for the floor people."

"After that, she gave me a lesson on how *not* to catch a case. She told me her mother would tear me apart in court and send me away for life."

"Is that right?" Lola stared the truth out of Grace.

"It's apparent you have taught your daughter well. Lucah Hunt is the name." Lucah extended his hand for Lola to shake.

"I'm sorry, if she was rude."

"I didn't take it as that. She is smart and assertive, which is a good thing in today's world. She had me scared for a moment. I was thinking about calling my lawyer." The two broke out in laughter. Lola's nose began to twitch. The scent in the air was more intoxicating than every bottle in the liquor isle.

"Allergies maybe?" Lucah asked as he smiled at Lola.

"No, something smells damn good. It must be some of those Whole Food shampoos or body oils. Love my Whole Foods samples, ya know." Lola wanted to knock herself over her head with a baguette for sounding so damn corny.

"Hate to boast, but I'm going to take the credit for this one.

It's my cologne, Le Hunt."

"Le Hunt?"

"Yes, I had it made at a perfumery in France."

"Let me guess, The Gallimard Perfume Studios in France?" Lola responded.

"You got it! I love that place. There is another, but I like Galliard's better."

"Excuse me, I'm hungry." Grace moaned as she pulled her mother's skirt.

"Hush up Grace and eat a pop tart. By the way, didn't I tell you to go see Mr. Danny in seafood and pick out three lobsters?"

"You mean *two* lobsters mommy. Daddy doesn't live with us anymore, you know." Lola burned holes through Grace for blabbing out their personal business.

"Do I need to put you in your place again?"

"No, I will ask Mr. Danny for *two* lobsters and see what he has for me. Sorry mommy."

"Yeah ok, you better be cool and stay in your place or you gone have a hard time pulling this shopping cart from your butt."

"That's mean, just plain old mean. Love you too moms." Grace smiled while shaking her head at her mother.

"I see that tough love working for you."

"Not all the time. I'm sorry, she's been acting out since the divorce. It's been hard on her, but that's why I keep her days busy. I do not want her to focus on any of this mess. I'm sorry for being rude; I'm Lola Jameson-Springfield." Lola almost lost the pasta sauce she was holding in her hand as she tried to shake Lucah's hand. An overwhelming amount of nervous energy traveled throughout Lola's body when Lucah shook her hand. She hoped security would not take her down for stealing looks of Lucah. In her rulebook, Lucah's a pretty boy, and Lola hated pretty boys. She felt they were trouble and up to no good, but for some reason; she wanted to burn her rule book.

"Wait, are you *the* Lola Springfield."

"Yes, now you gotta promise not to act a fool. You act as if I told you my name was Halle Berry."

"Truthfully, you look much better if you ask me."

"Ok, I'm not silly enough to turn down a compliment, so thank you!" Lola blushed until her ass cheeks grew warm. She and Lucah engaged in stress-relieving laughter. *Hell maybe these workouts with my trainer, and age-defying genetics are working for a sister.*

"Excuse me?"

"Oh nothing, thinking of my list. I always manage to forget something."

"It's ok. Listen. I am creating a new team to help me turn a few things around within my company and charities. I released a few people who disappointed me, and now, there is a lot of mess to sort through. I recently retained a new publicist, but I am currently searing for a new lawyer as we speak." Lola and Lucah turned isle four into a virtual office and it was clear they were not planning to break anytime soon.

"Wow, I would love to help, but I am on my way to take downtime. I'm not looking to take on big work right now."

"In all honesty, all I would need is someone to review contracts, proposals and *scare* a few people from time to time. You know- the *honest* stuff lawyers do."

"Tell you what, here's my card. Email me some information. To remain in the clear, a brief summary of your needs and plans will help immensely. I will be honest and let you know if I can be of service to you. Understand, anything over fifteen hours a week is pushing it. I'm trying to stay in tune with Grace right now."

"If you don't mind me asking, who's going to take care of you?" Lola paused and thought hard for about ten seconds. Lola couldn't believe how forward Lucah was. She smiled at the thought of throwing her battery operated boyfriend, out her bedroom window and using Lucah as a replacement. It was time for some *real* physical stimulation. It was time for someone to warm her up at night. No matter how much she wrapped herself up at night, the cold and loneliness still found a way underneath her covers.

"That was a hard right punch, Lucah. In all honesty, my shrink, Xanax and my good old B.O.B. is holding me down for right now!"

"B.O.B.? What is that?" Lucah asked as his face shifted to the shape of a halfway finished jigsaw puzzle. Lola laughed when Lucah's face.

"Listen to track number ten on Raheem DeVaughn's, *The Love and War MasterPeace* CD and give me a call. Let me know what you think."

"Well, my imagination is running on the wild side, because I know Brother Raheem doesn't play about his music and lyrics. The brother is beyond sexually explicit with his erotic poetry."

"Listen to it carefully!" Lola smiled with her bedroom eyes as she slid past Lucah. As she sashayed down the aisle; she tried to remember where Grace was. The fifteen minute meeting in isle four was now over.

"Thanks Lola, I will be sure to call you."

Must be sure to call her. My Lord, she is stunning.

Chapter 34

"Hello Gabrielle, sorry I didn't answer your call a few minutes ago. Is everything ok with you? Your message sounded as if you were sitting on the edge of a knife."

"Thank you for asking Lucah. Unannounced guests reminded me of my promise to allow them to use my gallery for a project. It totally slipped my mind."

"It's ok. How is the book coming along? Aren't you close to releasing it?"

"Yes, but I may have to delay things."

"Why? You stuck in a dry spell?" Gabby almost choked on her latte while speeding down highway forty.

"Uh- no."

"You sure you don't have writers block?"

"No, more like drama on the block."

"Oh, I'm sorry. Look, if tonight isn't great, I will understand."

"No, tonight is fine. Some fresh air would be good for me. I'm in a great state of mind to create. I would love to see your project ideas. I will sketch it up first, and we can create magic from there."

"Sounds great! I'm here at the market, would you like me to grab you something?"

"A nice Riesling with some fruit and cheese would be wonderful. Thank you for asking."

"I should be home in fifteen minutes. See you soon."

"Great."

Chapter 35

"**B**aby, you home? Gabby! You playing hide and seek with me woman?" Dale was anxious to see his wife.

"Baby, are you here? Woman, you must be in the mood! Promise you gone put it on me good." Dale wasted no time striping down. Into his second sip of wine, he saw a CD begging for play and a note from Gabrielle. Captured by the writing on the envelope and CD label; Dale turned violent.

"That lousy bitch!"

Not one minute into playing the CD, Dale's manic episode turned dangerous. Leaving nothing unturned in the house, he knew Gabrielle's letter was full of instructions regarding how long he had to vacate. It would be a matter of time before the storm returned and he did not want things to end with multiple news vans parked outside their home. The thought of living the best of both worlds was ruined by a bitter lover.

"Gabby, I'm sorry!" Dale cried into the phone.

"Dale, it's over. I don't need to hear it. I'm out for a while. Please have your items out before the end of the weekend. I'm sure your brother won't be too mad for having to help move you out. Tell him it's the last time. If he doesn't believe you, share the video with him! That will shut his ass up. We are done, do you hear me?"

"Wait, where you at?" The man in Dale came through. All his years of cheating made Dale paranoid. No matter how much wrong he stood on trial for, his wife had no business being with another man.

"Don't trip off what I do. Far as I am concerned, you stopped caring long time ago and tonight, I stop."

"You better tell me where you going." Gabrielle had no intentions on sleeping out tonight, but she wanted to prove to Dale that she was no longer riding him or dead emotions.

"Not at my mother's or my sister's. I don't need you trying to find me to explain how whorish you are. You had better check that bitch and tell her to stop fucking with me! Read her letter! She threatened to expose things that belong in this family, not the damn media! You better fix that bitch! She's happier with you. So, call her, tell her you asked for the divorce. Be sure she knows I didn't put up a fight. I don't want this out!" Lola disconnected herself from something she should have done long time ago.

Chapter 36

"Lucah, I've been on the sick side of the world, please give me some time to get back with you. I hope all is going well. Hey, do you own a floral shop? The arrangements you keep sending are wonderful! I must admit though, this last bouquet gave semblance to a funeral arrangement. You need to call and have them send the right one or refund you. For the record, my pussy sends its condolences. She sure does miss you. Oh well, soon as Lily gets better; expect another hot night in the sack! Talk to you soon!"

Chapter 37

"**M**r. Hunt, this is Isabella Valdez, we need to arrange a business meeting. I am ready to start your project. Thank you for sending your contact, and payment. I am free everyday this week except Friday. I'm leaving for Atlanta to spend time with a few friends, and I will not be back for two weeks. Have a great day!" Isabella stared at the phone as fantasies developed in her head. Lucah reminded her of Miguel and she was ready to tests the waters.

"Virginia! Glad to see you my love! Oh my heavens, where should I start with this hot news?" Isabella grabbed her friend by the arm to sit down on her office couch.

"How 'bout the end girly? I'm starving, did our food come?"

"Yes, it's on my counter. Now listen, should I try...well there's this client I wanted..."

"Fuck him!" Virginia yelled as she bit into her salmon.

"What? Damn you woman! Will you let me make the announcement first! I could have said he was blind and looked like a dead squirrel in the face with one nut hanging, and there you go talkin' shit!"

"If it salutes...aim high and pull it on in! Hell, and make sure you blow those cobwebs away with a blow dryer or something first! Brother don't want to play in a desert!"

"Well, you sound relaxed and bright! What or who shall I say, done blew in *your* rust pot?" Isabella quizzed while sipping on wine.

"Let's just say he's a colleague!"

"Aw Virginia, please tell me you didn't mess with that doctor you was trying to throw my way like a half-eaten chicken bone?" Isabella stomped across her office floor as she shook her head. She knew her best friend well and she was surprised to see how she crossed the line by dating her deceased husband's best friend.

"Yes I most certainly did." Virginia felt shame for sleeping with her deceased husband's best friend, but the feeling of newness sent shame on its way.

"Oh Lord. Oh well, it's done now. How do you feel?"

"I feel damn good! He's amazing in his own way! I did not want to compare him to a dead man, so I let go. I was not going to make that mistake Bella. Oh yeah, that damn Jada Pinkett-Smith did it on her show, *Hawthorne*."

"That's TV, girl. Oh Lord, that was a good lunch." Isabella fell back as she unzipped her pants.

"Oh well, art imitates life and all that other jazz."

"Yeah, you're right." Isabella sunk into her desk chair. Hearing Virginia's news afforded her the right to fantasize about her and Lucah. If her best friend was in the mood to date again, why continue prolonging her life. As far as she was concerned, she had been the best wife and widow she had known.

"You wanna tell me something about him?"

"Let's say he's thirty-two and full of life. I saw it dancing in his pants, and girl, I want it dancing inside me."

"Oh my! Can your fifty-two year old ass hang with that young man! Hell, he's Devin's age ain't he?"

"Fuck it, I'm gone die trying." Both women laughed tears.

"Well you do that. Be careful girl. Work with him and see where it goes. Bella let go and live life. Miguel set you up to live life in peace. Now if you do not mind, I am going to the spa before my date! That damn man almost threw my damn back out."

"Girl I don't wanna hear no more of that mess! Make sure you leave a foot between you and the headboard, that way, you reduce the chance of breaking your neck when he slams into the back of you."

"Good-bye!" Virginia grabbed her jacket, hugged her

friend, and headed back to her office.

"I got lunch next time." Virginia reminded Isabella. Isabella was excited to see what may develop between her and Lucah. For Isabella, she always warned her staffed about dating clients, but this time, she found herself breaking all the rules.

Chapter 38

"**O**h wow Lucah, your home is a fortress. I think I need to buy some art from you!"

"You sound pleased."

"Very pleased. It's wonderful to see someone who appreciates art. You must have millions invested." Gabrielle was amazed in Lucah's taste for fine art. From framed portraits to beautiful vases and other priceless forms of art, Lucah had a knack for detail and fine living.

"Glad you love it. Are you ready to whip up a new masterpiece?" Lucah quizzed as he poured Gabrielle a glass of wine.

"Do you mind if I do a few woo-sah's and listen to a few songs on my phone as I set-up? It's a routine of mine.

"Sure, would you like to connect your phone to my Wi-Fi speakers?"

"No, I'm good."

"Would you like to eat first?"

"That fruit and cheese tray looks nice. I've been on the go all day and eating heavy this late in the evening is a sin in my book." Gabrielle stated as she spun around in a circle.

"I understand. Well with all you have, it's worth preserving." Lucah gently flirted.

"Tell me what you have in mind, Lucah."

"It's a portrait of me at my best. I've always wanted a portrait of myself. I hope I don't sound conceited."

"Long as you don't start bragging, you're fine."

"Well take your time and enjoy the fruit and wine. Tell me-is this a good night for you. I know I asked earlier, but you look disturbed. You don't look too relaxed. You wanna talk?"

"Ok, pretend you are the bartender, pour me another

drink, and I will pour thy heart out."

"Another glass coming right up!" Lucah poured more wine and wiped the counter down with a white towel as he executed the role of bartender.

"My husband and I recently split. I stopped loving him a long time ago- he's a cheater. Yet, for some dumb reason I held on."

"Why hold on so long? Why allow the deceit, and the disrespect."

"Starting over is a bitch. I'm afraid of the future. I'm not interested in anything after this divorce. Great friends and casual sex will do just fine."

"Take time to heal. It's better not to become heavily vested in a relationship."

"I'm not over the hill, Lucah but I sure as hell refuse to be scouting clubs at the age of fifty-three. That stage of my life has been over years ago."

"I take it there are no friends using your gallery tonight."

"You got it!" Gabrielle confessed as pity sat on her face.

"How do you feel?"

"I'm ok, I couldn't stand to deal with him tonight. That's why I came to you."

"Your outlook on relationships will change. It gets better."

"I don't want to be tied down, fuck love. I need something new, and refreshing. I don't want another old ass dog playing the same old ass tricks. I can't understand why some people choose the role of, "player" for life. It has to be fucking lonely!" Gabrielle was allowing the wine to speak for her broken heart. Deep down, she always cherished monogamous relationships, but as of today, the idea of being in several open relationships was tempting.

"You're right, somewhere along the way, love and happiness left with Al Green and those hot ass grits! No sense in holding on when you're tired." Lucah confessed.

"Oh wow, you are funny and wise! I will be sure to leave a tip in your jar."

"I'm done with everyone else. It's all about me right now. I'm ready to slip into the role of freelance lover. I won't take on the role of being a player, but for now- variety sounds nice."

"How is that not being a player?" Lucah asked as he leaned on the counter.

"A player keeps secrets. They tell stories, and they are filthy dogs. Me? I will let them know that they are not my main man. I will let them know that I am not looking for shit serious. Now after that, they can choose to roll with me, or get lost. You men do it all day long." Gabrielle stated as she bit into a strawberry.

"That's colder than the North Pole." Lucah took a picture of Gabrielle's ugly side.

"Not to me. I want openness. I don't feel as if I should explain myself to anyone. I don't want to feel contained in misery. I want the freedom to do whatever I want. Keep pouring bartender."

"Stay single. Enjoy yourself." Lucah was aggravated by Gabrielle's reasoning on the subject.

"Yeah, give or take, I cheated a few times, but it was in retaliation for what he did to me."

"I see." Gabrielle kept getting uglier with each word."

"Love is dead. Whatever comes my way, hey- it's what I want it to be."

"You are indeed a woman in charge!"

"Well, I think I am ready! Where should I set-up? I will also need to check the lighting. It doesn't need to be super bright but lit well enough for me to see all the detail you want in the portrait."

"The master bedroom is where we will be. I think it's the perfect place for my portrait. My office is there as well." Without any thought of Lucah's requests, Gabrielle grabbed her items and headed to the master bedroom.

"Oh wow Lucah! I love the dome chandelier. It's beautiful. It's raining crystals in here. I thought I ran a clean and tight ship, and here you are living on the Ritz. My spot is begging for a total re-do." Gabrielle took a self-guided tour through Lucah's master suite. "Lucah your balcony is to die for. Who in the heck does your landscape?"

"Not sure. I have a team of people that set things up. I'm needed in so many places, so the less required of me makes my life easy."

"Must be nice."

"Do me a favor, and focus on the bed. I want it to be the focal point of the portrait." Lucah disappeared into his walk-in closet. The thought of biting Gabrielle was not a hard one. Her heart was an iced over road of regret. Her tongue was tainted and anger was apparent. Lucah felt Gabrielle was not telling the entire truth, and her views on dating, turned him off. She reminded him of Brooke- and it wasn't the sweet side.

"Ok, I know this is strange but at anytime you feel uncomfortable, please let me know so we can change things around.

"What are you talking about Lucah?" Before Gabrielle looked up, Lucah was rested on his bed, naked, resting his upper body on his left arm, while resting on his side. His position showed Gabrielle how blessed he was.

"Stranded in time?" Lucah teased. Gabrielle failed to respond and it did not look as if she was trying to remove herself from the awkward situation. After multiple attempts in getting her attention, Gabrielle responded on Lucah's last clap.

"Oh, this ain't right." Gabrielle laughed her embarrassment away. Her attempts to divert her attention elsewhere were unsuccessful.

"Should I kneel or praise dance, Lucah?" Gabby did her best to restrain her inner feelings, as her thighs gave way to a nervous tremble.

"It's kind of hard- no pun intended- for me to focus. I've never seen a subject as beautiful yours."

"You mean me or my dick?" Lucah requested clarity as he shifted his weight around in the bed.

"Your dick." Gabrielle stated as she took to her feet. The sight of Lucah stroking his blessing in a raw manner made it the sin she wanted to down like a calorie filled milkshake.

"Do you want it or not?" Lucah teased.

"To do the portrait, you mean?" Gabrielle asked as she tried to pace her breathing. Watching Lucah stroke himself sent Gabrielle into heat.

"You said no attachments, right?" Lucah reminded Gabrielle of her list of dating requirements.

"I never figured you to be a man with too much time to play games. It's obvious, you knew what you were doing. Now what you offer is something I have no problem taking. I will paint the portrait later- if that's what you want, Lucah." Gabby was ready for Lucah to bless her with his wondrous gift. With all the hell she had been through, she was sure a night with Lucah was a long and overdue blessing.

"Come join me, why don't you?" Lucah opened the covers as Gabby slid right into his arms.

"You smell good. I love that scent. Is that what you use to hypnotize your women?"

"You didn't smell my cologne when you saw my dick did you? You know what's going on. How long Gabrielle?" Lucah asked while combing Gabby's hair with his fingers.

"Sex wise, you ask?"

"Yes, what else could I be talking about?"

"What do your fingers tell you?" Gabrielle spread wide as a peacock.

"Wow, that long? A little moist and certainly tight. Works for me, you're a keeper."

"Are you done talking?" Gabrielle asked.

"I'm all in. Talk to me. Talk this scene out."

"Oh, you like to talk, huh?"

"Get me going. I'll talk back."

"Let me narrate. To see something so large - causes a shift in the way my body releases pleasure." Gabrielle purred.

"It's like that?" Lucah asked as he inserted himself deep within Gabrielle.

"Damn." Gabrielle gasped for breath between her wordings. Gabrielle thought her wildest feelings were reserved for paper; but Lucah proved she could do otherwise.

"While my body releases shivers that should be reserved for someone else; my heart skips a beat."

"You love what's inside you?"

"Yes, the idea of receiving pleasure by someone as sexual and free as me; excites and seduces me to report myself as a missing person." Gabrielle stuttered her wording as, Lucah provided the much needed maintenance she required.

"Don't worry, I won't turn you in. You're mine." Lucah promised as his strokes intensified.

"Damn, I never want to resurface when I know I can spend an eternity in a darkness laced with climatic moment's one right after the next."

"Damn you feel good!" Lucah exclaimed.

"You love it hard and fast don't you?"

"Go head, knock it the fuck out."

"Back it up!"

"Damn Lucah, right there- don't stop."

"Spread them knees out and dip."

"Harder!" Gabrielle screamed as she fell flat onto the bed. Lucah grabbed Gabrielle's thighs with a strong grip and shoved all of him deep within.

"Your dick promises soreness will follow but the thought of your long and powerful strokes causes my pussy to fuck pain right back in its face."

"Let me finish this off." The animal in him unleashed a hellfire moment Gabrielle would never forget.

Chapter 39

"Lola, its Lucah. I hope your few days off has served you well. I reviewed your plans and suggestions and I love them. Let's get together to talk out some of the terms in the agreement. If I am not asking too much, may I take you out to dinner? Now hear me out, I know exactly what you are going through and I feel you deserve a chance to relax and enjoy the other side of life. Do not burry yourself under mounds of work, woman. I will be free after three today. Leave me a voice mail or text. You pick the place."

Chapter 40

"Thank you for seeing me today Dr. Arlington. I apologize for being absent from our sessions but my career is quite demanding."

"Lucah, I see you are into giving more than you are taking these days." Virginia cited as she jotted down her notes. Virginia was still upset with Lucah keeping his past a secret.

"I have a lot to give away and my time is limited. As I stated, no one takes any part of the earth with them when the big man comes a calling..."

"Lucah, what are you preparing for? What is the rush? I did your doctor a favor by taking you in as a referral, but you have yet to open up to me. You never gave permission for me to obtain your medical records, so how can I provide a fair assessment of your mental health? I know you feel as if I am lecturing you, but this is how millions of Americans' are misdiagnosed with mental health disorders." Dr. Arlington lectured while frustration pulled her head from side to side.

"Listen, we are all on borrowed time. What promises do you see etched in stone proving that you, or I will be here the next second, day, month, or year?" By this time, Lucah was sitting on the edge of the chair with his eyes locked on Virginia. Virginia listened to Lucah's off rhythm jazz while his hand signage spoke another set of bitter words.

"My bitter ex-lover shattered every part of my world. She never gave me a chance to decide if I wanted to stay in the relationship after I found out about her *undercover* work. My doctor wanted me under therapeutic care to help me along the way, so I took his advice."

"Ok Lucah, you are here, but what are you going to do?"

"Look, I am not your parolee and I do not have to check in with you if I choose not to. I am in my right mind. No book or coping mechanism will get me through this. Time, that's what I need."

"No one ever said anything about you being on parole, Lucah."

"Stop acting as if I am and everything will be fine." Steam had reached its boiling point and Lucah was out of room for bullshit.

"Doctor, please feel free to write whatever pleases you. Save your coping mechanisms for those who need them. As I told the doctor, I stray from the danger, so no one should worry about seeing me on the news. I have too much to lose to do stupid things."

"What is that smirk for Mr. Hunt?" Virginia slammed her chart down. The look Lucah gave her was unsettling.

"I don't know. What do you think? Better yet, don't tell me- tell your fucking notebook. Our sessions are complete. I will pay any balance due on the way out.

"No, you pay by mail or online. I will send you a summarized bill for the final payment. No payments will be taken today. My assistant is out of the office right now."

"This was a waste of time." Lucah snatched up his trench and headed out the door without one single word.

Tell the book my ass Mr. Hunt. Your ass is darker than a bat cave and I intend on finding out what you have hidden in it.

Chapter 41

"Lucah, I am happy to see how satisfied you are with my agency's work. Please sit."

"Tell me about yourself Mrs. Valdez. I understand your husband passed away not too long ago."

"Yes, it wasn't the way one would expect, but it's been a close to a year. Still hurts, but life for me is one day at a time."

"I understand. I lost the love of my life about the same time as yours."

"I'm sorry to hear that Lucah."

"I felt like balling up and dying some days, but I had others to live for. I knew better was out there, but I knew I had to get through the bad first. It's life."

"Me too, but some days I feel lost. At times, I feel as if my purpose and passion died with my husband."

"Our lives have purpose. Sometimes we need help getting back on the road."

"My mother always said detours were the best teachers in life." Isabella stood close to her office window staring to the heavens.

"You can't keep good folk down for too long." Lucah said.

"I'm getting back into the swing of things. I must admit how the new world of dating; scares the shit out of me."

"How do you mean?"

"I mean, I never had to worry about all the crazy shit."

"Please explain." Lucah asked as he reclined back in his chair.

"The down low crisis has me nailing my front door shut." Isabella paused and thought if she was too forward with her conversation.

"Please go on. I would love to hear how you feel. It may help me. Trust me, I have heard everything there could be said, when it comes to men."

"Lucah, I'd rather die alone if I had to settle. I'm not settling with some woman's husband, I will not love a man who refuses to love me back, and Lord knows I'm not into loving a bi-sexual man."

"I understand. Keep going."

"As long as the good Lord allows me to keep both hands, and D batteries, I'm good." Lucah choked on his wine.

"Oh hell, I'm sorry. I did not mean to go that far."

"It's ok. You sure know how to tell the truth don't you?"

"Yes, I do. You're easy to talk to."

"People cross paths for a reason."

"Don't play dumb. Every girl needs a toy and with the way the market looks...I'm fine in the slow lane. Like I said, I'd piss the sheets if I found out my man was taking it from the back." Isabella placed her heart on the table.

"Hey, the same goes for me. If you don't mind me saying, women are no better."

"True, everyone has the potential of losing screws. The sad part- people never know when to stop playing games. Not everyone is on a mission to hurt, or destroy. I feel a good lover is one who knows how to give as well as take."

"Touché Isabella."

"Right now, I want my life to have quality, and ultimate fulfillment without commitment. I want things to mature from one point to the next in all naturalness. Anything else would be an added bonus."

"That is doable."

"Lucah, I never thought I would be looking for anyone outside of Miguel. If there is ever such a thing, we had our life planned to perfection. We knew when we were going to retire, and everything afterwards. Right now, bitterness is resting on my tongue. This isn't right."

"Why bitter?"

"I am bitter for being tossed into this mess of a world, as a single woman. The pickings are slim. I mean, I can't find a decent companion without him thinking about my money or my panties. Miguel is a hard act to follow."

"I too was bitter, but you know you will never be free, right? That bitterness is toxic and it's killing you on the inside."

"You're right. Pain kicks my ass on many days."

"Why are you still looking?" Lucah's questions posted Isabella dead center court. The buzzer to respond was counting down. Isabella's mind tried to create a defense that would not show her offense; but Lucah's playbook was better.

"I think I want something but in all fairness, I'm a bull-shitter. I'm just happy my girlfriends are happy. I enjoy hearing their stories. Why do you ask if I'm still looking?" Isabella turned away from Lucah.

"Looks like you need a friend. I'm sure you have room for a friend, right? I'm sure we can help each other along the way." Isabella held back tears as she stared at her husband's picture on her mantle.

"I need all the help I can get."

"Live- don't worry about all the bad stuff. You ever notice how we overlook the important things in the midst of our hunt?" Lucah's words sent chills throughout Isabella's body.

"You sure you have nothing up your sleeve, Lucah?"

"I come as honest as you could imagine."

"Never as honest as my Miguel." Isabella rebutted.

"You should try. Friendship is the perfect primer for any relationship. Not saying we would graduate to the next level, but friendship won't hurt.

"True, but I told you *love* is far from my mind."

"It's far because you haven't reached for it." Isabella thought back to the conversation she and Virginia shared. She knew it would be wrong to compare a dead man to the current man. Isabella smiled the answer Lucah wanted to see.

Chapter 42

"Lucah, its Lily. Please call me. We need to talk when you are free. I have left messages for you and I have even stopped by your home, but your security guard told me you were home in Greece. I hope all is well, but please- call me soon."

Chapter 43

"**L**ucah, you cheated! Slow down!" Lola yelled as Lucah blazed past her on his roller blades.

"Naw, you bragged and now you gotta eat my smoke. You knew dog gone well you couldn't speed skate like a pro."

"Oh now you wanna talk and skate? What a show off." Lola complained as she tried to pull back every breath escaping her body.

"Push hard woman, we got about ten minutes before we make it back to the car! Now push! Last one there has to serve lunch."

"I'll be damn if I gotta serve lunch, see you when *you* get there." Lola pushed hard to pass Lucah.

"Ha! Hurry up so you can serve me my lunch!" Lola cheered as she started removing her roller blades.

"Well, you showed me up, Ms. Lady." Lucah panted as he leaned against his car.

"A wonderful spring day, with a fine man serving me a wonderful lunch on the top of Art Hill is something any woman would die for." Lola smiled as she directed Lucah to his serving duties.

"Okay, chop-chop...a woman can't wait forever!" Lola rushed Lucah as she finished taking off her roller blades. Defeated with happiness, Lucah was obliged to serve Lola a champion's lunch.

"Oh wow! These strawberries look fantastic! Where did you get them?"

"Soulard's. I love going to the market on the weekends. Gotta get there early for the fruits or they sell out. I love fresh fruit.

"True you are." Lola bit into one of the strawberries while her eyes searched for heaven. "Okay, what else do you have in that magical basket of yours?"

"I have some homemade potato salad, mixed veggies in Italian dressing, a cheese tray, and a small platter of BBQ-grilled salmon and chicken breasts. I also have bottled water and a bottle of wine on ice. Sound good?"

"I am glad you have some pillows in the trunk. I am warning you now, I will *not* move until I have a thirty-minute nap."

"I got you! No problem, take as long as you want."

"Thanks for offering your friendship Lucah. I'm glad we are able to talk with each other. All of my friends are married, which voids them from understanding what I'm going through."

"Yeah, I feel you on that. I prefer to keep to myself. I only talk with my Pastor, and the good Lord. People have too much going on their own lives. Everyone is wrapped up in their own world."

"You know, my husband was nine years younger than me.

"Okay, and?"

"My mother always told me how it would bite me in the end."

"How Lola?"

"I'm forty-eight, he's thirty-nine, and a ten year old is more mature than he is. He's too busy living life on the edge, and does not own up to fatherhood. I know I can't worry about that, but I don't play games. He's dating a twenty-one year old."

"It's only a game if you play back. Once you are done with someone, learn the lesson and understand what tore the two of you apart. People make the mistake of getting back together for the sake of their children. Some feel the time apart served, provided enough 'air time' but the damn problem still exists. Remember the reason why the relationship went south in the first place. Trust me, the reason will remain in the air like smog."

"Ok, tell me I can hire you as my therapist." Lola joked as she took another bite of the salmon Lucah was feeding her.

"It amazes me how people always pick-up these *how to*

relationship guides, listen to Steve Harvey..." Lucah loaded sarcasm into his statement.

"Ha! You feel the same about, Steve too?" Lola giggled as she pumped her fist in the air.

"Yeah, he's over rated."

"Well hell, I'm not mad at the man for selling a book full of stuff that's been told in every language possible. Get rich where, when and while you can!" Lola cheered.

"Now you know some people prefer being stuck on stupid! I think some people enjoy setting themselves up for failure."

"True."

"Back to you, you have a lot going on woman. Don't waste your time worrying about him. Your daughter matters the most. She is enough, you must agree."

"You're right, that child is a little mini-me."

"You ready for your nap?" Lucah placed the pillow on his lap and motioned for Lola to rest upon it. Lola decided to free her mind of Baylor and all the drama.

"You got me, right?"

"No problem. Chill on out and I promise I won't let any of the Forest Park creatures get hold of ya." Lola nestled her head on the pillow. Her beautiful dark cherry, auburn colored hair covered Lucah's lap. As Lucah took pleasure in running his hands through her hair, Lola held onto his leg. Lucah refused to lower himself to the ground when it came to Lola.

She's the reason I want to live, Lord.

Chapter 44

"Lucah, what's been up my man?" Dr. Helton quizzed as he offered Lucah a seat.

"A woman- that's what's happening."

"Get out of here."

"Yeah, she's a great friend. Like me, she's fresh out of a relationship and she is clearly focused on getting through things. She understands how my relationship ended. I also explained my situation to her as well."

"Your situation? All of it Lucah?"

"Don't worry, we are building our friendship, and there's no talk of sex. We vent and comfort each other, and that's it. I have no intentions on hurting her. When I am comfortable, I will tell her about my diagnosis. In the meantime, I am enjoying our friendship. She told me she was not ready for a relationship."

"I see."

"It's been a long time since I have enjoyed the company of a woman." Lucah spoke with passion. His face was bright and his voice held strong. Lola was indeed resurrecting Lucah from hell.

"Have you thought about my son's story?"

"Yeah, every time I see, or hear her voice, I think about getting that second chance. She seems to play on level ground. She's honest and her heart is clean. I mean there are women who turn bitter, and become plain lousy after a bad break-up, but this one; she always looks for the good. She has her days, but hey, don't we all? Not to mention, she has a beautiful child also."

"Well listen, you give her the chance you never got. No matter what she says or feels about your situation, you do what is right."

"I got it!"

"Okay, up on the table."

"Give me some deep breaths. In, out, in, out. Good. How's the sleep been?"

"Well, I'm a night owl and I'm also an early bird, so what does that tell you?"

"You know you should be sleeping a lot more right?"

"When I'm dead."

"Well guess what?"

"Bang! You are almost dead! Your labs are saying otherwise. Your white count is awful and your blood count is low. Have you been losing blood through your stool or vomit, Lucah?"

"No, I haven't. What are you trying to say?"

"Have your assistant bring your bags; I'm admitting you in the hospital today. You will need a few pints of blood, a few scans, and an endoscopy and colonoscopy. I need to see where this loss of blood is taking place."

"Not a good week doctor."

"What? Not a good week to live? I am not having it; I am walking you to over the bridge to the hospital. Lucah, I don't want this problem to intensify. How are you walking around?" Dr. Helton, removed his stethoscope, and grabbed his pager and iPhone off his desk.

"Okay, but if it's nothing serious, I want to leave immediately. I have meetings, and events to attend. I can't afford to miss anything." Lucah knew he had Lily and Gabrielle to deal with. Lily was making more noise than a hen on a Sunday morning, and he knew Gabrielle was close to clucking herself.

"No problem. I will do what I can to get you taken care of. When was your last meal?"

"I had a full breakfast around six this morning, and I a bottle of vitamin water, an orange, and granola around noon."

"We will start the transfusion this afternoon, and you will receive a light dinner afterwards. Around six-thirty you will have to drink a prepped solution for the colonoscopy. No food or drink after your last meal Lucah."

"I got it doc."

"Denise, please take Mr. Hunt to room seven-sixty. It's a private room. Be sure to keep his name off the patient information list.

"No problem doctor."

"I will see you in the morning Lucah."

"Sure deal doc. Are you sure I can't do anything to change your mind about this stay?"

"Lucah, you know the answer. Now don't give the staff a hard time." Lucah waved his hands in the air surrendering to the doctor's orders.

"Juan, it's Mr. Hunt, I will be in the hospital for a couple of days, will you please bring my work bag, my other cell phone, and two days worth of clothing for here and a suit to wear home? Yes, bring the mail as well. Are there any messages for me? Who? When did she come by? Next time she does, instruct her not to come by until I request her. Was there anything else? Good, I'm in room seven-sixty."

Lily's persistence was pinching Lucah nerves. Not done with everything on his menu, Lucah found himself planning a way out of the mess he created with Lily.

Chapter 45

"Lucah, its Isabella, I need to speak with you about the next project on your list. I also need you to review your new website before we publish it. Call when you are free. Have a great day."

Chapter 46

"Lucah, I mailed the offers and proposal suggestions to your office. All worked except one of them. I provided my reasoning and documents as to why the merger would have been hell awful. Grace and I have several sporting events over the next few days and from there, we will be with family for Memorial Day. Talk to you soon."

Chapter 47

The next day came late as far as Lucah was concerned. Lily sent enough emails to compile into a book, clients never ceased calling him, and he missed Lola.

Continuous trips to the bathroom during the night cancelled sleep. The nursing staff never stopped taking vitals and the vampires in the lab seemed thirsty all night.

"Good morning Mr. Hunt. My name is Lisa and I will be your nurse for the day. We have a lot do. Lab will be here in about ten minutes to draw your blood, and you will be off to have your CT scan."

"You're the director." Lucah grumbled as he tried to make sense of time. "Will you please give me a few moments to attend to my personal hygiene?"

"Oh thank you! I love seeing patients tend to their hygiene first thing morning." Lisa chimed as she disconnected Lucah's IV lines.

"Why do you sound happy about that? Isn't that the normal thing to do?"

"You know, some of these patients can be disgusting. Just because they are in the hospital does not mean they should stop bathing, brushing their teeth and combing their hair. Even if we have to do it, we will; but they refuse."

"Oh now that's sad." Lucah laughed as he grabbed his shower bag.

"Some days I wanna tell them off. You're sick- not dead dammit!" Lisa vented as she leaned back on the moved about in the room.

"Well don't worry; I will be the picture perfect patient."

"I kindly thank you in advance. Allow me to review you chart over once more before you leave to have your scan. Marissa is your patient care technician for the day. Our information will remain on this patient board until the shifts end. Your new nurse and tech will introduce themselves at the start of their shift."

"Well I hope to leave right around the time you end your shift."

"Sorry to announce bad news, but you should prepare to stay for at least three days. Getting the bleed under control and making sure, we pump enough blood back into you; is high priority. We have to make sure your count stays within the normal range."

"You are full of good news beautiful." Lucah flirted as he shuffled across the room.

"See you soon Mr. Hunt." Lisa said as she left the room.

"Ok, thanks a lot Lisa." Sitting on the toilet gave Lucah time to think about Lola. Hurting her was a sin in his eyes and he refused to steal her chance at experiencing love again.

Chapter 48

"Dr. James, its Lily Lee. I need to know if I you have something available right now. I feel far from well and I am worried. Great, eight o'clock sounds good. I understand- no food or drink after midnight. Excuse me? Well I have this rash on my stomach, mixed with fevers, and the chills. No, there have been no trips overseas. Ok, thanks." Lily couldn't sit easy until she found her source of illness.

"Chef Danny!"

"Hey Lily. Is everything ok? You look worn out."

"It's all yours! I'm tired and I'm not well. I'm going home to rest and I will call your tomorrow after my doctor's appointment. I hope to be back tomorrow afternoon. If anyone gives you shit, send them home and I will deal with them accordingly."

"No problem Lily. Who's driving you home?"

"I called my assistant, she will be here soon. In the meantime, will you make me some soup?"

"What you got in mind?"

"Anything, I need to feel whole again."

"Coming right up." Chef Danny scatted from Lily's office to the kitchen. Out of the twelve years Danny worked with Lily, he was never able to give testimony about seeing his boss in a weakened state.

Chapter 49

"Lucah, please pay attention to your body. When you vomit, you have to look at what you throw up. I'm sure had you looked you would have seen coffee ground-like particles. You had a few tears in the lining of your esophagus as well."

"What happens now?"

"If you go into a vomiting spell, keep an eye on it. Your throat will be sore for a few days from the endoscopy, but that's about it. Call me if anything alarms you. I also wrote a script for some iron tablets. That should help with your anemia. Make sure you follow up with a high-fiber diet. The iron tablets will cause constipation, Lucah. Oh yeah,"

"What?" Lucah growled, as he grew tired of doctor's list of irritating instructions.

"Stay away from that damn *natural from the earth* lady! She is no doctor! Until those *natural earth people*, attend medical school; they are NOT licensed physicians."

"Now you let me be. I believe in some of that stuff. I will consult you before I try anything new- is that better?"

"I thought my son was hard-headed. I guess it will have to be your way, or no way at all. Take care of yourself."

"Whatever you say doc."

Chapter 50

"Lucah, I am too happy to see you!" Lola yelled as she dropped her case files.

"Whoa woman! I didn't know you jumped that high." Lucah was surprised by Lola's welcome. The two held onto each other for hours it seemed.

"How was Memorial Day with Grace and the family?"

"It was great! Good music and food always pumps a party up! Baylor tried to piss the day away, when he showed up with his half dressed ratty tease; to pick up Grace."

"How did that go? Lucah quizzed as he took off his suit jacket. He loved watching Lola and Lola loved the way Lucah's eyes danced with her. The two had grown fond of each other.

"Grace spoke her mind. She told her dad off. She told him she wasn't ready for the other woman to be in her life. She misses him and she made that known. I was proud of her. I had to calm her down afterwards but she was fine."

"She's winning cases early. Your mini-me is making her mark; get her ready for law school."

"Oh hell no- anything but this!" Lola pointed around her messy and chaotic office.

"Where have you been hiding Mr. Hunt? Lola quizzed as her outlined Lucah's face with her finger.

"Who wants to know?" Lucah smiled as he and Lola's lips played like magnets.

"How about I kiss you?"

"I'd love that!" Lola whispered into Lucah's ear, as she hid Lucah's lap, with her backside. A kiss meant to greet Lucah; ended up being a kiss long enough to show how deep her affection for him, came to be.

"Wow, and to think he willingly messed his marriage up. What a dumb ass."

"It's ok, you're showing me where I need to be." Lola whispered back.

"You don't say." Lucah was happy to see Lola looking to the future instead of her past.

"I know my worth Lucah. It never left my conscious. I guess my will to love myself at one-hundred percent, overshadowed my duties in my marriage. I admit- there were times, where I should have done more for him, but there were times where he should have done the same. I don't have the extra space to have a big ass, *man-baby* in my life."

"Ha! A *man-baby*? What the hell is a *man-baby*?"

"It's a man who acts like a damn baby. It's a man who whines about every fabric of his life while he sits by and does nothing. I know there are plenty of women living in misery with these types of assholes."

"True, but you know that goes both ways, right?"

"Well this is about my way, right?"

"You are right about that. Anyway, why bother talking about him when you could be kissing me?" Lucah felt drawn to Lola and he did not know how to slow the reels from spinning. Before he knew it, he was engaging into the dark, murky waters.

"Kiss number two, and kiss number three, and..." The two locked their lips and settled into one passionate kissing session.

Chapter 51

"Lucah, I never thought I would see you again. Where you been hiding?" Isabella quizzed as she escorted Lucah into her study.

"Greece. I went home to visit family. First, I planned a business trip, but my sister intercepted my plans and *begged* me to come home earlier than planned."

"How was it? Greece may be where I take my next vacation. Working full-time at the agency has broken this woman down!"

"Hush your lips." Lucah pleaded as he reached out to hug Isabella. Isabella's guilt diverted her attention from watching her husband's picture on the mantel. As Lucah's hold on Isabella grew tighter, her eyes searched for reasons to deny Lucah. She hoped moments shared with Miguel would dance in her eyes. Maybe the thought of Miguel's touch, or the way he whispered in her ear; would tear through the emotions she felt for Lucah.

"Lucah, I want say something." While avoiding eye contact, Isabella pulled away from Lucah. Her nervous energy worried him. Lucah's hands started to perspire and he started pacing her study floor.

"I'm not looking for a relationship. I miss my husband and that's it. I know in my heart there will never be another man to replace him. I have no idea what you are looking for Lucah, but I feel it's fair for you to know what can and cannot happen." Lucah did not know how to digest Isabella's truth. At first, her rejection stoned his heart, but by the next beat, Lucah knew he had to finish what he started.

"Lucah, did you hear what I just said?" Isabella questioned as she placed her hand on Lucah's shoulder.

"Listen Isabella, I am here for you. Use me how you feel, I'm here to provide. That's what friends are for."

"Lucah, I never said *use* you."

"I know what you meant and I'm fine with that. Look, everyone has lost something great in his or her lifetime. Knowing one will soon win the chance to enjoy something new after a loss is a great reward. I hope you take the time to look at life as for what it can be and not for what it is."

"Lucah that's beautiful." Isabella responded with tears in her eyes. If only she knew Lucah's dick was hard three lines ago, her feelings may have changed. Regardless, Isabella wondered if the tears tracking her face were for Miguel or for Lucah's consoling prose. At heart, Isabella was a passionate romantic drunk on hope. Lucah knew his gift of being a great wordsmith would ignite Isabella's desire to let drunken hope spin around until it found what it was looking for.

"Love is both a beauty and a beast! If you continue to beat on love, it will turn into a hell awful beast. That beast is something many fail to take the blame for."

"What do you mean Lucah?"

"Love is sweet, both people are happy until one starts to think for both. Soon, there are no more conversations, and the accusations begin. No more sharing and caring. Once the beast is large enough- it rips the relationship to pieces! Lo-" Lucah stops in his tracks as his thoughts of Lola surface.

"Huh? What were you going to say Lucah?"

"I'm sorry. I meant, Lord knows peace and happiness is what I wish for your life. I am not here to complicate your life. Given the fact I'm your client, maybe it is best we remain professional."

"I don't want that." Isabella spoke as thoughts of letting loose circled her head. "*Live life, let go, and enjoy yourself.*" The words of her friends invaded her thoughts. Isabella planted a hell fire kiss on Lucah. The heat between her legs signaled global warning, and Isabella's thighs separated and welcome newness to lay between them.

"This feels good." Isabella cried as Lucah caressed her

smooth skin.

"It's time for you to let go." Lucah watched Isabella cry blindly. Too shy to look Lucah in his face, she followed every touch placed upon her body. Her long golden hair swept the carpet, as her arms extended above her head.

"Let me do this."

"I wanna feel whole again." Isabella cried, as Lucah tasted every section of her body.

"You feel that?"

"Go slow." Isabella pleaded hoping to lock every moment she and Lucah shared into her memory. Lucah introduced himself to Isabella as emotions oozed from her body. Lucah pulled her legs into the air and worked them like a pair of scissors against his smooth chest. Isabella darkened her blindness, by placing both hands over her eyes.

"Look at me. Open your eyes Bella." Isabella sat up on her elbows as he she stared Lucah dead center. Lucah rolled his neck from side to side, as he bit on his lip without any interruption of his intense sexing. As the rooms ambiance settled to a quiet hush, Isabella's feeling of renewal allowed her to climax not one, not two, but three times.

Chapter 52

"**V**irginia, I see a lot of changes with you and I hate them." Raymond announced as he sat in his office seat.

"Look Raymond, I told you all about this mess. Two of my good friends are going through hell and my desk- fuck it. I'm sinking." Virginia confessed as she blew out steam.

"Sweetheart, you know I'm here for you. Look, if you were anyone else, I would tell you the same thing."

"What would that be Raymond?" Virginia quizzed as she unbuttoned her blouse. Raymond's blue eyes danced around Virginia's hefty cups.

"Ah hell, let it wait. Get that bra off." Raymond teased as he nosedived into Virginia's breasts.

"Virginia, take some time off, catch up on your paperwork, and stop taking new clients for about two months. Focus on the ones you have. If you have clients who are non-compliant; discontinue them." Raymond stated as he pulled away from Virginia.

"Yeah, you're right." Virginia sighed as she grabbed bottled water from the refrigerator. Virginia and Raymond's relationship flourished over the last few months. Numerous dates and trips down memory lane proved to be the much needed therapy and second chance at life they both deserved. They knew what it was to have loved and lost someone special all in the same breath. Virginia, Raymond and her husband attended Yale together. At a time in her life, Virginia knew her husband was the one, and never questioned it. But as her world turned; she often wondered if Raymond was the one all along.

"Ok, I will slow down after I help my new patient who was recently diagnosed with HIV, *and* help a friend with post-divorce episodes. At least Isabella's glow is back on!"

"Oh wow! That is great news! Hmm, let me check the news.

Where's the remote baby?" Raymond searched the office for the TV remote.

"The news, I thought we were going to..."

"Hmm, both of you aligned at the same time... something in the universe is about to blow!" Raymond joke.

"Quit playing!" Virginia pinched Raymond on the neck."

"There you go playing all rough."

"Ok, I'm sorry, let me kiss it."

"Nope! You have done enough!"

"You big old baby."

"Now you know there's nothing babyish' bout this man here! You know this white boy will throw down at the sound of a zipper. Don't act crazy V-."

"Ok, let me stop. Listen, have you ever heard of Lucah Hunt?"

"Can't say that I have. Why?"

"He was referred to me by Dr. Ted Helton."

"Ok, I know Ted. Cool dude. We played in a charity golf tournament about a month ago.

"Well Ted never gave me any of his medical history. He told me about a traumatic event altering Lucah's state of being-mentally speaking, and I agreed to take him on."

"Well, what's the deal?"

"I figured the more we consulted with each other; he would eventually open up, but it never happened. On his last visit, I informed him on my needed to know more about him and the issues complicating his life. I told him I could not help *him* until he opened up."

"What happened?"

"Well he got pissed at me for reminding him on how I operate my practice. I informed him about being unhappy with the lack of cooperation on his behalf and that's when he clicked."

"See Virginia, you did enough. Don't add stress. Note things for what they are and move on. When they step out of line the *third* time, cut your ties.

"Raymond, that guy was crazy!" Virginia pleaded her case. "He went from normal to extreme psycho within seconds. The glare in his eyes made me so uneasy."

"Call Ted, tell him the deal, and let him handle it."

"I plan on it, but in the meantime, I'm going to see what dirt I can dig up on his ass. There is something dangerous about him and I'm not going to stop. You know he had the nerve to flirt with me a few times?"

"You mean to tell me he didn't see the icy throne you sit upon?"

"You so funny, I'm going to pass on laughing. Any who, I guess him sitting there biting his lip while rolling his head from side to side; was the key he needed to get me turned on."

"What exactly did you say to him, V-?"

"I informed him that I was a professional, and that his little act was not going to help slip my panties around my ankles."

"Yeah, you tell Ted about that nut case. He needs to know. In the meantime, find something better to do with your time. Leave that man alone."

"Well doing you sounds nice right about now. Let's go home. Are you done for the day?"

"I am sure am!"

"Good, I can finish putting hickeys all over your body!"

"Ok, I want you to focus on one area though."

"You are beyond nasty Raymond."

"I know."

Chapter 53

"Gabby, what are we going to do about this book? I have left message after message and you have not returned any of my calls. If I do not hear from you by tomorrow evening, I am flying out your way! Oh yeah, expect a hell hot slap across the face! You got me popping' pills bad, and this front lace is looking like I got stitches going cross my damn forehead! Now you know how jacked up that must look! Call me Gabby! I am worried about you!"

For the last few weeks, Gabby managed to turn her once bright home, into a hell cave. Lights off, closed curtains, and dead silence shown no resemblance that the world still existed. With most of the furniture in the house gone, the sound of a broken home was on the forefront. Dale came and took half the home with him and this time- he took his entire wardrobe. Gabby dared not play with the idea of a possible reunion with him; so she broke a few of his cherished workbenches, to stain his heart. Her bed swallowed fifteen pounds from her petite frame, and her bout with depression, pushed her to the edge of death.

"Gabby?"

"Gabby, say something. Child, why are you hiding?"

"Mom, leave me be. Please leave me be!"

"This place stinks worse than hell. Oh Jesus, praise Jesus! I am glad I told your father to stay home! Baby, look at you!" Gabrielle's mother cried as she ran to fetch a face towel. "Why does this house smell like this?" Gabrielle's mother did her best to navigate through her daughter's torn bedroom.

"GABBY! This bathroom is horrible! How long have you been throwing up? There's blood on the floor *and* carpet! Oh Lord, I'm calling 911."

"Mom don't! I don't need a scene. You can help by getting

me get dressed and driving me to the hospital. I do not need nosy ass people meddling in my business. I can't deal with this shit right now!" In a frantic, Gabrielle's mother ran around her daughter's home packing and cleaning at the same time. She sprayed a shirt with perfume, and wrapped it around her face, to help mask the circulating scent of death.

"The only damn thing missing is a vulture circling your bed!" Gabrielle's mother cried. Gabrielle looked as if death was piggy backing her right to hell without escape.

"Mom, be sure to call Jill. I know she's going to fly in tomorrow, if she's not already in flight. I know she's mad at me for not returning her calls."

"Okay love, here, put these clothes on. Baby, you got a lot of explaining to do. You knew I was going to come around sooner than later. Are you trying to kill yourself again?" Gabrielle's mother lectured and interrogated her daughter non-stop. "Oh Lord. Child, where in the hell did you find a subject as such?"

"What are you talking about mom?"

"That man on the portrait. Good Lord, does he have it going on like that Gabby?" Gabrielle's mother could not help drooling lust onto the plush carpet.

"I need my glasses on- wait, no I don't."

"Baby if you took four away from his six-pack, he still got it going on. Hell, it would take a lot of bad shit to make a man that fine, go bad."

"Yeah, well something tells me he's not as sweet as he looks." Gabrielle evil eyed the portrait she painted of Lucah.

"What that mean child?" Gabrielle's mother asked.

"Nothing mom, forget it. I'm ready, are you ready?"

"Yes, let's go love."

Chapter 54

"Lucah, how are things going?" Dr. Helton asked as he charted notes.

"I'm fine and you?" Lucah felt uneasy about his appointment with Dr. Helton today. He had no intentions on discussing anything except his health.

"Look Lucah, I can't continue to ignore the fact that there's something going on with you. I heard about your last appointment with Virginia."

"She was damaging my nerves."

"You told me you would share your diagnosis with her and you also told me you were going to be open-minded about therapy."

"She was too pushy. She was nosy and judgmental. I told you, I do not like people who look down on others. She's a damn basket case herself if I may add a few grand of my own."

"Oh, and now you're playing the doctor, huh?" The tension between the two men increased. Eye to eye, both men stared each other down without the intent to blink.

"Lucah, do you want to get better? Do you want to live a long life? Do you have any hope man? What happened to the woman you met not too long ago?"

"She's fine! Why are you asking about her?" Lucah snapped as he took to his feet. It was obvious Dr. Helton struck a nerve when mentioning Lola.

"Why on the defense, Lucah?" Have you had any partners since your diagnosis?"

"My answer to that is still no."

"Look Lucah, I am here to help. God knows I am a private man. The story I shared with you about my son was between you and I. I felt compelled to share the story with you, because your eyes resembled my son's, the day he found out."

"My companies are busy, my family is worried about me, I'm traveling too much, and sure- it would be nice to have a love to call my own; but I'll make it work. Please note- my actions are worthy of praise- not condemnation."

"If you are into this woman, tell her the truth."

"I know what kind of friend I have. She's wonderful. There is always a smile in her voice, and her heart is golden. It's a shame she was taken advantage of. Understand that if we move outside of friendship, she will receive the chance I never received."

"Listen Lucah, many people are HIV and they are able to live productive and happy lives. They are in relationships and many of them *live* for the cure. Lucah, I do not want to start preaching because I know you know better."

"I won't mess up. I will talk with her. In the meantime, I feel fine. Please keep your crazy ass doctor friend out my life. She's barking up the wrong tree."

"I will smooth things over with Virginia, but promise me you will attend a support group or private therapy. I will email you a list of male psychiatrists. Maybe things will be better with a man."

"I agree. Please keep my diagnosis private. I did not authorize you to talk about my health to her."

"Good. I will call you when your results from the lab come in. In the meantime, here is a list of new doctors to check out."

"Thanks Doc."

Chapter 55

"Dr. Arlington, Ms. Lee is here for her session."

"Thank you Mac, send her in." Virginia made a last attempt to clean off her desk. Clutter bug at heart, she never wanted people to see her outside the standards she designs for her patients. Virginia had a knack for masking her imperfections.

"Hello, I'm Lily Lee." Lily appeared lifeless. Her body language modeled a ghost in passing.

"I'm Dr. Arlington, but please, call me Virginia."

"Thanks Virginia."

"Okay, start where you want to start."

"As you know, from our phone conversation, I was recently diagnosed with HIV. It hit harder than a ton of wet cement. Brain freezing pain and paralysis set within. After three more lab tests, I gave up denying truth."

"Have you thought about harming yourself or anyone else?"

"Well not myself, but the asshole who gave this to me- yes! My ex and I have been apart for three years. He was on the down low, just to throw that out there. For the first year post divorce, my blood was tested every three months and none of my tests came back positive. Plus, he's not positive for the virus. We've talked and I shared my diagnosis with him."

"I see. How many men have you been active with since your divorce?"

"Two. One operates on batteries and the other, a smooth-ass operator."

"Have you tried to contact this man?"

"I've tried calling him, no answer. Been by his place, but no response."

"Why not, might I ask? Virginia asked in shock as she scooted towards the edge of her seat. Virginia removed her glasses and reached out to grab Lily's hand."

"Lily, you have to report this man. I'm sure you feel defeated and out of wind right now but it's important you report this guy as soon as possible."

"Not until I see him face to face to give him a chance to tell the truth. Maybe he doesn't know he has it." Lily opted for hope. If she found out Lucah was low enough to inject his poisonous venom in her, she was dedicated in escorting him to the gates of hell herself.

"Are you two exclusive? When was the last time you have heard from him?"

"Three months. He is a busy man and he is always traveling. I left him a message asking to meet soon. I told him if he failed to meet me, it would be his funeral announcement across every media channel possible."

"Don't make excuses for this man. He's failed to return your calls and now you have to *threaten* him to return your call? You do the math Ms. Lee."

"I know." Lily cried regret.

"Ok, you have two days to find out his deal. From there, you need to notify the local Center for Disease Control and the police."

"That's fine. Can I see you here this Thursday at eleven?"

"Yes, I will write you in. Do you need any medicine to help you with your depression Lily?"

"Write the script, and I will take it if I need it. I'm taking so much medicine right now; I'm not interested in taking anything new."

"That's fine. Once you start taking them, journal your feelings. I need to see how you are reacting to the medication and to also monitor your moods. Also, call me when you start the meds, if the adjustment period goes fine, I will set up your auto re-fills."

"No problem. Thank you, you are so kind."

"Lily, I want you to come to this support group next week. I have some phenomenal women living with HIV that will inspire you to move forward with life. Here is my private number. You call me anytime. It's no rush right now. I totally understand, but the group is there is you need it." Virginia felt Lily's pain and did the best job possible to hold her tears back. Virginia was great at what she did, because she cared about her clients.

Chapter 56

"What in the hell is wrong with Gabby, Renee?"

"You had better lower your voice before I knock hell out of you. Your guess is good as the next. All I know is that the house was a mess Dale. When was the last time you two talked?"

"Three months. She made it clear that she didn't need me in her life."

"Well you're damn right! Where in the hell do you get off thinking she needs you? There you were living the good life and you fuck it up by loaning your dick out to anything with a heartbeat!"

"Renee! Enough!" Gabrielle's father yelled.

"I could give a damn about you right now Dale, but I tell you what, you better make things right with my daughter. I know Gabby has her issues but,"

"Yes, issues *your* wife caused Richard. If you think, an alcoholic drunk who beats on children produces great results; then you are as fucked up as your wife! Your daughter was a terror! All the verbal and physical abuse done by your wife's hands was too much! You two knew she had problems, but I guess if you felt if you prayed super hard; she would be ok! Mental health issues are real! The devil ain't got shit to do with shit mental!"

"Richard don't do it!" Gabrielle's father punched Dale clean across the waiting room floor.

"If you ever project bullshit images of my wife and my daughter to the public, I will drag your ass to the cross myself!" Gabrielle's father yelled as he loosened his tie. Never in all his years had Gabrielle's father allowed holiness to escape his body. Through witnessing his daughter's pain, Gabrielle's father remained silent and respected his daughter's wishes. A pain buried deep within his heart, Gabrielle's father blamed himself for allowing his wife to abuse Gabrielle. Being a man of the cloth, this shamed her father. Standing proud on Sunday mornings preaching to his congregation about sin, love, peace and forgiveness and here he lived in a mansion of hell. Truth left his heart a long time ago and the validation of being a true disciple of Christ seemed it would never see resurrection day.

"Please Richard, stop! Lord knows we don't need this mess right now. Please sweetie, come on, and let's grab some coffee."

"I'm sorry, did I walk in on something? Dr. Helton asked as he paused in his steps.

"No, we are fine." Everyone gathered themselves while eyeballing each other.

"Are you the parents of Gabrielle Withers?"

"Yes we are. How is our daughter doing?"

"May we talk in private?"

"Wait, what about me? I'm the husband." Dr. Helton ignored Dale and looked at Gabrielle's parents for confirmation.

"He is but they are going through a divorce."

"As long as they are married, he has legal rights, plus he needs to be present for this news."

"What news?"

"I apologize for you having to witness that. What is going on with Gabrielle?" Dale questioned.

"Dr. Helton's head hung low as he pondered on how he would tell the family the news, all of which he's told all too many times.

"Gabrielle is HIV positive."

"Lord I feel faint." Gabrielle's mother searched for seating.

"I got her, please continue on Doctor."

"In the beginning, we ran a battery of tests on her, and came up empty on the first round. Her electrolytes were off, and her blood count showed she had a severe infection, and dehydration was present because of the severe spell of vomiting and diarrhea."

"That explains all the blood in the bathroom." Gabrielle's mother whispered.

"We are treating those issues right now. In the midst of trying to pinpoint Gabrielle's problem, she daughter admitted being involved with a man that she opted not to use protection with."

"Lord NO!" Gabrielle's mother cried. Gabrielle's father held onto his wife as they continued to listen to Dr. Helton.

"What is going to happen to her? My child, my child- is HIV positive?" Gabrielle's mother sobbed.

"I know this is a lot to take in, but advances in science have made it possible for one to live a quality life. Many people live twenty plus years with the disease. It is all about being proactive in one's healthcare. Right now, she needs all of your support. She needs your love and understanding."

"She has the support, but what about her health? What will this medicine do her body? I've heard a lot of horror stories." Dale quizzed as he shook his head in disbelief.

"It's tough starting out. The body will experience a number of side effects from the medication, but it is important that she take everything as prescribed. No missing doses, no discontinuing medication without my permission. We want to help her immune system as much as possible."

"We understand. May we see Gabrielle now?"

"Yes, but please limit your time with her. We gave her some medicine to help her rest. She is currently on IV fluids to help hydrate her system. She is also on oxygen but that won't be for too long. I referred her for psychiatric services as well. The doctor is Virginia Arlington, and she is the best I know. Try to get Gabrielle to meet with her soon."

"Ok, is there anything else doctor? Do I need to take off work, or make special care arrangements?" Gabrielle's mother asked in guilt. All the years of abuse she pained her child with came forth in her mind. Grown and all, Gabrielle would always be her mother's baby in her eyes.

"She's coming home with me Renee. That's not up for discussion. You can stay at the house to help, but she stays home. She has my total support. I'm there for her."

"Let's see how Gabrielle responds. Just take it one day at a time. I know Dr. Arlington has a few HIV workshops and therapy groups coming up. I know your wife would benefit greatly if she attended. The important part is to help Gabrielle through the process of acceptance and moving forward. That alone is one big hurdle to cross."

"We understand and we will do everything we possible." Gabrielle's father stood to shake the doctor's hand.

"Did you give it to my daughter?" Gabrielle's father asked Dale as he rolled up his sleeves.

"Richard, not here!"

"Look, your daughter and I are both guilty of cheating. After I left the home, I went and got myself tested for everything. All of my lab tests came back negative. I think we need to worry about this man she's been seeing."

"Well, we want to see your results, then."

"That's no problem. In the meantime, we need to focus on Gabby. Can we agree to that?"

"Dale, we can't forget this, but we will do anything for our daughter; even if it means you being with her. You make sure you stand by her side." Gabrielle's father pleaded.

"I'm here for her."

Chapter 57

"What's going on Isabella?"

"Now why do you have to start our conversations as if, I'm one of your damn patients?"

"Ok freak, what you been up to? You giving that young boy of yours lessons on how to make it *all right* for ya?"

"How trifling must *you* be, trick?" Isabella laughed.

"Girl I'm just messing around with ya. Hell, I wonder what a young buck would do for this old girl."

"Not a damn thing. You know your nerves too bad for that." Isabella giggled.

"You damn right." Virginia snapped her fingers in the air.

"Anyway, I'm glad to see you glowing and shit. Damn, did you lose a couple of dress sizes, Isabella?"

"Sorry it's been a while since I saw you. In between work and being sick on and off, I had to take some down time. I was close to going to the hospital, but it went away. Lisa really takes care of me. Back to my new man, he is amazing! I want to cut his back open to see if he runs off energizer batteries. He can't stop and *dayum*- I cannot stop him."

"Well enjoy it girl. Raymond and I are enjoying the hell out of each other right now."

"Really? And to think you was trying to push him off on me."

"Yeah, I know. You know the funny thing about it all, is how I find myself questioning if all this was meant to be."

"You gone eat the rest of that cup cake?" Isabella cased Virginia's cup cake as she finished hers.

"I *love* Cakes by Nette. I have to tell myself I can only go three times a month. If no, I will be looking like a cupcake!"

"Just count it as happy weight!"

"Thank you for that! I certainly will."

"Bella, who is this mystery man? I wanna meet the man that's responsible for my friends glow!"

"You know he's a client of mines right?" Isabella stated as she looked over her shoulder, hoping to hush her friend's voice.

"So what- you keeping secrets now?"

"No, but you better keep your damn mouth shut!"

"Look, I know you not schooling me on confidentiality. If anyone knows about confidentiality, it's me! Even though there are days where I wanna put all my crazy ass patients on blasts to the world; I turn from sin. Bella, there are days where I wanna sign my damn self in. The stories I hear are enough to make the strongest person slice their wrists!"

"Ok. His name is Lucah Hunt." Virginia's face turned as ivory as a seashell. With every second passed, joy faded from Virginia's face.

"Virginia, what's wrong? Do you know him?"

"Girl, that man is a *devil*!" Isabella was scared shitless by Virginia's statement.

"A colleague of mine referred him to me for treatment. He told me that Lucah had experienced some *life-changing* event. It appeared to be so bad that he was blocked up with depression."

"Well what the hell is his problem?" Isabella was scared.

"He never let me in. When I reminded him on how important it was for him to open up, girl some psycho showed up and I was like fuck it all! I ended my sessions with him, and told him I would mail his final bill."

"This doesn't feel right Virginia." Isabella's relaxed stance switched to a defensive one, as she thought of the worst possible circumstances that hid behind Lucah's glitch free swagger.

"Did you find anything weird about him, when you took him on as your client?"

"Not a damn thing. You know how I fine glove potential clients. I do my best to avoid train wrecks." Isabella replied with her head cradled in her hands.

"I'm going to call Dr. Helton and demand he provide information about him. I need an excuse to get him to divulge his medical history."

"Tell his ass the truth. One of your clients is in therapy because of him. Tell him how nuts he became when *your client* wanted to slow down on the relationship. You better tell his ass something!" Isabella spat fire as she paced the office floor.

"You got some wine? This shit starting to get on my nerves." The blaming session in Isabella's mind had taken control, and regret was close to moving in.

"Yeah, it's in the fridge. Just keep the whole bottle out." Both women pondered over a millions of ideas as they emptied the bottle.

"The thought of me and Lucah being something special is starting to turn into the worst thing I have ever done."

"Fuck it, here goes!" Virginia dialed the phone and turned on the speaker.

"Hello Ted, its Virginia."

"Hey there, how are you doing?"

"Wish I could say well, but things are kind of crazy in my court."

"Sorry to hear that."

"It's ok. I invite most of the shit in, so I guess I gotta deal with it."

"Hey Virginia, I'm glad you called. I have a young woman, who was recently diagnosed as HIV positive. I gave her your information because she really needs therapy. I spoke with her and informed her about the workshops and groups you have."

"Does she seem to want the help? I'm not interested in big top acts right now. I'm trying to relieve my own stress *and* case load right now. I hope you understand."

"Yes, I do. She is there and as you know, the acceptance process is something she is trying to swallow. I do believe she will come around in time. She has a lot of support."

"Great! I will take her. What's her name Ted?"

"Gabrielle Withers."

"Wait, are you talking about best-selling author and international artist, Gabrielle Withers?"

"Yes, I hate to say it." The sadness on Isabella and Virginia's faces stretched their frowns a mile long. No matter the person diagnosed with a disease, one would be inhumane not to feel sympathy for the inflicted.

"Wow, my prayers go out to her. She will be the second woman this week I have taken in for my workshop. Oh Lord when will this madness end?"

"I know it's sad."

"Hey Ted, I called you to discuss Lucah Hunt."

"You know I can go only so into discussion about him Virginia. You know about patient privacy."

"I do, but Ted; I have a client who I am servicing who has *dealings* with Lucah."

"How Virginia? Dealing how?" Dr. Helton's voice became heavy with the weight of curiosity.

"Well she and Lucah are involved in an open relationship. It's been going on for about a close to three months now."

"Ok."

"Well after they slept with each other, she informed Lucah that she was not looking for anything serious, nothing long term and he flipped out on her."

"Oh hell."

"What is it Ted?" Virginia's voice talked as if it was queasy and on the verge of vomiting fear.

"What the hell is it? Speak now dammit!" Isabella yelled as she took to her feet. "Fucking say it! What in the hell is wrong with the bastard?"

"Virginia who is that?"

"It's my client. She's the woman who's been involved with

Lucah."

"I'm sorry to say but, Lucah Hunt is HIV positive. I ask you ladies not to speak on this, because I'm wrong for telling you this."

"What?" Isabella and Virginia screamed in unison. Isabella grabbed her chest as she fell back into her chair. Isabella's breathing mimicked a woman in labor.

"Isabella, are you ok?" Virginia screamed as she ran to over to Isabella. Virginia proceeded to take Isabella's vitals.

"Come on baby, put your feet up. Raise your head. There, rest on back. Let's get this jacket off."

"Mac! I need you now! Get in here!"

"What the hell is going on?" Mackenzie panicked not knowing where to start helping. Seeing her boss out of control caused Mackenzie to pop a few Xanax for herself.

"Ted, we have a lot to talk about! You need to find Lucah Hunt and you need to alert the authorities. I feel this man is knowingly transmitting HIV."

"I will call him and I will go to wherever he is. Please keep this private until we meet. You set the place and we will come."

"I'm giving you little time on this. Keep us informed please. This man has a lot of explaining to do! I'm getting Isabella to the hospital."

"Is she ok?"

"No, she has blood pressure and heart problems. Also, now that you ask, she's was violently sick with the flu for a week. I think trashing the thought of her illness from last week being a spell of the flu, would be the right thing to do, right?"

"Let's get her tested first, and we will go from there. I will be to the hospital in about forty minutes. Traffic on forty is getting thick, but I can pull it off. Tell them I will be treating her. Who's her cardiologist?"

"James Anderson."

"Thanks, I will talk to him as I'm driving."

"Good." Virginia felt paralyzed as she watched her best friend's health turn against her. With everything she had been through, Virginia doubted if her friend had enough perseverance left inside.

"Did you give her two aspirin Mac?"

"Yes, a few minutes ago. I placed a few cool towels on her forehead and neck."

"Good, cancel my appointments for the next week. Call Dr. Benson and inform him that I had to take an emergency leave. Tell him I will call him tomorrow with details."

"Got it."

"Bella, can you hear me sweetie? The paramedics are on the way. You are doing just fine, hold on. I can't have you croaking in my office. I be damn if you come back haunting my ass." Virginia tried to get Isabella to laugh, but fell short.

"Girl, I can't believe this shit. The one time I open up, I end up regretting it. It's not fair." Virginia cried in pity.

"Hush now. Getting to the hospital comes first. We have to remain positive. No other way of looking at it right now. We will deal with whatever when it comes our way."

"I love you Virginia. I pray this shit is not what it seems. Do me a favor and call the kids. Call Lisa and have her meet us at the hospital. I think she's off work today."

"Ok. Relax until the paramedics arrive." Virginia felt guilty for relaxing in her pursuit to finding dirt on Lucah. Now both women sat and shivered in regret.

Chapter 58

"Hey there, long time no see Mr. Man. I missed you tons."

"I'm sorry." Lucah apologized as he opened his front door.

"What's going on here? Why are you packing?" Lola was worried because Lucah never mentioned anything to her about moving. With all the time Lola and Lucah had spent together in the last three months, Lola felt their relationship had formed a great foundation.

"I'm sorry. Truthfully, everything has grabbed me by the tail and I haven't stopped spinning as of yet. The unit here in St. Louis is not doing well. I spend more time traveling to the West Coast, it seems moving closer seems to be the right step. I am going to operate from Greece while leaving a team of key people here in the states; to be the face of my firm. It was time to make some executive changes."

"Well what direction will those changes shift us in Lucah?" Lucah ignored Lola's question because fear blinded him. Lucah was not ready to lose Lola, but it was a chance he was willing to take in order to remain a free man. He knew his freedom ticket would be in jeopardy once the other women reported him. He had stopped all contact with the women and they all refused to let up on him.

"Sit down Lola. I need to talk with you." A teary-eyed Lola reached for Lucah's hand as he navigated her through the mess in the hallway.

"Lola, I was hurt in my last relationship. I loved her and she loved me- at least I thought. Sadly, fate played me one hell of a dirty hand. At first, I was numb with fear and shame. I felt all alone and naked to the world."

"Lucah, what's wrong?" Lola's hand cupped Lucah's chin as she lifted has face to hers. Lola saw Lucah's pain and all she wanted to do was comfort him. Lola was shocked to see Lucah's strength in a vulnerable and debilitating stage.

"Lola, the woman who left me, gave me HIV."

"What?" Lola released Lucah's face and sunk into her chair. Lola stared at the floor as if she was staring through glass. Without looking at Lucah, Lola talked to the glass floor.

"You mean to tell me, you didn't have the respect, the common courtesy to inform me of your status? Did you not see me falling for you?"

"Look, I was scared Lola. I never had any intentions on sleeping with you. I would have never allowed things to go that far."

"Lucah, things have gone far enough. Why didn't you tell me up front?"

"I was afraid of you rejecting me. I was afraid of losing your friendship. My goal was to show you that hope still existed. I didn't want you to give up on love and happiness."

"Lucah, I would have come around. Time heals all wounds. I'm a grown woman. Hell, I'm not the first to go through a divorce."

"Lola, you helped me and I pray I have helped you through your struggles."

'It's been great Lucah."

"Lola, I do not anticipate you jumping on board to fly away with me. I understand you have a life, and a wonderful daughter." As Lucah talked on, distance had taken its space between the two. Lola's avoidance of eye contact confirmed Lucah's thoughts.

"Lucah, I will be here for you. We started as friends and we will remain so. I was looking forward to a relationship, but this news- the way you went about things changes everything."

"I understand Lola. I'm not upset and I respect your feelings."

"Lucah, taking risks happens on every avenue of life but when it comes to my life-, I try to reduce risks as much as possible."

"Lola, I see where you stand and I have to respect that. Please know that I do not want to lose you as a friend. It's tough out here and having a good friend is a necessity."

"Come here you." Lola stood and welcomed Lucah to an overdue hugging session. Although things had not turned out the way Lucah wished on the outside, deep down in his heart, he felt good about the idea of him and Lola remaining friends.

"I will call you once I'm finished packing. Maybe we can catch a dinner and a movie. I want to share more with you."

"I would love that."

"I will also give you my new address and other info. I hope you will bring Grace for a visit to Greece. I want you to meet my family."

"Ok, make that date soon. I'm always up for a vacation." Lucah and Lola hugged once more. The chemistry between the two may have fizzled, but the way they felt about each other as friends, remained intact.

Chapter 59

"Dr. Arlington, its Lily Lee. May we speak soon? I thought about what you said and I have come to term with many things, but there is one thing- well, one asshole that I am nowhere near forgiving. I avoided giving you his name because of his stature. Well, as of today, that bastard has a name. His name is Lucah Hunt. I have been going out of my mind as to what I need to do. He will not return the phone calls, nor will he acknowledge the visits I made to his home. I have done everything possible to gather his attention. Please help guide me through this mess. I will have my phone on all day. I hope to hear from you soon."

Chapter 60

"Hello Mrs. Withers."

"Whatever." Gabrielle sighed.

"You are looking much better today. I'm Lisa and I will be your nurse today." Lisa announced as she opened the blinds, and tended to the patient board on the wall.

"Oh please with those blinds. I'm not ready to wake up to the world."

"Can't sleep always Mrs. Withers."

"I can if I put you out of my room."

"I won't let you. Now come on and sit up. I'm going to prepare the shower for you."

"No thanks, I will do that later."

"Ok, as you wish. Just to inform you, this board contains phone numbers for me and your tech assistant. Just call us if you need us. I will provide your medicines and assessments. Your tech will monitor your vitals and help me keep an eye on you." Lisa sat a small tray on Gabrielle's bed table. On it, paper cups looked as if candy were placed inside them. Gabrielle stared at the tray in a confused manner.

"Why all the pills? What's wrong with me?"

"Do you remember anything from yesterday?"

"I can't say that I do."

"We sedated you yesterday after your doctor came in the room to talk with you. You were weak and dehydrated when you came to the hospital with your mother. Your family visited yesterday, but you much slept through of their visitation."

"Ok, but that doesn't explain what's wrong with me. Do you know, or is there someone else who will tell me what is going on? I'm not taking those pills until I find out what the hell is going on." Gabrielle pushed the tray away from her.

"May I sit?" Lisa pointed to the side of Gabrielle's bed. Lisa took hold of Gabrielle's hand and patted it hoping it would help ease the pain related to the bad news she was close to delivering.

"Mrs. Withers, after several lab tests yesterday, the doctors came to a blank. The physician informed you that they were going to run more test after you confessed to the doctor that the last man you were with, you opted out on protection. With that information, the doctor ran an STD panel. Your feelings- well they confirmed your HIV status." Gabrielle sunk back into her pillows and screeched an awful cry. Gabrielle shook her head from east to west as she fought denial.

"Your level of shock was extreme. You suffered several anxiety attacks, spells of vomiting, and shortness of breath. The doctor placed you on a heart monitor and placed you on oxygen. In the end, the doctor felt it was best to sedate you for a while.

"Oh LORD! What's going to happen to me, Lisa?"

"Ms. Wither's, I'm not in your position, but please allow me to fill your spirit with some hope. I look at HIV the same way I do any other disease. There is treatment and there is enough advancement in medicine where one has the ability to live a long and productive life. You have to be proactive by educating yourself about the disease."

"Hope? I hope this shit is wrong! This is too much to bear. I didn't deserve this and this shit you're throwing at me sounds too scripted. Would you believe in the shit you just told me if the show was on the other foot?"

"I'm sorry, but I am sincere in all that I say. No one should have to die from this, or any other disease for that much."

"Hell, that would mean hospitals and funeral homes would be fucked. People gotta die, and there's no getting past it."

"We're here to nurse you to wellness and that's what we intend on doing."

"Quality of life... gone, another chance at love... gone! What am I suppose to do?"

"Fight! Fight Ms. Withers!"

"Fight my ass. I wanna shoot the lousy bastard that did this to me. I'm too old to be fighting shit like this. What are these pills for?"

"It's your daily cocktail. You will have to take another cocktail in the evening as well. All of these medicines will work together in helping your immune system combat the disease. Your educator will be by later today to provide you with some information about the medications. Side effects and other topics will be discussed with you as well."

"Cocktail? Hell, from what I hear, those medicines fuck you over worse than a pimp. Hell, if I wanted a cocktail, I would have ordered one!" Lisa felt powerless and was close to running out of inspiration.

"I'm too tired for this!" Gabrielle whined.

"I'm not going to allow you to take me there. Sit up and let's get going. I don't need to know my patients long before *tough love* kicks in." Lia commanded as she pull the covers of Gabrielle.

"You are too much. When does the next nurse get here?"

"You got a while to go. Now that I have you sitting up, I'm going to get your breakfast tray here. Here is some literature for you to review. I know it's too much to remember, but the more you learn, the more it helps."

"You're damn right, this is too much to remember." Gabrielle bitched as she flipped through a booklet.

"Will you promise to do your best? I suggest you keep a journal once you start your medications. It helps your doctor keep track of your side effects and progress."

"Who is my doctor?"

"His name is Ted Helton. He is one of our best."

"Hell, if he's the best, then he must have the cure in his lab coat."

"Oh now that would be ground breaking." Lisa smiled as

she poured Gabrielle a glass of water.

"Take your time taking the medicine. I have apple juice, sprite, and crackers to help you down some of your medicines. I'm going to chart, change out your IV fluids and bring in more flowers that were left at the nurses' station for you yesterday. If you feel sick, there's a pan on your side table and a few wet and dry towels."

"Trash the flowers. *Get well soon* is a damn joke, don't you think? Wellness comes after I'm dead and gone."

"Understood. Do you mind if I donate the flowers to those less fortunate?"

"Whatever you wish."

"Thank you. I will deliver them to other rooms. Thank you for your kindness. I will bring the note cards to your room, since they have your name on them."

"Thanks Lisa."

"You're welcome. No problem at all. Ma I ask you a question?"

"Shoot."

"Did you ever tell the physician who you slept with last?"

"No, they didn't ask. I was kind of glad, because I'm going to be dealing with the piece of shit on my own once I get out of here."

"I think it's important you provide his information. I's important that h is contacted right away."

"Good luck with that. I haven't been able to contact him since the night we had sex."

"Doesn't that make you wonder?"

"It scares and pisses me off at the same time. If Lucah Hunt did this to me on purpose- he is a dead man!"

"I see. I will alert the physician about this man. Please write his information down. We will work on trying to contact him."

"Good luck with that!" Gabrielle laughed. Lisa loved her job but it was moments as such, where she wished she worked in a different field.

Chapter 61

"**H**ello Virginia."

"Ted."

"We have a mess on our hands and right now, there's no way we should continue holding off on involving the authorities."

"I agree, but I want things done the right way."

"Aren't you late for doing shit the right way?"

"Look, don't give me attitude like that. I'm sorry, but as far as I was concerned, he communicated with me. Sure, he was stubborn about coming in at times, but he still showed. He still proved to be compliant and in his right mind." Virginia sat far from sold and stepped closer to committing murder.

"Virginia, right now he's allegedly accused of infecting three women. We can't go any further until we locate him."

"Three women?" Virginia was shocked.

"Yes, my nurse just informed me that the count is up to three. Gabrielle Withers, the new patient who I referred to you..."

"Yes..."

"She slept with him also."

"And you still think he's innocent? You must be sick *your* damn self! Take your ass to the psych ward and sign yourself in."

"You can be pissed all you want, but there's no need to talk ignorant!"

"There is no doubt that your patient is the devil. What kind of sick fuck walks the earth doing shit like that?"

"Virginia lets remain calm on work on a resolve."

"Whatever. I talked with Isabella after you left her room and she dispatched a friend at another agency to help with PR. Her brother works for St. Louis County and she's filed her case against Lucah. The warrant is in the making.

"I see. What about your other client, Lily Lee?"

"She's filed against him too. I'm holding a meeting with all the ladies today. No more waiting. Ted, this is going to be a mess, you know this, right?"

"Yes, I do. I guess he can kiss his freedom goodbye real soon."

"I can't wait to see that lousy bastard. I've got more than my mind to give him." Within twenty-four hours, the life Virginia once knew evolved into darkness.

"I'm afraid to see how many more will surface." Ted said as he leaned on the counter behind the nurses' station.

"Do you see the pattern here?" Virginia asked as she jotted down some notes on a sheet of paper.

"What- this fool spiraling out of control and infecting women all across the city, maybe the country with HIV?"

"No, the pattern is that he chose women who are rich, successful, and are over the age of forty-five."

"No, he loves older women. He mentioned that to me on several occasions. Younger women were never his thing."

"He may love older women, but I'm sure if you chose to focus on more than the obvious, you will see his pattern. Your patient has a severe case of Cougar Fever."

"Really? Cougar Fever? Those women *had* to do something to him."

"Ted, who in the hell deserves payback like that? Are you sure you not high or something? What you said is absurd. That's like saying all rape victims deserve to be raped."

"It's not what I meant Virginia."

"What do you mean?"

"I meant what if they did something that sent him over the edge."

"What? Oh, how about rejecting him? How about telling him that they prefer career over love?"

"Ok, I'm sorry Virginia. I'm just shooting ideas out."

"All I'm saying is your boy is off the leash and someone

needs to put his lousy ass down."

"Damn!" Ted yelled as his hand hit the counter. "There has to be a reason why he's doing this!"

"Oh, what happen to *allegedly*?"

"Ok, you're right." After several minutes of combing his beard with his fingers, Ted's eyes locked on the paper Virginia was using to take notes.

"I'll be damn! It's making sense to me now. The woman, the woman who broke his heart, was much older than Lucah. He adored the ground she walked on. I mean it was a serious relationship."

"Stop pacing Ted, you making me nervous. Sit down. What went wrong? Does anyone know her whereabouts?"

"She became a dust particle for all I know. He told me about the reports he made against her, and that she lived in another country. He spent over a few hundred grand searching her out. He even showed invoices from the private investigation firms he used to track her. At that time, I had no reason to say anything because he showed no form of bad behavior. Yes, he was bitter, but who wouldn't be?"

"I see." Virginia paced the nurses' station with her thinking cap on tight.

"We need to gather the women to discuss this in privacy. We need to orchestrate a plan to lure him to a common ground." Virginia suggested.

"I find that a hard thing to do. He has failed to return any of their calls. Hell, Lucah barley calls me when I request it. Virginia, do you think he's going to meet us somewhere to have lunch, and discuss why he did what he did?"

"No, but we have to find something, or someone that will draw him in. The news is going public soon.

Let's see what happens after his handsome face graces every news channel on air."

"Ok. I am going to make a few calls. Let me know if you were successful with Mrs. Withers."

Chapter 62

"Gabby, baby you ok?" Dale wiped his wife's forehead down as he consoled her. "I am sorry for all I have done Gabby. You did not deserve any of it."

"Dale?" Gabrielle was still in a blur and shocked to see her husband sitting bed side after all they had experienced. The cocktail of medication was taking hold of her body.

"I'm here, you relax yourself. I talked with your parents and we all care about you. Your mother is moving in to help you out."

"Dale, who were you cheating with after all this time?" Hesitating to respond, Dale's head extended to the floor. "How long you two been intimate, Dale?" Gabrielle tried her best to read her husband but she came short. Anger, disgust, hate, and fear circled her gut. Sitting easy was an impossible chore, when knowing someone she loved had violated her body and trust, in a vile manner.

"Answer me you dumb fuck!"

"Why? Why does it matter Gabby!"

"Because I'm HIV positive! That's why you ass!" Gabrielle threw her water picture at Dale. Not aware of her strength returning with supernatural power, she hopped took to her feet. No matter what she grabbed, she did her best to make contact with Dale's body. Once again, the monster deep within his wife, surfaced with a sickened vengeance. Dale tried his best to duck and dodge all she threw.

"Damn! Stop it Gabby! Look at my face!" Gabrielle fell to her knees and began beating her frustration into the tile. Dale worked without halt to stop the bleed on his forehead. Absent of what he's walked in on, it was clear his wife's pain, was created out of his inability to remain faithful. Dale snuck up on his wife and covered her with a blanket. Gabrielle surrendered, and folded on the floor, moaning cries of regret. With his wife crying to the tile, they both prayed for answers.

"Talk to me Dale. Are you HIV positive? What about that woman you were with?"

"No, I am not positive and she isn't- at least as far as I know- positive for anything." For the first time ever, Dale was honest with his wife.

"How did this go down Gabby? Who were you sleeping with? Was it while we were married?"

"I met him over three months ago. His name is Lucah Hunt. It started out as a working relationship. Right away, he expressed great interest in my work. After talking with him a few times, I saw nothing wrong when he wanted to hire me to paint a self-portrait of him. I've done work like that a million times before."

"Ok, but how did you two become intimate?"

"It was on the night I put you out. I was alone and my vulnerability set me up as prey I guess. I visited his home and Dale- I had no idea that I would be painting him in the nude. My head was foggy from our last rift, and the three glasses of wine did not help. After he delivered his nude self to me- well, I'm not going into details."

"Why would you do something like that?"

"I guess for the same reasons you did. Emotions were everywhere. I was on empty from our last fight. I felt as if someone else was breathing for me. Living didn't feel natural, and for the moment- I needed something new. Every time we had sex, it felt like a make-up session, nothing special. We were having sex for the wrong reasons. We never fixed a damn thing."

"Baby I'm sorry."

"Huh, not as sorry as I am."

"What is going to happen next?"

"Will you help me up please?" Gabrielle looked Dale over and realized the cut above his eye was still bleeding, and she called for help.

"I'm sorry for hurting you Dale. My state of mind is all fucked up. All I think about is how this mess will hurt the girls. I got Jill and the fucking media to deal with. I'm not even sure the publisher is going to extend the deadline. Plus, the promos have started for the book release and tour."

"We will get through this Gabby. The rest of that shit can wait. This is all about you right now."

"*We*? Are you planning on hanging around in this shit storm? Why would you stay?"

"You'd be surprised to see what I would do for you. You're still my wife and I still love you." Dale took hold of Gabrielle's hand. Even in the midst of hell, the two were able to find peace as their common denominator.

Chapter 63

"Ms. Jameson, you have three new clients needing your representation. Do you have time to look their files over right quick?"

"David, it may be a few days before that may happen. I'm closing on two cases, both of which need all the attention I can dish out. Place them on the counter. In the meantime, let them know my status. If they choose to wait, that's fine. If they need services right now, send them over to Michael Frazier please."

"Got it. But you may not want to sleep on these requests."

"Ok, I promise to look them over. Hey David, toss me the remote off the bookshelf please." Lola looked over the city's skyline and allowed her thoughts to travel back to her last session with Lucah. *Why did he have to lie? Why did he wait so long to let me in?*

"Here you go Ms. Jameson." Lola's afternoon was busy. Every day between two and five, Lola spent time checking local and national news channels to sift through all the crime in motion. Although the majority of her clientele came from referrals, a small percentage of them came from the news.

As she watched the news, Lola shook her head in disgust. As usual, enough crime had circulated though St. Louis to help the city hold its number one position of being the most dangerous city in America.

"We are breaking into your normal broadcasting to share breaking news. Today, around noon, St. Louis County prosecutor, Ted Phillips, filed charges against successful financier and entrepreneur, Lucah Hunt. Hunt is allegedly accused of knowingly transmitting HIV to several local women. The women, who wish to remain anonymous, have all presented the authorities with substantial information regarding Mr. Hunt and his activities." Lola was breathless. In an instant, Lola was relieved that things between her and Lucah never progressed. Praising Jesus for his protection, she cried for the women involved. As much as she wanted to have sex with Lucah, she refused to allow him in. Her heart was all he penetrated.

"Oh Lord, who in the hell have I been dealing with?" Lola grabbed her phone and clutched it in fear as she continued to watch the reporter blast Lucah.

"The authorities are asking for the public's help. If anyone has information on the whereabouts of Mr. Hunt, visit the stations website, or call the St. Louis County Police Department. We will have more information on this story as it develops. Here in downtown Clayton, this is Jeff Cummings for New Channel Six."

"David! I need you now!"

"Yes Ms. Jameson, what do you need?" David asked as he juggled paperwork, and a cell phone.

"Cancel my day. Email me today's itinerary. I left my office cell at home and I need my office to be mobile today. Just call my personal cell today."

"What time will you be back?"

"I don't know. I will call you when I figure things out."

"No problem. Be careful Ms. Jameson. You need some coffee? You look floored."

"No, I will be fine. Keep your phone on for me." Lola flew from her office with phone in one hand, handbag on her shoulder, while trying to slip her jacket on.

"This is attorney, Lola Jameson-Springfield, give me the prosecutor's office right now. I have information regarding Lucah Hunt."

Chapter 64

"Lucah, its Lola! Please call me. You are on the news right now and it's not in a good way! I'm speaking in my attorney voice right now. I don't know what happened, but I need to hear it from you first. I'm not in the position to judge, but don't leave room for me to assume the worst. As you know, I cannot represent you, but I know a whole pound of badass law dogs that will fight the battle for you. For your sake Lucah, do not delay coming forth. We need to work fast before the six o'clock news. You know how stupid the media gets, once the stories make it to the media." Lola prayed the message she left Lucah would prompt him into trusting her. After all, what other friends did he have?

Chapter 65

"Ladies, I'm Dr. Virginia Arlington. First, I want to extend how sorry I am that we are not meeting on better terms. I called this meeting to gather some sense of the role Mr. Hunt played in your lives. Please, provide me with a quick snippet of your history with Mr. Hunt." Virginia was careful with her wording. Her focus was to find a resolve, not start a riot between the three devastated and heartbroken women.

"I'm Lily Lee. I met Lucah about three months ago, when he lunched at my restaurant one afternoon. After he was finished with his meal, he requested my presence. I obliged because people always want to express share their experience; good or bad. For some reason, as I approached Lucah, his look stated that he wanted something that was not on the menu, and truthfully; I was ready to serve him. When I saw Lucah, he did a great job in making me forget my ex-husband and any other man that did me wrong. I mean damn- I forget about my ex-husband hanging around on the down low block. That well-groomed man seduced my mind into thinking slutty thoughts before I shook his hand. I admit; I was intrigued with him. He was confident, smart, and well off, money wise. We had a lot in common. His reasoning for calling me to the table was to join a partnership for charitable causes. It was a great plan. Even though he was talking business, I was half way done fucking him to death, in my mind." Lily stared out the window with a smile of regret.

"Good Lord. You too?" Gabrielle asked as she stared at the blank television screen on the wall. Gabrielle's face was also smeared with a smile of regret. Virginia allowed the women to keep the meeting as casual and relaxed as possible. Three women in the same room, discussing the same man they had all slept with was one hell of a symphony to conduct.

Lily laughed and continued. "Yeah, he was too smooth. For

the next three weeks, we worked together, but the night I decided to get personal, he took it to the next level without pause. I was numb. His smell, his talent, and his ability in making you feel as if you were the only woman he had allowed in his world; completed me. Not too long ago, I became ill."

"Ok, thank you Lily. Mrs. Withers? Would you care to continue?" Virginia was busy jotting notes. She wanted to gain as much information on Lucah as possible.

"I guess. I met Lucah at the Bistro about two and a half months ago. I was having dinner with my PR team, discussing my next book project. I decided to step outside to catch some air, and that's when I bumped into- wait, when his cologne darted up my nose. I found him by his wondrous scent. His scent was powerful enough to make a whole mall of women horny. When I saw the face related to the smell, he gave a new definition to getting wet."

"Oh damn, you right. I thought I had to go back in time to get that wet again." Isabella chuckled as she shook her head. The entire room erupted with laughter. The women were ill with a toxic humor as they held their mid-sections. Virginia shook her head at her best friend. She was happy to see Isabella smiling, even though the occasion called for the sadness of a funeral.

Gabrielle took back control of the room. "I'm serious! I swear I was pissing on myself, but my stuff...it failed to listen to me. I was thinking about the numerous positions I was willing to do for that man." Gabrielle confessed.

"Oh yeah, honey. I mean I'm too old for some man to be talking 'bout back my damn thang up! When messing around with them young ones; you have to leave about a foot or so between yourself and the head board. All it takes is one hard knock and you done snapped yo damn neck! Now how the hell would I look, walking around with a neck brace on?" Isabella belted another dose of humor into the ring.

"No, that's when you gone head, shut on up, don't say one-damn-word, and let folk think you were in a car wreck." Lily said as she held her head stiff, while using her peripheral vision to eyeball the room.

"Oh my goodness, it's nice to know that we are all a bunch of old freaks." Gabrielle teased.

"We chatted on and off about two, maybe three weeks before we hit the sheets." Gabrielle confused through laughter.

"How'd he get you into the bed?" Isabella asked.

"He offered a large sum of money for me to paint a self-portrait of him, and I took the job. I met him at his home that evening to view his private collection of artwork, and to take in the space where he envisioned his portrait to be created."

"That bedroom made you wanna take your panties off the moment the lights came on didn't it?" Lily teased.

"No. It was when he walked bare butt naked past me. Then he got in the bed, and pulled that snake from beneath the cover, I started shaking like a crack-head. Now that's when I was serious about getting naked!"

"I know, what a monster." Isabella shivered.

"I asked him if I should bow or start praise dancing. The thing was huge! It did not help that my husband and I were on bad terms. For once, I wanted to have sex without feeling sorry about something. On the flip side, I didn't know that my last screw would have me sorry for the rest of my life."

"You mean *us*?" Isabella cleared the air to remind Gabrielle that, Lucah had bitten them all.

"Lucah delivered himself to me. I saw him in the hallway of my building. He claimed he was looking for my PR firm." Isabella felt uneasy about making her personal life public, but she knew she was no different from the other women who sat in the room with her.

"Our meeting was brief, but I will not lie. He awakened every part of this old body. I have to admit that he's good at what he does, but he played the wrong damn game on the wrong bitch!" Isabella wasn't about to take her diagnosis light.

"It sounds as if Mr. Hunt was working on a tight deadline. Listening to you all has convinced me that he knew exactly what he was doing."

"Has the news gone public yet?" Lily asked in a hushed tone. Lily fought hard to recover from being married to a husband on the down low. With new gloom in her lap, she was back at square one; nowhere to go.

"Ladies, I have to ask one question."

"Go head." Isabella urged Virginia as she drank another sip of her tea.

"Did anyone use protection?" The room was quiet enough to hear a cricket tap dancing on cotton. All the women looked at each other as if they all shared the same answer. "Hello? Will someone answer that for me?" No one said a word. It was as if shame had sealed their mouths'.

"Ok, raise your hand if you used protection." Not one single soul lifted their hand.

"What in the hell is going on ladies? You mean to tell me he was *so* good, that you risked your life for a man- a *young man* at that?" Virginia jumped from her seat and paced the floor as if she had to deliver an executive statement.

"Ladies come on! *Really*? In these times?"

"I must admit, it sounds stupid now, but I'm done with my child bearing years! I haven't had a partner in years and- I guess the moment took over." Lily confessed with shame as a tear fell from her face.

"I'm sorry ladies. Please understand that I am not trying to make you feel bad. This kind of shit happened when we were young and dumb! True, we are out of our child bearing years, and yes, we experience enough hot flashes to induce global warning; but we should never stop using protection. Old age does not exempt us from catching shit!"

"Don't you think it's too late for that talk? I mean what the fuck!" Gabrielle was irritated. "What in the hell can be done now? This is something we will live with for the rest of our lives. I know there will be plenty days full of depression, but right now; I'm focused on fucking *his* life up!" Gabrielle punched at the air.

"Oh Lord, I feel sick to my stomach." Gabrielle complained as she reached for her pan.

"Are you ok?" Lily asked as she rushed to aide Gabrielle.

"Just nauseated. These meds are a bitch, but hey- I meant what I said! I am *stuck* on making his life a living hell. He does not deserve a second chance at shit!"

"That's what I'm talking about." Lily co-signed. Since meeting, Lily and Gabrielle had formed a tight bond. Both dogged by men they thought they would love until the end; gave them a certain pain to share.

"Ladies, we must keep this meeting confidential. The press has no idea who you are and your personal records remain private. Thank you for allowing us to meet in your room, Gabrielle. I wanted to give you all time to allow things to settle, but nothing will settle until Mr. Hunt has his dose of justice."

"Sorry to interrupt your session Dr. Arlington, but Ms. Lola Jameson is here to see you."

"Oh yes, please send her in."

"Isabella, it's time to take your medication. Would you like me to bring it to you?"

"Yes, please Lisa. Oh yes, will you bring the juice container from my room?"

"Sure, be right back."

"Ok ladies, we are about to meet the woman that may be able to help us locate Lucah."

"What? Who in the hell is she?" Isabella, worried about who was about to gain access to their secret meeting took a defensive stance. Lola made her entrance into the room. Every woman in the room locked their eyes on Lola.

"You are too beautiful. Let me guess, Lucah got to you too." Gabrielle tossed her funky assumption into the air.

"Not the way he got to you ladies."

"Oh and *you're* special?" Lily asked as she took to her feet. One hand on her hip and the other on her chin; Lily was hard at work speculating Lola's position in the game.

"Lucah and I are- were friends. I met him at a local supermarket. He was nice. Right away, it seemed as if we knew each other."

"Entertain us with something else beside bullshit. All he knew is that he was undeniable and that older women were looking for a ride." Gabrielle snapped. Lola was not too pleased with Gabrielle's loose brand of ignorance, but she carried on.

"We became each other's keeper. We talked about our relationships, and we spent a lot of time together. We went on several dates and he even met my family. I had no idea that I was dealing with a monster. He said he was exiting from a bad relationship and during that moment, we both were living life from the same chapter."

"Where is he at?" Isabella was sold that Lola and Lucah had not shared a bed. If she had, Lola would have shared her regret for falling prey to Lucah as well as reminiscing about his dick, within the first minute of meeting the group.

"Not sure. He closed his St. Louis office along with several others, to move back home to Greece. He told me his sister wanted him home, and that he was choosing to leave satellite offices on the West Coast, and I think a few on the East as well. His home was boxed up and the movers had taken close to everything out of his home."

"If the two of you were close, why didn't he tell you about his moving plans?" Virginia asked as she continued to take notes.

"I stopped by his house and caught him in the middle of packing. He told me about his diagnosis. He admitted that he was HIV positive. I was floored, because I fell hard for Lucah. I I was happy with starting something with Lucah."

"Sounds sweet, but as you have heard, none of us have experienced such a happy ending. You *have* to get him to come to you!" Lily snapped. It was evident that every woman in the room was jealous of Lola and Lucah's relationship. Lucah had never exposed himself to Lola like he did the other women. He consoled them, inspired them, but he never allowed them to explore his mind and feelings the way he allowed Lola.

"I might have a plan, if you ladies are willing to participate." Lola shared as she pulled up a chair.

Chapter 66

"Lucah, its Brooke. I'm sure you thought I was dead, but good old Brooke had a change of heart. As much as I wanted to die, my body just kept going. I see you have made a mess of things. I told you no brand of revenge was strong enough to heal your wounds. I listened to your voicemail and read your email over a million times hoping and praying your ill words were based on anger alone. Lucah, I have a jet touching down at Chesterfield Airport in three hours. Give them the name Daniels and a chance at freedom is yours. I'm not looking for much. Maybe we can take the time to mend things. I owe that to you.

The flight to destination *unknown* will be a long one, so prepare for it. Please, do not bring electronics for they may be traceable. I know you are accustomed to rolling in style Lucah, but catch a cab to the airport. A package with information and credit cards will be at the airport waiting on you. Trust me; I'm pretty good at falling off the radar. I promise no one will know it's you. I guess I will see where your heart stands in about three hours." Lucah stood as lifeless as a mannequin. Thoughts of being apprehended, and shoved behind jail bars; gave Lucah a migraine.

The mess Lucah created was big enough to ruin him for life, but he refused to go down easy. Knowing time would be borrowed after creating boatloads of hell; Lucah took time to set up multitudes of banking accounts. Lucah always preached charity. But the thought of living life on the run with limited funds buried that sermon. Lucah knew it would take more than good looks to live a life on the run.

In the midst of planning his run-away, Lucah tried to redeem himself as much as possible. He hoped with releasing over two-hundred faithful employees from service, with one year of severance pay; would help them move forward without hardship in their lives. Before closing out his last account, Lucah donated five-million dollars to five of his favorite charities.

Chapter 67

"Lucah, its Lola. Look, the media is having a field day with your story. *The Cougar Killer*? Is that how you want to go down in history? Lucah, as I said earlier, I cannot represent you, but I have the best of the best, willing to help. Help me understand why you have failed to respond to the women you slept with. Please don't be ashamed. You know I am not into judging folks." Lola pleaded as she recorded her plea video with her phone.

"You never judged me and I won't judge you. Lucah, deep down, I refuse to believe what is going on. I *know* you!" Lola started to tear up as she continued to speak her heart into the camera. "I've had time to be with you and this isn't adding up. Look at me, don't you dare take your eyes off this video! I have thought about so many things since we last saw each other, and I'm sorry to admit this so late, but Lucah, I love you." Lola held her head down as she cried.

"I didn't know what to do when you told me about being HIV positive. I still care about you, you are a great man in my eyes. I would be a liar if I said different." Lola poured her soul into every word she brought forth.

"Lucah, meet me at my home in about an hour. No one knows that I am talking to you. I want to see you. I want to hear what you have to say. I want to make sense of this all. If you give yourself a chance, I may give us a chance."

Chapter 68

 Frozen in his tracks, Lucah contemplated his next move. Thoughts of him and Brooke escaping to whatever paradise she had in store with him, puzzled his mind. Within the next blink, visions of him and Lola living life together made him reach for hope. Now that Lola's video was on constant replay; maybe there was a way for him to survive the mess he created.

Chapter 69

Lola rushed through crazy traffic to make it home in time enough to freshen up. Lucah agreed to meet with her. Nervous about Lucah's reaction to her video, Lola prayed for strength.

Lola checked her make-up about a thousand times and sifted through dozens of outfits; hoping to distract Lucah from her nervous energy. A combination of butterfingers and bad nerves caused Lola to drop her perfume bottle when the door bell rang. *Five, four, three two, one, oh shit, I need some vodka to get through this!*

"Lucah!" Lola cheered as she pulled Lucah into the house. "Did anyone see you come by? Were you followed?"

"No."

"How did you get here?"

"By taxi." Lucah responded as he removed his jacket. On edge and guarded, Lucah sat by the front door.

"Please, come into my study. I promise; it's just the two of us. I think you knew that ahead of time, or you wouldn't have shown up."

"May I have a kiss, a hug, or something?"

"Sure handsome." The butterflies dancing in Lola's stomach kept her on the line of queasiness.

"You feel good Lola."

"You too. Let's sit." Lola took Lucah's hand and escorted him to the couch in her room office.

"This office is beautiful. You have all of Forest Park staring right at you."

"Yeah, it helps me clear my head. Alright Lucah, what in the hell happened? Is what's circulating in the news true?"

"I thought you believed in me?" Lucah stated as he took to his feet.

"Baby, please sit down. I'm sorry; I am out of order for

talking to you like that. Help me understand." Lucah always found solace in Lola's voice. To him, her touch was an offering of unconditional love. He loved the way she was able to soothe his mind.

"Lola, I loved that woman. This all started because she was bit- if you want to call it that, by a man around the same age as myself. Lola, the transmission of HIV ruined me. I experienced many emotions during that time. Sad part, no emotion ever rendered hope or any peace." Lola poured Lucah a glass of vodka as she listened.

"Lucah, did you infect those women on purpose?"

"I prayed and thought hard. I visited my Pastor on many occasions to get help with my feelings. As much as I danced with the devil, it would have been okay to say he owned my soul. Hell- not life- existed in my heart. Yes, I did it. Yes, I infected those women." Lucah admitted his ugly truth.

"Oh my God Lucah! Why, why would you do that?" Lola felt shaken and within that moment, a cold divide separated them. Today was the first day she wished she never met Lucah.

"To be truthful, they were random. The media is wrong by saying I preyed upon them. I didn't."

"Well not turning yourself in, leaves plenty of room for them to say whatever the hell they want to say, Lucah."

"The thought of spreading HIV was premeditated, but the women- it happened in the order I met them."

"You mean the *victims* Lucah." Lola said in a cold voice.

"I thought you loved me. I thought you were thinking about giving me a chance." Lola kept her distance from Lucah.

"Look at me LOLA!" Lucah roared and the monster Virginia described, appeared before her eyes. Lucah looked at his watch to see if he still had time to catch the jet Brooke sent for him.

"Is this, the monster they were talking about?"

"I see you and I are through. I saved you, because I saw how much you loved life. I saw that no matter what flew your way; you knew you were going to push forward. I also thought of your child, and how awful her life would be if her mother became one of my victims. Do you know how much I needed someone like you in my life?" Lucah reached for Lola but she snatched away from him.

"The rest of those bitches meant nothing to me. I told you, it happened in the order in which they came into my life. I did not need their money, their love, or anything. I lost my sanity. I lost my life and someone had to pay!"

"You're damn right you lost your mind! You told me that you were upset because you were never given a choice. All that shit about you being stripped and left naked for the world to see; was some bullshit! How in the hell do you think those women feel?" Lola felt Lucah's coldness across the room.

"Had you came along before them, they wouldn't even be a part of my misery."

"What?" Lola shrieked as she pulled her approached Lucah.

"You are not going to put guilt into my head about this shit! You are the reason for all this drama going on. Fuck the idea of us meeting earlier in *your* fucked up life! Fuck being the one that could have saved those women! You will *not* include me in your bullshit!"

"You love me and you damn well know it Lola!"

"Yeah, I'd love for you to get what the fuck you got coming your way! You messed up when you tried to play, God! How dare you! Don't you understand that vengeance is the Lord's?"

"To hell with God!" Lucah's soul condemning words froze Lola in her tracks!

"Oh wow! You know, I think it's time you say your good-byes!"

"Goodbye to who? What in the hell are you talking about? Bitch, you better get back in here and talk! You owe me!" Lola ran from the room crying.

"Hello Lucah." Three familiar voices echoed. Lily, Isabella, and Gabrielle stood behind Lucah. Three pissed vixens looking for revenge was the last sight Lucah wanted in front of him.

"Lola! Get back in this room right now! You bitch! I can't believe you set me up!"

"Get over it Lucah. Your end is near." Lily said as she pulled a knife from her jacket. Isabella punched Lucah in the stomach with her Louisville slugger. Out of breath and in much pain, Lucah fell to the floor.

"Look Lily, put the damn knife up! I said whip his ass, not fillet his ass."

"Sorry, every chef brings a good knife to a fight party. Plus, why not fillet his dick." Lily didn't have to be hungry to slice Lucah's penis and fling it on the grill.

"Leave me something to do." Gabrielle begged as she bumped Lily to the side.

"Oh counsel," Isabella sung. "Will you please come into the room? We need you to advise us on what we can do without getting in trouble with the law."

Lola re-appeared into the room showing obvious signs of frustration and anger.

"Ladies, if you want to live life without the possibility of parole being denied, call the police and let the system deal with his lousy ass."

"Listen here, you better come up with something different. He's not leaving here without getting his ass whipped or cut, first." Lily snapped as she unzipped Lucah pants. "I'm taking *his* shit into my own hands!"

"Lily stop!" Everyone including Lucah screamed. Lucah's Eye balls fell out his head. Isabella towered over Lily and forced her to the floor. When the knife fell out her hand, Gabrielle retrieved it.

"I'm not leaving without doing something to him. We don't have to cut that monster off but we gotta do something." Lily screamed in frustration as she pulled her hair into a pony tail.

"Why Lucah? Why did you do this to us? Did you ever care?" Isabella was desperate to probe Lucah's head. "I have never seen this side of you." Now held hostage, Lucah had no choice but to open up.

"I will say it again. Things went down as they occurred. I did not hunt any of you down and I was not stalking anyone. In the end, the urge to put out what was done to me; won the battle."

"That's some lousy shit Lucah." Gabrielle used the sharp end of the knife as a pointer against his chest. Everyone froze in fear while watching Gabrielle toying with Lucah's life.

"All my life, I was a giver. I was the one doing for everyone but myself. I never meant all the vile words I spat in my husband's face. I never took pleasure in cheating on him when he had wronged me. What about my life?" Gabrielle pointed to her chest with the knife. She cried her pain into Lucah's face. "What about *me* having the chance to rise above everything that was placed on this earth to rid me of my faith and love for the Lord?" Gabrielle cried as she swung the knife at Lucah.

"Oh God! Someone get her." Isabella screamed.

"Back off! I swear I will cut whoever tries to come near me." Gabrielle returned her attention to Lucah. What about my life you bastard?"

"What about it? I can't take shit back! You women- wait- *you cougars,* have all the nerve. What's wrong with dating someone your age? Why do you need a younger man to help you feel alive? What does having a younger man on your arm mean?"

Isabella took her bat and charged every ounce of strength she had into pressing it straight through Lucah's abdomen.

"My turn!" Gabrielle yelled as she shoved Isabella out the way.

"Look here, that cougar shit might be a joke to you, but I don't see those young boys turning *cougar pussy* down! It's the same way for the sugar daddies and the rotten pieces of eye-candy they run around town chasing." Isabella spoke truth into the air. Lola returned to the room looking as if every bad element on earth had raped her.

"Damn! What happened to you?" Lily gasped as she rushed over to Lola. Lola was empty and the glare in her eye was dead.

"What did you all touch?" Lola asked in a dead tone as she stared at Lucah.

"Wait Lola, what's wrong? You're scaring me" Isabella's nerves started rattling. Afraid, Isabella tried to distract Lola's look of death.

"Oh shit, *Death Wish Six* is in the room. This bitch got Charles Bronson beat. We need to get out of here." Lily said as she grabbed her handbag.

"Lily, take the vodka bottle and the glasses in the kitchen and clean them down. Make sure you clean the sink and dry it with a towel. I have some bleach wipes on the counter, be sure to wipe down everything you touch with them. Afterwards, there's a trash bag on the kitchen counter; put any trash you make in that bag." Without asking any questions, Lily went about her prescribed duties.

"Isabella, dust this floor up. I want this house to look undisturbed." Lola pulled a gun from behind her and sat on the couch next to Lucah.

"Oh-hell-no! Lola, please put the gun away!" Gabrielle pleaded as she tried to negotiate with Lola.

"Sit-on-the-other-couch! We are going to get this story right before I put you all out." Lola's decision was final. It was time to put Lucah to rest.

"Ok, the kitchen is squared away. All glasses have been cleaned and dried, wipes and kitchen towels are in the trash bag." Lily announced as she paused in the doorway. Lily was shocked to see Lola holding a gun.

"Everyone sit down!" Lola's voice turned cold. With hate and disgust frosted on Lola's face, bitterness was the taste that burned her tongue.

"One question- do you want the justice system to serve this asshole, or do you want me to do it?" Lola asked.

"We can do it together Lola." Gabrielle responded as she reached for Lola's hand.

"No, you all will have enough to deal with. Your doctor appointments, your families, your careers, and dealing with the shit, this asshole ushered into your life." Lola kicked Lucah in his groin.

"Can you imagine spending the rest of your life in prison, receiving poor ass healthcare, while missing your families because of *this* asshole?" None of the women answered but their looks proved how Lola's reasoning made plenty of sense.

"I've worked in the justice system for years. I've seen scum come and go, but this shit right here will walk away laughing. He has too much money and too many connections. He will flee before his trial starts. What happens if he gets out and infects other women?"

"She's right." Lily co-signed.

"I don't know if I can live with this. I mean I'm pissed, I'm hurt and I'm at a lost sometimes, but this is someone's life." Isabella battled with right, and wrong.

"I tell you what..."Lola closed her eyes and lowered her head to help pace her thoughts. "None of you were here. The last time we saw each other was at the hospital. We met to help Dr. Arlington create a profile on Lucah. We were there for therapy. The only thing I spoke about was my relationship to Lucah. I promised Dr. Arlington that I would try to get Lucah to meeting me at my home to discuss what was going on. I will take the rest from there. I suggest you all share the alibi of being at home. It does not need to be anything different from that.

"Are you sure this will work?" Lily asked as she pondered Lola's plan.

"I'm positive. I work this shit all day long. I know the

questions they are going to ask.

"Bitch you better be a damn good shot!" Lucah snarled as he motioned toward Lola.

"Sit your ass back!" Lola kicked Lucah in his chest. "I meant what I said when I told you nothing would come to be for us." Lola lowered herself to Lucah's level as outlined his face with the gun.

"What? You thought you were going to fly away laughing? I mean, what did you really think?"

"I should have tagged your ass too." Lucah confessed as he tightened his lips.

"Spit on me and I cut your fucking lips off!" Lola yelled as she placed the gun in Lucah's mouth.

"Ok, we're going home." Isabella gathered her jacket and handbag. Lily took no time trailing Isabella to the back door.

"Have fun in hell Mr. Hunt." Lily sang over her back without one last glare at Lucah. "You deserve it more than my ex!" Lily exhaled joy as she danced out the back door.

"Thank you. I mean it Lola." Gabrielle thanked and hugged Lola.

"I question at times if he hurt you more than he did us. I guess we all lost something, huh?"

"Don't worry, we will be fine!" Lola consoled Gabrielle.

"I agree with your reasoning. It would be a sin to let him out on bail until his hearing. I would never rest easy knowing the system let him free. I trust you and thank you." Gabrielle kicked the hell out of Lucah before she left Lola's house. "Enjoy hell you dog bastard."

Chapter 70

"Lola, its Virginia. Have you heard from Lucah?"

"Yes, he's right here at my house." Lola was close to ending Lucah's safari hunt.

"Why there?"

"I lured him here. I wanted to talk with him. I wanted to hear things for myself. Truthfully, I didn't think he was going to show up."

"That's dangerous Lola."

"I'm ok. Trust me."

"Are you near him?"

"I'm in my kitchen. I have to get back in my office. That's where I have him tied up."

"What? Tied up?"

"I'm calling the cops. Give me your address."

"5511 Lindell. Hurry up, he's getting antsy!"

"Ok, doing it now. I'm ten minutes from your home. Do the best you can to keep him calm." Lola said a quick prayer begging for forgiveness. Lola didn't tell Virginia the whole truth.

"You ready to bite this bullet?"

"Why are you doing this Lola? You talk about me, but this isn't you. I know you."

"Huh? Look Lucah, no one knows much about the other person these days! I mean, my husband's midget fooled me bad. That shows just how much I didn't know him. You don't fucking know me." Lola was disgusted with Lucah.

"You grown enough to live with this?"Lucah tried everything possible to avoid meeting death.

"Oh, I'm very grown. Right now, I'm going to prosecute my damn self."

"I'm sorry."

"You should have said you were sorry to those women."

Lola loosened the ropes on Lucah's hands, and freed his feet from the ropes. "Get up, walk to the couch, and sit down. Lola threw the rope into the trash bag. Lucah was slow to move.

"Massage your wrists and ankles. Get the circulation going, I don't want any sign of you being tortured." Lucah's breathing was hard and heavy. Sweat fell by the pound from his face as he readjusted his clothing.

"I know I hurt you. I don't want you to live with this Lola. Taking a life is not as easy as you think."

"Lucah, I have spent most of my life helping the rich get away with shit, in the court of law. There were days where I wanted to end my career because there were many restless nights. I might be a bitch in the courtroom, but I'm human at the end of the day. I can't let you walk."

"I see. Why add to what you are dealing with?"

"Oh no, I'm no longer adding. Today is the day where I stop turning people's wrongs into rights." Lola laid her gun down and picked up the knife.

"Lola, please don't. I love you so-,"

"**BANG**!" A loud gunshot rang throughout the room. Lola looked down and saw her gun missing. She turned to see who fired off the shot.

"Virginia? How did you get in?"

"The back door. The police will be her soon. I called them after I pulled up."

"Why did you shoot me you lousy bitch!" Lucah yowled as he held his stomach.

"One, you deserved it, and two, I wasn't going to trust anyone but myself to put your ass down." Virginia fired off another shot into Lucah's chest without the blink of an eye.

With the gun still smoking, Virginia started drilling Lola.

"Ok, here it goes, I came in about five minutes ago. I saw the two of you fighting in here. He knocked your gun out of your hand. As he ran towards you, I picked up the gun and fired it off twice.

"Ok." Lola was white as a ghost.

"Hurry up and toss this office! Where did this knife come from?"

"It's Lily's."

"Put it in your kitchen drawer now!" Virginia zipped through instructions as she tossed Lola's study around.

Thinking like her old self, Lola finished perfecting their story.

"Ok, he came to talk right as you were calling me. I told you he was here and you came as fast as you could. While waiting on you to come, he turned on me, and we started fighting. I pulled for my gun out my drawer, he kicked it out my hand and that's when you came in."

"Make the shit stick. Don't fuck up! I wanna enjoy what's left of the summer as a free woman!" Virginia snapped as she scanned the area.

"Here, let me rip your dress a little. I'm going to mess you're your hair up and pull a little out! I need to put some between his fingers.

"No you're- OUCH!!! That shit hurt, Virginia." Lola patted her scalp to assess her hair loss.

"That's more than a little of my hair!"

"You still got edges, shut up!"

"You go smear your lipstick on his lips and shirt. You can say he tried to force himself on you and you pulled away."

"WHAT!!! Now you need to be shot! You're nuts! This isn't right, Virginia."

"I'm not listening! Start screaming!" Virginia instructed Lola to liven the scene.

"Yes, I called five or so minutes ago, and the police have not yet made it to 5511 Lindell. We need an ambulance- and from what it looks like, the coroner too!" Virginia motioned for Lola to keep screaming.

"What? Operator I can't hear you. Please Lola hush, he's not moving its ok."

"Oh my God, I can't believe he turned on me. All I wanted to do was talk. Oh my God, please no!" Lola screamed loud enough for the operator to hear.

"Damn it! Get those cops here now!" Virginia screamed. "Lola you should have never trusted him! The whole world is looking for him, and you hoped he was going to sit and reason with you? Are you damn nuts?" Virginia ended the call and both women smile at each other as they checked the crime scene over once more.

"Are you ready?" Virginia quizzed Lola.

"Ready as I can be. Virginia, what made you come to my house?"

"Isabella called me. She told me the deal. She had doubts about you. She wasn't sure if you were strong enough to kill him."

"She's that good at reading people, huh?"

"You see me here don't you?" Virginia spread Lucah's arms apart and pushed his chest inward on the couch.

"It's the cops!" Lola squealed as she jumped to her feet. It was time for the real ordeal and Virginia looked Lola over to check her confidence.

"Sit down! You are the victim! I will do the talking! Talk when asked! Don't fear the cops. You didn't do this shit for a living! Be the fucking victim! Get your face on!"

"Got it." Lola shoved Virginia off. She sat on the floor in a corner with her head tucked between her knees. As she rocked, she remained focus on the plan.

"Father God, forgive me. I knew exactly what I did, and I ask you to forgive me. I know you say vengeance is yours, but-forgive me father. Lola lost words to give to the Lord. She knew the act she and the women committed was wrong, but it was too far in the game to start over. As Lola tried to pace her breath, she peered at Lucah's lifeless body with tears in her eyes.

"There she is!" Virginia pointed to Lola as the paramedics came over to access her injuries. The paramedics checked Lola over and Lola went along. The other paramedic checked Lucah for a pulse. He shook his head left to right. His partner knew Lucah was dead.

"I think my shoulder is dislocated." Lola imitated pain as she leaned to the right. The paramedic placed a sling band around Lola's arm to help stabilize it.

"Mrs. Springfield, are you able answer a few questions? We have collected information from Dr. Arlington, but I need to ask you a few questions? The detective asked as he pulled up a chair.

"I can give a general statement. Anything outside of that, I would like to have my lawyer present."

"No problem ma'am."

"Virginia, call Baylor? Let him know what happened, and tell him to get here fast. My phone is somewhere on my desk. He's on speed dial number two."

"Ok. What hospital will you be taking her to?" Virginia asked the paramedic.

"Barnes Hospital." The paramedic responded as he finished checking Lola's vitals.

"Thank you." Virginia ran off. It didn't take long for the media to swarm Lola's home.

"Ok, where do you want me to start?" A battered Lola asked.

Chapter 71

"**O**kay! Who's ready for the first round of drinks?" Lola cheered as she delivered a tray full of drinks by the poolside.

"Damn, this vacation is long overdue! The press has been on our asses like tattoos." Gabrielle confessed as she batted the heat away while stretched out on a lounge chair.

"Ok, who's ready for my chicken?" Lily took orders from the grill. Lily never understood the word vacation, so there she stood over the hell hot grill. We always joked about how many armies it would take to kick her ass out the kitchen. Since her diagnosis, Lily threw herself into her business more than ever. I guess you can say it was her way of working through things.

I thought the women would have become statues after finding out about their illness. Hell, little did I know they would prove me wrong. Their strength and devotion in redefining their lives was beautiful and priceless.

"Well, you know how we *Cougars* get down right!" Isabella shimmied across the patio decked out in a large sun hat, a neon-pink, two-piece with black licorice stilettos, all by Chanel of course. There was nothing that could ruin my day. Seeing the girls living with vigor and happiness motivated me to do the same. I often question if I would be as strong as they were if it happened to me.

"Break that shit down." Isabella danced across the patio, trying her best not to fall. Never has a day arrived where I felt trusting the legal system was the best thing to do. I think I would have shot his ass on the way into the courthouse, had it got that far.

"Girl, yo ass gone break your tail bone! You better come on over here and eat and take them damn shoes off." Lily teased Isabella as she delivered the rest of the food to the table.

"I'm going to die a diva! Flats are for little girls; quit hating on me *Mz*. Lee." Isabella picked up a grilling fork and challenged Lily to a fight.

"Oh Lord, what about relaxing? Y'all play too damn much." Lola muttered. It appeared the alcohol had taken effect.

"Ok ladies, let's catch up! Come on round the table!" Virginia called.

"Open that bottle up!" Lola barked.

"Look bitch, if you drink one more thing, a live intervention is going down right here! Here, drink this damn water." Virginia tossed Lola a bottled water. Lola looked at the water as if it was bottled sewage and tossed it in the pool. "You gots to be shitting me right?" Lola peered over her shades forgetting to take her next breath.

"Get over it sister! Eat something!" Lily pushed Lola's face into her plate.

"Ok ladies, may I have your attention? Gabrielle tapped her glass with a fork. *"The Cougar Killer"* is still sitting at number one for its tenth week!" All the women cheered at Gabrielle's news. "Who wants to guess what Lucah's paintings sold for?"

"You mean the one of him naked or the one of him as half-man, half-cougar?" I was curious to see how much Lucah was worth in death.

"Both of them! A woman from Belize contacted me at my gallery. I 'bout shitted myself when she made the offer."

"Damn Gabby, why you gotta talk gutter when I'm eating?" Lily complained as she pushed her plate away!

"Twenty- million- damn -dollars, is what I tell you, no lie!" Gabrielle jumped into the air while holding her double d's down! We all screamed and fell onto one another as if we won the world's largest jacket pot.

"Do you know who she is?" I asked while finishing off my potato salad.

"Her name was Brooke. That was all I remembered. My

accountant handled the deal. We talked for a few moments. She went on to talk about how she enjoyed the book and that she was proud of me when she saw me on Oprah telling my story.

"Brooke?" That name rang every loose bell in my head. "Brooke? Hmm that name sounds familiar. Damn, I'm getting old!" You know how shit sits right on your tongue and for some reason you can't get it out?"

"It will come to you." Lily said, while going through her second piece of chicken.

"Yeah, she expressed her sympathy for us all. She was so nice."

"Did you keep our names on the low?" Lily asked without blinking. The rest of the girl's remained adamant about keeping their names private.

"Do I look like a dumbass? It took a lot of prayer and humble pie to bring this story to life. At first, I wanted to publish the book I did a re-write on. But when I thought about the women and men, who never came forward to press charges against their assailants; I had to step up. I would be wrong to not share this story with those in pain. It's others out there just like us."

I always said how I wanted my last book and painting to free me for the rest of my life. No more writing or painting as a career. Its official, writing and painting are just things I enjoy doing. No pressure, no deadlines and no stressing over bullshit reviews. I want time to focus on me and my family." Gabby gleamed as she thought about the endless opportunities her new found wealth delivered.

"I love you all! I decided to give each of you a gift." Gabrielle handed an envelope to each of us and here we sat, ripping through the envelopes as if our freedom papers were inside each one of them.

"Gabby!" Lily screamed with her hand over her mouth! "You are giving us *three* million dollars! Are you nuts?"

"Oh Lord, woman you *are* nuts!" Lola was in shock as she stared at her check.

"Nope! She's fine! Gabby, you have done well by me darling!" Isabella bounced around with her check stuck to her forehead. "Check me out bitches!"

"Isabella Valdez, as your shrink, I am ordering you to take your medication!" We all erupted into sheer laughter.

"That's ok, I'm legally crazy, so talk what you want!" Isabella retorted. I could barely contain my laughter.

"Oh Lord, this kind of laughter will cure any illness. We need this laughter, like we need the need cure to AIDS. In the midst of it all, we are blessed." I love these women.

Lily, how is everything in the restaurant business?" Right now, if I can get Lily to put her food down, I might be able to get her to answer one question.

"Well if you must know- I'm pregnant!" We all took a moment to die on the inside. No one knew what to say.

"What are you going to do?" I asked.

"Virginia, I don't want *it*. I'm going to have the abortion next week. I can't take the risk of *it* getting sick, I can't stand the thought of dying while *it's* growing up, and truthfully; if *it* looks like Lucah, I will kill *it* my damn self!"

"Damn, that's harsh! I would say if you going to keep on calling the baby '*it*', it's wise to abort. Why do you have to be so mean about this Lily?" Lola was disappointed to hear Lily's cold tone. It broke the fun of the summer day.

"Was Lucah a warm and sunny guy? Uh, *hello*? I don't hear any takers on that shit right there! The decision is final. I will be fine. I survived Lucah Hunt, and there is nothing that can hold me down!" Lily resumed eating as if food would never be available after tonight.

"Call me, and I will go with you." Gabrielle hugged her best friend. The bond between Gabrielle and Lily was special. The strength each woman delivered to the other; delivered them from the pool of blues, on many days.

"Lily, you know we are here for you. Just keep us involved. You don't have to do a damn thing along."

"Thank you Virginia." Lily sobbed as she laid her head on Gabrielle's chest.

"What about you Bella?"

"Family wise, a lot of shit went down. My children grieved. The boys were so upset and hurt. My sister ad brothers are there for me. There were moments where I felt ashamed."

"Why Bella?" Bella never disclosed this with me when we were in session.

"Do you know how many times I called myself stupid, or an old whore? When I think back to my reasoning for not using protection; slicing my wrists or a quick hanging seemed to be a good idea."

"Do you feel that way now?" I asked in my shrink voice as the other women sat back crying their own pain.

"No. God gives me peace. I made the decision, I have accepted the outcome, and I look for the message." Bella spoke through her tears. "I told my family, if I chose to live; then I expected them to do the same. Shit, I'm living for a cure- not the end of life!" Isabella proudly stated.

I was surprised to hear of Isabella's boys accepting her decision to live on. I'm sure had I not pulled the trigger on Lucah; a new wave of crime would have flooded the streets of St. Louis. Judge me if you want, but I stand by my act.

"Getting to the good stuff- I turned my agency over to baby girl and she is doing the damn thing! I am so proud of her."

"Looks like all of that schooling and on the job experience paid off." Lola stated as she sipped on her umpteenth drink.

"It did indeed. But wait on this... Devin has settled down!" Isabella gleamed with joy.

"What woman's world is that boy about to turn upside down Bella?" Virginia was in shock.

"Remember my private nurse, Lisa?"

"You don't say! I thought she was a good girl, Bella."
Isabella had nothing but good things to speak when it came to,
Lisa. She spoke many times in the past on how it would take
death to slow Devin down. I'm glad it was Lisa, and not death.

"To my surprise, they've been messing around since I was
in the hospital the night of the accident. Devin bothered the hell
out of her until she folded. That's why she quit working for me,
and returned to the hospital."

"Your *good* nurse has been medicating your son real good."
Lily teased as she snapped her chopsticks at Isabella.

"Hey, I'm happy if he's happy! I must admit, she is a fine
woman and I am relieved to know, handling Devin is not a
challenge for her. Devin has calmed down a lot. He's taken true
form of his father-" Isabella's smile matched the warmth of
summer as she peered over Miguel's memorial.

"Bella, does Miguel's memorial site in the yard a bother to
you or do you think it's helping you to move forward?" I asked
because she spent countless hours there.

"In the end, this is where we planned to be. We planned on
growing old together here at *Southern Comfort*; and here, is
where he will remain. The funeral was for closure, but I wanted
him cremated. I know there would be no other place he' rather
be. Now stop worrying, Virginia."

"Whatever keeps that glow on your face makes me happy."
I refused to let my friend retire to the south alone. After
Raymond and I married in a private ceremony two weeks ago,
we packed up and moved to Georgia. Raymond's good for me, so
why wait? I'm blessed to say that I've had the chance to say that
I've had two great men in my life. I know my husband would
have wanted me to move on.

"Gabby, how are you and Dale? You two work things out?"
Lola asked as her attack on the vodka continued.

"It was rough at first, but we worked things out. I was

surprised when fell onto his old ass knees to beg for a second chance."

"You don't fucking say!" I was shocked when I heard the news of Gabby taking Dale back in. I was bitter for all the shit he'd done to her. On the other hand, I can imagine how tense things may have been for Dale; knowing his wife was HIV positive.

"He's a new man!"

"Are y'all fucking?" Lola blurted out. The lawyer in Lola never saw the stop sign. It was one interrogation right after the next.

"We ain't holding hands all the time! Is that good enough for you Mz. Lola? Gabrielle gleamed as she popped her neck.

"You like it, I love it!" Lola smiled.

"Not sure what direction that whore bitch he was messing around with went, but things have been quiet!"

"You sure you didn't kill her?" Isabella was serious with her questioning. Gabrielle ignored Isabella.

"Does anyone have regrets?" It was silent for a few moments.

"Yeah, I wish I would have worn a thong instead of this bikini." Gabrielle whined.

"Look, we've all talked about this more times than I could give a damn, but the cards were dealt; and we played the best hand possible. There are no losers here! Life showed us what a bitch she is, and guess who won the fight?"

"Come on girls, let's sit poolside." Lola pleaded. I have something to say." It was if the celebration turned into a wake.

"It's time to put this shit behind us. Yes, I admit, I cared about Lucah. But the pain I saw in each of your eye's made me want to kill him ten times over. He didn't hurt me physically; but he crushed my heart." Lola cried into a napkin as she sat poolside. We huddle over to Lola and held onto our sister.

"I'm all alone, Baylor has moved on and I'm scared to

death about starting over." Lola clenched onto Isabella's hand. "What Lucah did, has paralyzed me. How do I know the next man won't be like him?"

"You don't, but you live and you learn. Your fear is paralyzing you Lola. Count your blessings and move on. Just take some time to find what Lola wants." I knew it would be a while before Lola gave her heart to another man. You just don't bounce back onto the dating scene when something like this happens.

"You can't allow Lucah to hold you back love." Lily said.

"I'm leaning on the Lord, to reveal my destiny." Lola responded as she dabbed her tears away.

"Fall in love with, Lola! Do what makes you happy. Find your center and focus on peace. Peace is the perfect form of balance. It's what moves us from day to day. Take the time to walk with the Lord and share your intimate thoughts with him. Lord knows he's answered many of my requests." Isabella spoke with the inspiration of a motivational speaker.

"Lola, if Lucah were still here, peace would be absent from your life."

"I know."

"That's why I shot him. You needed me there. I love you all, and I could not stand by and watch you all lose your lives over trash. Lola, you have worked hard all your life and you have too much life ahead of you. I know you hate to think back, but Lucah was right. You are smart, and deserving of a life of happiness. Live, learn, laugh, and repeat the cycle till the Lord calls you home."

"Thanks Virginia!" Lola hugged Virginia.

"Oh yeah ladies, if anyone feels bad for Lucah Hunt, I have no problem with burying you on top of him."

"Are you serious?" Lily asked as she pulled away from the group hug.

"Naw, I'm playing." Virginia laughed.

"You are wrong for that. I thought your ass was for real!" Lola laughed Virginia's wicked joke off.

"Lily, turn the radio up. I wanna get my groove on!" Gabrielle yelled while doing her version of the stanky leg. The sound of happiness returned to the party and we continued our new birth celebration. More drinks were poured, and the radio blared as we danced the day away.

Now if you think I fell asleep on that bitch Brooke, then I guess you really don't know how me after all. Like Lucah, Brooke shall soon meet her maker. Without her, none of this drama would have occurred. There's a bad cougar on the loose and the bitch needs to be put down.

I hoped you enjoyed this book.
Feel free to comment on my
Website at: www.londab.com
or email me at: talk2me@londab.com
Until Virginia finds Brooke, check out my other titles:

Who's Loving Me?
My Soul Desires…
One by One;
Portraits of Mental Illnesses in America.
Why Don't We Get It? Jan 2017 Release Date